Been
in
Love
Before

ALSO BY BRYAN MOONEY

Christmas in Vermont—A Very White Christmas

Once We Were Friends

Love Letters

A Second Chance

A Box of Chocolates

INDIE

The POTUS Papers

Eye of the Tiger

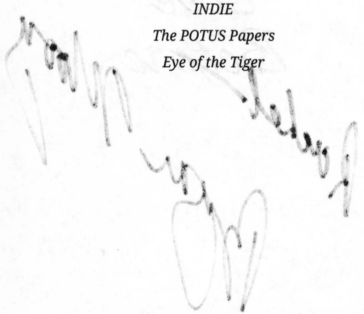

Been in Love Before

A Novel

BRYAN MOONEY

LAKE UNION
PUBLISHING

Text copyright © 2016 Bryan Mooney
All rights reserved.

Published by Lake Union Publishing, Seattle

www.apub.com

Amazon, the Amazon logo, and Lake Union Publishing are trademarks of Amazon.com, Inc., or its affiliates.

ISBN-13: 9781503937314
ISBN-10: 1503937313

Cover design by Janet Perr

Printed in the United States of America

To my loving wife, Bonnie. Thank you for all your patience.
To those who have loved,
to those who have lost love,
and
to those who have rediscovered the wonders of love.
To all of you—never give up hope.

Chapter One

Robert James Macgregor, the eldest of the three Macgregor brothers and the patriarch of the family, stood tall at the front of the old Boston Whaler aptly named *Scottish Pride*. His floppy Hemingway hat covered his long, dark hair, revealing just a few wild, curling wisps of gray peeking out from underneath. His eyes scoured the water in front of the slow-moving craft, searching for his treasure. It was a hot and humid June day, with the Florida heat scorching his back, as the sun began to set below the purple horizon. On the water there was only the slightest of breezes. His mind wandered while his eyes searched in front of the boat. A hot shower, a cold beer, and a fresh-grilled fillet would be something to look forward to at the end of the day, he thought to himself.

His son, Bobby, stood high above him on the captain's perch; they were both scouting the shallow water for the same thing—cobia. The elusive fish, nicknamed "the fighting king," would often swim in these sea-blue waters off Key West.

It was their last day on the water. Father and son had been on the boat since early afternoon and had come up short in their quest. They had caught three small pompano earlier in the day, but they had been too small to keep. Within the last hour, the two fishermen had caught four barracuda, great fighting fish but hardly edible. That might explain why the other fish were nowhere to be seen: no fish liked to swim with barracuda around—too risky. The sun was setting, and they were both tired and hungry. They were determined to catch their dinner for that evening, but it would soon be time to head home.

At last the younger Macgregor stood tall and grinned, shouting, "Starboard side, a hundred fifty yards out, in deeper waters." He pointed excitedly to a spot in front of them as he throttled the powerful Mercury engine into position. The outboard sprang to life and covered the distance quickly. He loved the responsiveness of the engine. His father had salvaged and rebuilt the abandoned motor until it growled like a tiger. The younger Macgregor swung the longboat around, slowed the skiff to a crawl, and waited for a signal from the deck below.

His father baited a large fishhook with a flopping sardine. When the boat came to a slow troll, he waited, then shifted his old cap around for a better view of his target. There ahead in the clear, blue waters was what they had been searching for all day—cobia—a large one.

"Forty-pounder!" Bobby shouted eagerly from the bridge above.

"Fifty, if not more," responded his father. "Bring her around, son, nice and slow. And don't spook 'er." The elder Macgregor readied the huge rod as the boat pulled into position and, with one long, deliberate motion, cast the baited hook far beyond the boat, well past the scavenging fish. Robert was in for a battle, and he knew it. These were fighting fish, and they did not give up easily.

He reeled in the bait, steady-like, near the large, cautious fish. There was an art to fishing, a certain patience, a rhythm that one had to learn in order to be successful. An ebb and flow, just as in life. He had mastered it years ago, and he felt the rhythm as the boat began to gently rock from side to side. He held the fishing line loosely in his fingers, letting it out patiently, waiting for the slightest movement. He continued to let the line out, slowly. *Wait . . . wait . . . wait . . .*

The bait drifted past the cagey creature, which appeared to take no notice; then without warning the enormous fish turned and took the bait. The fish struck it hard. Robert was pulled forward. A lesser man would have landed in the water along with the fish, but the Scotsman was about to show this fighting king who was boss. Robert held on tight as the hook sank deep inside its mouth. The mighty fish ran for the safety of the dark-blue deeper waters; it was running and pulling hard, but Robert knew it was only a matter of time. The shiny, silver-white fish jumped high in the water, signaling its defiance, then jumped again, fighting for its life.

Robert's strapping shoulders and muscular arms pulled the massive fishing rod back with long, steady movements, his hand turning the reel at the same time. With each measured stroke, the fish battled closer and closer. The fighter continued to struggle against all odds in its losing battle. The regal fish was defiant to the end, even as it was hauled aboard and weighed.

"Fifty-six pounds," said the elder Scotsman, proudly hoisting the bright-silver delicacy with his portable scale. The older man held it high in the air before he gently set it down in the boat out of respect. Robert was all about tradition, for he felt that without it there could be no life worth living.

He bowed his head, saying, "Cobia, master of the deep, we salute you and your valiant effort," paying homage to his worthy adversary. The ritual over, he looked up, put his hat back on his sunburned head, and said, "Come on, son, let's head ashore and have dinner. Take us home."

"Aye-aye, Captain," Bobby said and jumped to the wheel. He gave the boat its lead and opened the throttle, and the huge engine replied with a sudden surge of power, leaving a frothy trail of white water churning behind them. They headed for the dock, the salt air blowing in their faces as the afternoon sun brought back some not-so-distant memories from Robert's past.

He remembered the times he had been on this very boat with Tess, his wife and best friend of thirty-five years.

Tess had lectured him repeatedly—it was time to retire. She was right, as usual. He was going to try to enjoy life and retire in the fall; October was as good a time as any to retire. He liked the fall. He decided it was time to turn over the family business to Bobby.

It was then he had made another decision, without telling Tess, and secretly placed an order for two new matching sports cars, a huge extravagance for any man, but unthinkable for a Scotsman. A retirement gift for the both of them. He chose his car in a dark British racing green and ordered hers in a bright ruby red, her favorite color. It had always been her dream car.

She had retired three years earlier from her position as a nursing shift supervisor at Saint Mary's Hospital and immediately begun to encourage Robert to do the same. They were going to enjoy life while there was still time left to do so.

In October of that year, Tess was healthy, a ten-year cancer survivor, and they were going in for her annual checkup before they drove to their weekend cabin in the Florida Keys. They were going to spend some time together to regain some balance in their life. Tess was giddy about their upcoming time away together. For two whole weeks, he would be all hers, and she was going to make the most of it. They had always had a life filled with family, work, and, of course, doctors, tests, and numerous medicines. Now all that would be changing; now it would be just the two of them, just as when they were first married, and both of them could hardly wait. They were like kids on the last day of school. Life was good for the Macgregors.

At the doctor's office came the bad news: the disease had returned and spread to her lungs, her hip, and her blood. The oncologist gave her six months to live. He was wrong; she had lasted only four. That was two years ago.

"Goddamn the world," Robert had said in anger at the funeral. "Goddamn the world, and those who have to live in it."

Robert missed her more than anything. He missed her smile, her laugh, her companionship, her humor, her crossword puzzles, her constant teasing, her quirky humor, her mumbling in her sleep to someone named Harry, and her color-blindness—her inability to match any of her clothes. (They clashed regularly about her choice of clothes to start the day. To make life easier for her, Robert finally sewed labels inside her clothes listing the colors.) But most of all, they were comfortable together, and now that was gone from his life. He had put his plans to retire on hold and decided to work part-time.

"Prepare to come about," his tall son boomed overhead, breaking the mood and bringing him back to reality.

Bobby had pushed him for this week away together, before the baby came. His wife, Patti, was due soon, just about the time of Mary Kate's upcoming wedding. After that it would be tough to get away from the store for a whole week. Mary Kate was getting married in two weeks, and time would be at a premium as the wedding approached. This would be his and Bobby's last time together at the cabin for a very long time, and they both knew it.

Bobby needed his father's strength, as always—the whole family did—and they relied on him and looked to him for direction. He was their moral compass. Now Robert was hurting, and Bobby felt helpless, watching the proud man struggle with the loss of Tess. He too missed his mom, more than ever. She had always been someone special in his life.

Friends said "Give it time," but things were only getting worse for his dad. Gone were the generous smiles, the hearty laughs, the pranks, and the humor of the big man. Bobby needed to talk to this stubborn Scotsman. He needed to do it soon, before it was too late.

The boat slowly pulled into a secluded cove just north of Key West. Robert had bought the overgrown homestead some fifteen years earlier, along with the dilapidated old cabin, creaking dock, and sunken fishing boat. He loved to fix things, and this had been a perfect weekend project.

He bought the property for less than the cost of a used car from the family of the old man who had lived there. The deceased owner's relatives arrived from Minnesota, and after the funeral, they visited the property and decided they had no use for it. "Get rid of it before we have to pay any more taxes on it," the heirs told the Realtor after their rental car became stuck in the home's muddy driveway.

Robert spent most weekends over the next five years clearing the land, draining the mosquito-filled swamp, paving the road and driveway, redoing the plumbing and electricity, fixing the sewer and water systems, and rebuilding everything from the cabin to the boat to the dock. It was a beautiful bit of paradise on the water, it was all his—and Tess's. She loved the place even more than he did, when she was alive. Now she was gone.

That was then, but now—and Robert would never admit it to anyone—he was lonely. His son came down regularly to help around the property, fixing things, but after Bobby got married, those visits became fewer and farther between. Bobby's second wife, Patti, was not really a water person, so he saw his son less and less, except at the store. He loved her like his own, but Robert understood—either you had salt water in your veins or you didn't.

"Look alive there!" Bobby shouted, and his dad sprang onto the dock, grabbed the tether ropes, and secured the boat to the newly rebuilt wooden pier.

Once ashore, Robert quickly filleted the fish like an expert, carving out huge steaks from the once-proud prince of the sea, as Bobby fired up the outdoor brick pit grill to cook it. They ate well, gorging themselves, with plenty of fish fillets left over for later.

Bobby sat back to proclaim, "That was the best. Nothing like a fresh-caught fish, hot off the grill."

When they finished, Robert cleaned the plates and table and grabbed a couple of beers from the outdoor cooler. He looked around with pride at the property he had brought back to life, filled with so many memories. The tall grasses at the water's edge swayed in tune with the gentle breeze. Handing a can to Bobby, he sat back in one of his newly refurbished Adirondack chairs to watch the sun set. A gray-blue heron glided by overhead, looking as if it had nowhere to go and was in no particular hurry to get there, but that was typical of life in Key West.

Last summer Robert had learned that a neighbor had abandoned some chairs at a nearby cottage, and the Realtor was going to pay someone to haul them to the dump. So he rescued them from the trash heap and refinished them, then gave them a fresh coat of paint. They looked brand-new. Robert was handy that way, and that was how he made his living. He could fix anything, and the name of his store said it all: the Frugal Scotsman. Robert owned the largest secondhand variety store in South Florida. The store was immensely popular and had tripled in size over the last fifteen years. He had kept adding on to the original store and had then hired his son, Bobby, to help manage the place. Bobby had also expanded the store's offerings to include more newer, high-priced items, much to the chagrin of his father.

"Bobby, do you want any of those fillets to take home? I can't eat all of 'em," his father said.

"No. Thanks anyway, Dad. Patti doesn't like when I grill fish. She says it stinks up the house."

"Well, use the damn outdoor grill, for Pete's sake."

"Can't, it broke last week. Patti was going to the store to order one while I was away and have one of our guys deliver it tomorrow."

"Hell, don't do that. I can fix it. I'll come over and take care of it when I . . ."

He held up his hand. "Dad, thanks, but Patti wants a new one. The old one was over ten years old, and she wants to have neighbors over for barbecues this summer. She wants to show off a little bit. It's fine, really. "

"Well, if you say so, son, but don't throw the old one out. I'll come by and pick it up, no problem. Maybe I can fix it?"

"Dad, I already set it out for the trashman before I left. Patti insisted."

"Okay, okay, it's your life and your family, and I'm not about to interfere. No big deal. Besides, I got enough old damn barbecue grills around the store to last a lifetime. And those new ones are selling really well at the store. Thanks to you."

Bobby smiled. Selling the new grills at a separate grill store had been his idea, which his stubborn father had fought every day, saying they would never sell. He grinned in triumph as he sipped his beer.

"I'll ice down the rest of the fish and take 'em to your uncle Eian tomorrow. You know him; he'll eat anything." When he was done, the older Macgregor looked away to the changing sky and sighed. Sailboats glided by on their way home to the downtown port. He sat in silence watching the orange-and-amber sun set on the calm waters, just as he had done when his Tess was still alive.

Bobby reached out to touch his father's arm and said, "I love you, Dad."

His father looked back at his only son, a tear swelling in his eye. "I love you too, Bobby." He paused for a moment before continuing, "Hey, hand me a beer, son."

"Sure." Bobby looked at his father. Even at his age he still had a full head of hair, dark as coal like his brother Eian's, with only wisps of gray on the sides. Sitting beside him now, Bobby could see the thick, bushy eyebrows protruding over his father's penetrating hazy-brown eyes, which were lost in thought. He could make out the determined chin that told the world that once his father made up his mind he wanted something, there was no stopping him.

After taking a large gulp of beer, his father proclaimed, "The thing you really need is more space . . . or a bigger house. That old two-bedroom of yours is going to be cramped once the baby comes along. Tell you what, we can put on an addition if you like . . . and if Patti approves, of course. We can add some more space for you two. What do you think?"

"Sounds great. Let me talk to Patti." Then, changing the subject, "Hey, what's your meeting with Mary Kate about tomorrow?" he asked, taking a big swallow from his beer.

"Graw said she wanted to meet with all three brothers. I'm sure it has something to do with her wedding. Only got two more weeks, but you know, sometimes I can't understand my brother Ryan. She runs his home even though she's living elsewhere. That daughter of his goes wild, especially now with her mother, Grace, gone," he said with a knowing grin.

"Now that was a pistol, that little Gracie," he continued. "She was a fiery one, red hair and all. And that Kate, she's just like her mother, red hair and an awesome temper to match. But I miss that Gracie . . . yeah, she was something special," he said philosophically, his eyes drifting out to sea. That famous Scottish twinkle returned to his eyes as he recalled the times he had spent with the family. He was sad, and it was heartbreaking: all three brothers had lost their wives over the past two years.

It's just not fair, he thought to himself. *The Macgregors lost the best women in the world.* But he had his son, Bobby, to keep him company, to work with him and keep him sane; that was all he needed.

Bobby reached into his back pocket and pulled out his wallet. *Now is as good a time as any,* he thought. *Let's get this over with.* He found what he was looking for and handed the business card to his father.

"What's this?" Robert asked.

"Dad, you remember you asked me to get you the name of the volunteer who heads up the senior social counseling programs?"

"I remember your Patti saying I should call them. She said she would get me the name and phone number of the person who runs it. That's what I recall," Robert said, his voice rising, his face turning slightly crimson as he fingered the card. "I tried programs like this once before already, remember?"

"Dad, listen, the last thing I want to do is to fight with you or argue with you. This has been too nice of a week. I don't want to spoil it. It's been like old times. There's the card; do with it what you want. Call them or not—it's up to you. Patti says this one is different. It's supposed to be more like a social program, primarily geared to older folks who have lost their spouses. Her uncle went there and had nothing but great things to say about it. And about the people who run it." He paused for a moment to watch his father.

"You need to talk some things out, Dad. Maybe meet some people, get out into the world. Hell, go out on a date. Do stuff other than retreat down here every weekend. You need to talk with people who are grieving just like yourself. I know it can be a little scary and you may not want to embarrass yourself . . . but it's up to you now. I'm out of it. Hand me another beer."

He could see the wheels spinning in his father's head as he was silent until he finally said, "Embarrassed? Scared?" Standing, he turned to face his son. "You think something like this would scare me?" Bobby could see the bravado rising.

"This is Robert James Macgregor you're talking to, named for your great-great-grandfather Robert Jeremiah Macgregor, longtime descendant from the MacGregors of the Scottish Highlands in the Cairnwell mountains." His face turned crimson. "Tradition? I am named for him the same as you are, the same as you will name your son, and don't you ever forget it. Me, scared? Hell no. The only thing that scares this Macgregor is the fires of hell."

Bobby just looked at him, nodding his head, watching, knowing that sometimes he had to let off a little steam. He had to tell him. Soon.

"Dad, sit down, please," he whispered calmly, not really wanting to venture into this discussion.

Robert sat and took a gulp from his beer, and the heaving in his chest began to subside.

His son waited a few minutes before he asked, "You okay?"

"Yeah, I'm sorry. I just miss your mother, that's all. It hasn't been easy without her."

"I know, I miss her too, but we're all just trying to help."

Robert stopped, then gave a small grin. "And if you really must know, I was out on a date just last week," he said with pride.

"Oh yeah?" Bobby queried, more interested than ever. "Where did you go? With whom?"

"Beth Ann McGuire."

"The librarian?" He had to hold himself back from laughing.

"Yes, and she's very nice. So keep a civil tongue in your mouth."

"Dad, she's very old, she must be close to . . ."

"Never you mind how old she is. We had a very nice time. I went to a charity book reading at her house. Had cookies, coffee, and I met some very nice lady friends of hers."

"Oh," Bobby commented and decided to say nothing further about the "date."

He took in a deep breath. It was time to discuss something he and Patti had talked about together for weeks; now it was time to finally talk to his dad about it. Gently. "Dad, I've been meaning to ask you . . . well, Patti and I . . . wanted to know . . . what if we didn't name the baby Robert? Would that be so bad?"

"Why wouldn't you call him Robert? It's a tradition," he said, his eyes and nostrils flaring. "Then you can call him Bob, Robbie, or . . ." He stood before him, his eyes narrowed, drilling his son as he awaited his response. Robert Macgregor was a traditionalist, especially when it came to anything Scottish. Tradition was life, at least in a Scottish family.

"Well, you know . . . Patti . . . she . . . we . . . were thinking, you know . . . maybe to try a different name . . . like David or something . . . or maybe Bruce or Scott. That's another good Scottish name. Right? That wouldn't be so bad, would it?"

"What? The boy's name is Robert. It's a Macgregor tradition, lad."

"And Dad, what if it is a girl? Unfortunately, we've had two sonograms, and they still can't tell us whether it's a boy or a girl."

"It'll be a boy. I promise you, it'll be a boy. I know these things. Stand tall, you're a Macgregor."

"You're right, Dad. I'm sorry I brought it up." He shook his head and took another drink from his half-empty beer. Silence descended again on father and son.

Minutes passed before his father whispered, "Bobby, what did you mean when you said . . . I might be embarrassed?" His father stood looking at him.

His son didn't really want to venture there, but maybe now was the time to clear the air. "Dad, sit down, please."

The old man's chestnut-brown eyes flared again before he took in a deep breath and sat down. He was a true Macgregor, including the temper.

"How can I say this?"

"Spit it out, Bobby. We got no secrets 'tween us."

"Okay, for one thing, Dad . . . your clothes."

"What's wrong with my clothes?" he asked, looking down at the fishing outfit he was wearing.

"Dad, your white T-shirt is gray and has so many holes in it that it looks like Swiss cheese. And your ancient deck shoes are wrapped in gray duct tape, and everyone knows it's meant to cover the holes in the soles of your shoes. And look at your jeans! They're filthy and they must be ten years old. Throw them out and buy something new. I know it goes against the grain for you to spend money on what you consider frivolous, but . . . it's up to you. Or let me buy you some clothes. Patti would love to take you clothes shopping just like Mom used to."

"I appreciate that, Bobby, but I don't care what people think of me. Besides, the tape on the soles of my deck shoes gives me added traction on the boat. My friends and family are all I care about, and that's the end of it." He took a long drink from his beer bottle, but Bobby watched as his father's left hand went down to caress the soles of his threadbare shoes. Bobby could tell he was thinking, wondering.

Finally his father's voice softened as he asked, "Let me have a look at that card again." He squinted, and then said, "Damn, Bobby, I don't have my glasses with me. Can you read it to me?"

His ploy had worked. That was the only way he could get his father to go, if he made him view it as a challenge. That had been Patti's idea.

"It says on the card, 'Coleen Callahan, Regional Bereavement Volunteer/Social Coordinator.' It lists her regular business phone number in Boca Raton. She's apparently a CEO of a big real estate company and just volunteers with this agency. The phone number is at her business office."

He rubbed the card between his fingers. "Tell you what . . . I'll give her a call if it'll make you happy." He looked closely at the card, then paused as he reflected. "I used to know a young lass in school named Coleen McGrath. Spelled her name the same crazy way, with one *l*. I really liked her. We dated for a while, feisty young thing, but she moved away and I never . . ."

His son smiled as his father tucked the card in his pocket.

His dad reached for the tray on the table he had brought outside and picked up an old, nearly empty whiskey bottle and two smudged whiskey glasses. It was a pint of thirty-year-old McClintish Scotch whiskey. He poured them each two fingers and then raised his glass high over his head in a proper salute. "To the Macgregors!"

With a smile Bobby gave the traditional response, "Long live Scotland!"

Chapter Two

Damn him. Damn him to hell. I'm an honors law school graduate, newest lawyer at my law firm, and I'm not going to have any man rule my life, no, not anymore. I need to know—and need to know now.

"Mickey?" she said from the kitchen as he poured her after-dinner drink in the other room.

"Mickey?" she shouted again.

He came walking in and snuggled up behind her. "You called, my dear?" he said, reaching his arms around her.

"Don't. We need to talk. Did you speak with your parents? The wedding is in two weeks, and I need to know if they are coming. Surely they've finalized their travel plans by now."

"I spoke with my father today, and he is in some very serious discussions with a firm in Australia. Very delicate negotiations, and he may have to leave at a moment's notice to go there."

"Well, just have him say yes, and if something comes up, I'll understand. What about your mother? Is she coming?"

His shoulders slumped, his head drooped. "Red, I just don't know what's going on with them. Believe me . . . but I promise you I'll get an answer for you by tomorrow."

"Promise?"

"I promise."

She slung her arms around his neck and kissed him. "Why don't we stay in tonight? Just you and me. What do you say?" she asked, sipping her drink.

"You want to give up attending the new art-gallery opening in Delray?"

"Pass."

"Free food."

"Double pass. I just want you, that's enough for me."

"I love you, Red, always have. We're soul mates." He paused and looked up at her. "Don't ever leave me."

"Never." He was one of the strongest-willed people she had ever met, but he had certain ideas about family that she had never understood. For some reason, people leaving scared him.

"Let's stay in, then," he said, wrapping his arms around her. "Maybe do some popcorn and watch some horror or mystery flick on TV?"

She pouted. "How about *Casablanca*? B&B—Bogart and Bergman, doesn't get any better than that." Or *Sleepless in Seattle*? Or *Love Affair*? Or *The American President*? What do you say?"

He pulled her close and whispered, "Hummm, a nice romance movie? How about a compromise, say—*Rear Window*?" He kissed her neck.

"Jimmy Stewart and Grace Kelly. Romance-mystery, the best! I would love that," she said, kissing his ear. "Unless . . ." She smiled and kissed him again, then turned out the lights and led him upstairs.

Mickey softly squeezed her hand. He felt guilty. How could he tell her without hurting her? Damn him. He had to tell her soon. *Tomorrow. I'll tell her tomorrow.*

Chapter Three

Eian Macgregor awoke to a bright Sunday morning with the Florida sunshine pouring through his bedroom window. He looked at the clock: eleven thirty. He had been up late the night before, and now his hangover was telling him he was getting too old for this kind of foolishness.

His long legs draped over the end of the bed, but he was used to it at this point in his life. When he had traveled while playing professional baseball, he would always ask for a longer bed. After a while he just stopped asking because he always got the same response: "Sorry, sir, none available." The coffeemaker in the kitchen signaled with a loud beep that his morning java was ready for him. He picked up his shorts and T-shirt off the floor, dressed, and lumbered into the bathroom to brush his teeth.

He stopped to grab a handful of the pink terry-cloth robe that hung on the back of the bathroom door. He pressed it to his face and breathed in deep, smelling the all-too-familiar sweet lilac perfume of his late wife Alice. She had been his second wife, and they had been inseparable for the last fifteen years before she finally lost her six-year battle with Alzheimer's.

He cursed the dreaded zombielike disease, which robbed people not only of their identities but also of their dignity. The last two years had been a living hell: she did not know him, or anyone else, except for those rare moments of recognition when he had carefully brushed and fixed her hair, applied her makeup, and dressed her just the way she had always done herself. It took him over an hour. When he was finished, she lifted her eyes to his, and sometimes he saw a flash of a thank-you coupled with the thought of *I love you* drifting across the wasteland of her face before she returned to the darkness of her own world. God, how he missed her, and he realized that no amount of alcohol would ever bring her back.

She had been in and out of three different health facilities when he needed help and could no longer manage her, but he always brought her home with him. It was where she wanted to be, home with her Eian.

He cried and grieved for her when she was gone. It was almost a relief that she died; her suffering was over. Now he was doing what everyone told him he should be doing, getting on with living, after having had six years carved from his life. But he didn't mind; he had loved her until the very end. He loved her now, and he missed her more than anyone could imagine.

Eian heard the front door chime alert and female voices in the background. He grabbed his coffee mug and went to investigate who would barge in on him without knocking or ringing the doorbell. He had a sinking suspicion as to her identity.

"Hello? Hello? Who is it?" he shouted.

"Oh, Eian, you're still here?" came the puzzled reply.

He recognized the high-pitched tone. It was the last voice he wanted to hear on a lazy Sunday morning. It was the voice of his stepdaughter, Laura.

"Yes, of course I'm still here. Where else would I be?"

She came into the living room, accompanied by an older woman dressed in a business suit.

Laura was always dressed in the latest fashion from her regular shopping trips to the New York boutiques. Shoes—expensive. Handbag—expensive. Watch—expensive. Her makeup and hairdo were impeccable. She worked with her father at his advertising agency, and part-time as a Realtor. She spared no expense on her clothes or on entertainment for friends or clients. She just never seemed to have time for her mother. *Her damn loss now,* thought Eian.

The woman accompanying her reached out her hand and, after introducing herself, said, "You're Eian Macgregor, the baseball player, aren't you? I listen to your radio broadcasts all the time."

"Yes, I'm Eian," he said, instinctively turning on the Macgregor charm. He smiled and held her hand as he looked her in the eye.

"I've seen your commercials on television, but I must say you are much more handsome in person."

"Thank you."

"But I've heard you do quite a lot of other things, at least that's what I read in the newspaper last week."

"I have my own sports marketing firm and work for the radio show broadcasting the Major League Baseball home games. I also work as an agent for other players, do personal appearances, autograph signings, and a lot of charity work."

"How do you manage the time to do all of that?" asked the woman, obviously interested.

The woman started to say something else but was interrupted by Laura. "I see you're still womanizing," she interjected. "I'm sorry, but I'm going to have to cut short this lovefest. We have things to do."

His first marriage, after college, had lasted only two years. Her youthful carousing when he was on the baseball circuit, coupled with his constant traveling, was too much for his new young bride. She left him while he was on the road in Kansas City, leaving only a note and a stack of unpaid bills. It was a messy divorce, and he swore he would never again lose someone he loved.

Eight years went by, and then he met Alice Cummings at an autograph session. They were married a year later. Her daughter Laura was from her first marriage. Eian had met Alice's ex-husband at a funeral years ago and had not been impressed.

"Careful of him. He's a real weasel," he remembered Alice telling him later. Laura was more like her father than her kindhearted mother. All she was ever interested in was money.

Eian turned his full attention on his stepdaughter. "I never cheated on your mother, never. I dated a lot before we got married, but I never cheated on her. And at the end . . . I was with her day and night, which is more than I can say for the likes of you."

"Believe what you want if it makes you feel better, but I know different. Besides, I had other things to do than to hear Mother tell me the same story over and over again," said Laura. "And now I don't have time for this; we have work to do."

"What do you mean, work? What's going on here? What are you doing here?"

"Well, if you'd open your mail every once in a while, you'd know what I am talking about. I'm selling the house, and you have to vacate."

"What do you mean? Selling? Vacate? I don't understand."

"The house is in mine and my mother's name, and now it belongs to me."

"Are you sure about that? I'm the spouse. And in Florida the spouse has . . ."

"As the spouse . . . you're entitled to a portion of the proceeds of the sale but only after all the house sale expenses. Of which there are many."

"Laura, I have certain legal rights. Besides, I never received any show cause or any other legal notices."

"You were sent orders to vacate the premises multiple times over the last two months, and you were supposed to have all of your things out of here by last week."

"I get all my mail, and I never got anything like that."

Her voice rose, as usual when she did not get her way. "You have one hour to pack up and leave or I'll call the police."

"Go ahead and call 'em, you little twit," he told her with a smile. "It was nice to meet you," he told the awestruck Realtor with his melting charm, and returned to the kitchen to read his newspaper and call his lawyer on his cell phone. His attorney's voice-mail message said, "Leave a message at the beep, and I'll get back to you when I return from vacation, or feel free to call my office and speak with my assistant, Amy. Have a nice day." *Sunday. Damn.*

He turned to look in the living room and saw Laura pull out her cell phone and dial a number. The police arrived at the house within ten minutes.

Laura stood by the front door, her hands on her hips, and greeted them with an angry frown, pointing at Eian, who was leaning against the door frame, drinking his coffee. "Get him out of here. Here is the vacate directive from my lawyer and the courts," she told the two officers. She folded her arms in a sulk, waiting for the officers to do their duty. The senior officer read the court order, folded it, and walked toward the kitchen. Eian sat down at the table to drink his coffee and finish his English muffin while reading the newspaper.

"I'm sorry to have to do this, Mr. Macgregor. I'm such a big fan of yours, but according to this paperwork, she does have first rights to the property. It doesn't seem right, making a man move from his own home, but according to this court order, I'm afraid I'm going to have to ask you to leave, please."

Eian wiped his mouth with his napkin and approached the small group assembled in his living room. "I see, Officer. I know you're just doing your job, but you see, my wife, the late Alice Macgregor, wrote up a life estate trust on this property before she passed away. That means that I can stay here for as long as I live, and no one can make me leave until they carry me out on a stretcher with a sheet over my head."

His little grin irritated his stepdaughter, who was fuming at being delayed in her quest to oust him. Eian had never cared for her much. All of Alice's friends came to visit, but she rarely came to see her failing mother other than call to ask her for money for some project or charity donation she was working on. And, of course, his sweet Alice always obliged.

"He does have a point, ma'am," said the older, paunchy cop.

"That document would allow him to stay here," continued the younger cop, a short-haired, brown-eyed officer in a heavily starched blue uniform.

"I don't believe it. My mother promised me this house before she died. Where is this so-called document, Eian?" she asked defiantly.

"It's in my safe-deposit box at the bank, where I keep all of my important papers." He grinned again.

"Well, let's just trot on down there and get it," she proclaimed with her hands on her hips, now smiling herself, thinking she had called his bluff.

The older officer interceded. "Ma'am, I'm afraid we'll have to wait until tomorrow to do that. It's Sunday, and the banks are closed today."

Her face grew redder and redder as she stomped her feet and spun around to leave, her real estate agent running to catch up.

"I'll see you tomorrow, Eian. Count on it!" she ranted, and slammed the door shut behind her.

They all watched her leave until the older cop turned to look at him and smiled. "You don't have any such paperwork at all, do you?"

"No, sir, I don't, but I wasn't going to give her the satisfaction of seeing me leave here with my tail between my legs. I'll be out of here before the morning and then let the lawyers straighten it out; they always do."

The younger cop blushed and asked, "Mr. Macgregor, I feel awfully funny asking this . . . but would you mind giving me your autograph?"

"Sure, I'd be happy to do that."

Eian went into his den and pulled out of his desk a promo picture from the local sports radio station he worked for in Boca Raton. In the picture he was wearing his baseball uniform. He signed it for the young cop.

"Thanks, Mr. Macgregor. Thanks a lot."

Eian walked them to the door, and the older cop stopped and asked him, "Why didn't you ever get your wife to sign something like that? You could have avoided all of this nonsense."

"Alice always said she was going to have the lawyers write one up, but I don't think she ever got around to it . . . and toward the end we had a lot of other more important things to worry about."

"I understand, but Mr. Macgregor, as a squatter we can't force you to leave the property. You have certain legal rights too, you know what I mean?"

"Yes, I'll have my attorney deal with her tomorrow."

"We won't have to be coming back here, now will we?"

"No, Officer, no problems here. Until I talk to my lawyer, I guess I'll bunk over at my brother Ryan's house for a bit."

"I am sure he'll be happy to see you."

"I'm sure; he has tons of space. Have a good day, Officer."

In the past he would have crashed on his sofa at his office in Delray, but he had hired his old friend Rose Gilardo, an interior decorator, to remodel it and make sense of the old boxes, files, and memorabilia, along with the hundreds of baseball bats, gloves, and balls. The sofa was gone. *It should be finished this week,* he thought. *I hope.*

He packed, finally tossing Alice's pink robe over his shoulder. He was ready to leave, and turned to look around his homestead one last time. "Good-bye, baby. I'll miss you, sweetie," he whispered, closing the door behind him. He loved that house.

It was only a thirty-minute drive from his home to Ryan's house on the beach. He drove up State Road A1A from his house in Lauderdale-by-the-Sea and marveled at the huge mansions going up seemingly overnight along the beach thoroughfare. The city straddled the ocean roadway, with the ocean on one side and the Intracoastal Waterway on the other.

He and Alice preferred living along the restful Intracoastal Waterway. Sitting at the breakfast table, they would occasionally see the gentle manatees slowly gliding along the water, heading south to Fort Lauderdale with only their dark-brown, leathery backs breaking the water's surface. He headed north toward his brother's house in Boca Raton. *This should be interesting,* he thought. They had not lived in the same house . . . in a long, long time.

As he drove toward his brother's beach home, he made a detour through his old Delray neighborhood, turning left onto Atlantic Avenue before making another left onto South East First Avenue. He pulled to the curb, stopping before an oversize three-acre plot of vacant land, which still had a gray, weathered **FOR SALE** sign posted at the corner.

He looked over the lot with fond recollections of his and Alice's plans to build on it. *This is where we are going to build our dream home, just for the two of us,* they would say to each other. Now it was filled with bittersweet memories. *Should I just sell it and get rid of it? Plenty of time for all those decisions later.*

Eian noticed the grass was very high and that someone had dumped some old tires and discarded a refrigerator on his property. He made a mental note to contact the property-management company to come by and take care of it. He said his good-byes, started the car, and pulled away from the curb to drive the short distance to his younger brother's house. He and Ryan together, this was going to be like old times, he thought to himself.

Chapter Four

Dr. Ryan Macgregor sat on his large patio overlooking the beach in front of his large white stucco house in Boca Raton. It was an ultra-modern three-story house with a four-car garage and so many bedrooms he had lost count.

Sitting by the pool, he was going through the motions of reading his outdated professional magazines. He bought the house because Grace loved to swim. Then he had lost her when she was biking down A1A and was killed by a hit-and-run driver. Now he sat by the pool and thought of nothing but her.

She had called him that day from the side of the road, and he remembered she had told him, "Chill the champagne, Ryan my sweet, I beat my best biking time this morning. Today is a good day, I can tell." Her voice had faded away. Then, talking with an edgy laugh, she said, "You won't believe this guy, baby . . . he's driving like a maniac. He's crazy or drunk," she shrilled. She talked faster as the fear rose in her voice. And then he heard her say, "Oh no! Oh my God! No! . . ." There was static, and then the line went dead. *Dead?* From that moment on, she was gone from his life forever.

Now he sat by the pool he had built for her, catching up on his reading, skimming through past issues of *Psychiatric Journal Review*. He knew that as a psychiatrist, he had to keep up with the latest in his field, but he could no longer tolerate the incessant medical bulletins. In addition, he was not interested in their conventions, even though they were usually held in some remote island paradise or on a luxury cruise ship. He had a good practice with another doctor, and he was good at what he did, but he could not face the truth: his Gracie was gone. As a psychiatrist, he was at a loss. What could he do? Talk himself out of it? He had lost the love of his life. It wasn't fair. Life wasn't fair.

He looked at the still water of the pool beside him and wondered how long he would have to stay under the surface before he would die . . . and join her.

What if I take the rest of the sleeping pills and just lie on the bottom and never wake up? Maybe I could just take the pills I have in the medicine bottle upstairs and just fall asleep . . . and never wake up? That should be enough to do the trick. Just lie in our bed, with thoughts of Gracie. Why wait? She is only a breath away. She would be there waiting for me.

Grace had always said he was a procrastinator and afraid to make a commitment. They dated for years until she gave him an ultimatum— get married or else. *I could join her at the bottom of the pool; it would only take . . .*

"Hello?" he heard a familiar voice call. Again, it sounded through the air: "It's me; I'm home."

"Oh my God, Gracie?" He was dozing, and his eyes began to tear as he looked into the sun at a figure approaching him.

"Dad? Daddy? Oh, there you are," said his daughter, causing his recurring dream to once again disappear in an instant. A tear still hung in his eye, unable to fall. His Gracie was gone.

"I was calling for you, Dad. Didn't you hear me?" said his tall, independent, red-haired daughter. She was the image of her mother, temper, iron will, and all. She had taken charge of everything since her mother died. In a way Ryan was glad to have her help. He was lost and adrift without his Gracie.

"Hi, Mary Katherine. I must have dozed off here by the pool. I didn't hear you come in."

Only her parents called her Mary Katherine; everyone else called her Mary Kate or clung to her childhood nickname, *Graw*, given to her by her paternal grandfather. When her grandfather first saw the screaming red-haired baby, who was delivered at his home, he said in his heavy Scottish brogue to her mother, "Hell, woman, don't worry about it, she'll *graw* out of it!" She immediately stopped crying, and the nickname Graw stuck.

Her eyes narrowed as she examined her father in the early-morning light and guessed what was going on. "I miss her too, Daddy." She kissed him on his forehead.

"What was that for?"

"Do I need a reason to kiss my only father?"

"No, no, you don't. What's up?"

"I thought Uncle Eian and Uncle Robert would be here waiting for me."

He squinted, looking up at her into the hazy morning Florida sun. "I left them a message, and Robert called back saying he would be here, but it would probably be much later in the day. He and Bobby were down in the Keys fishing. And I'm sure your uncle Eian will be here soon; it's Sunday, free food and free drinks, and he never misses a game on TV when he's not in the broadcast booth."

"Like always. Daddy, can you call them and make sure that they are here later today, definitely? I really need to talk to them and to you today." She kissed his forehead again and said, "I'll see you later, Daddy.

I am off to meet with the caterer, and then I'll come back here before I go to the office and meet a new client."

"It's Sunday, Mary Katherine. Don't they give you time off?"

"Yes, Daddy, they are very good to me there at the law firm, even though I am new there. I love my job. However, I have work to do. But make sure to call them, okay? I'll be back later. Bye, Daddy. Love you."

She kissed his cheek and, like a whirlwind, was gone.

Chapter Five

Sunday morning Robert Macgregor sat on the old wooden chair on the porch of his seaside bungalow and sipped his coffee as he watched the glory of the beautiful sunrise over the Keys. Bobby had left hours earlier, but the elder Macgregor was lingering as long as he could. He didn't want to leave.

He secured the boat to the dock for rough weather, shut off the hot-water heater and the main water supply for the small house, locked the doors, and closed the shutters at the cabin. *Time to go,* he thought. Then he started on his long drive home to Boynton Beach, some five hours away.

The narrow two-lane road leaving Key West had but a few cars heading north from the southern Keys. He loved life in the Keys. On the drive home, he had a long time to think about *his* life.

Maybe I should just move down to the cabin permanently and then head north for family events. Bobby can run the store. I have everything I need here at the cabin. I can hunt and fish anytime I like, and the town of Key West is only minutes away. That makes sense. Yes, that's what I'll do. I'll just wait until after the wedding before I tell everyone. There is plenty of time. Time to get on with my life. He could always come up for a few days to see everybody, including his new grandson. Now content and with a plan formulating in his mind, he began to hum an old Harry Chapin song, "Mail Order Annie," a familiar tune from his childhood. *It was one of Tess's favorites. Yes, that is exactly what I'll do.*

Five hours later Robert turned off I-95 at the Boynton Beach exit and headed west on Boynton Beach Boulevard. He passed a golf course and a country club and then a canal, and finally a cornfield. He made a sharp turn onto a narrow, dusty road running beside the canal, which led to his home. At the end of the dead-end road, he stopped in front of a solitary house with a view of the seventh fairway of the nearby golf course on the other side of the canal. He liked to tease his younger brother Ryan, the doctor, because he too had a waterfront home. The only difference was that Ryan had paid millions of dollars more for his.

Robert's two-bedroom cottage was small, with a porch at the front and the back. The front entrance featured a leaded glass door, which he had salvaged from the demolition of an old mansion nearby. He had also secured matching twin French doors for the rear, off the living room. There was a broad expansive deck off the back, with a boat dock and a fishing pier in the canal. He had everything he needed right here and knew he would miss it when he moved to Key West.

"I'm home," he said aloud to the empty house as he walked inside, and upon hearing no response, he repeated himself. "I'm home!" A mouse scurried from the mass of discarded cartons of Chinese food in the corner of the kitchen.

The pungent odor of half-eaten pizzas, emanating from a pile of pizza boxes stacked high on the kitchen table, welcomed him as he entered. Inside, the floor of the house was littered with newspapers, dirty clothes, fast-food containers, beer bottles, fishing gear, and soda cans. It was hard to tell the color of the carpet underneath all the clutter inside the house. The kitchen sink was filled with half-empty soda and beer glasses, and stacks of plates with strands of spaghetti still clinging to them.

The master bedroom contained an unmade king-size bed with the bedsheets bunched together at the end of the mattress. Pillows were scattered about the floor. The bed was pushed against the window, the heavy, dark mahogany headboard still stored in the garage attached to the house.

He looked around the small house and knew what Tess would say if she saw it. Since she had passed away two years earlier, he had kept meaning to clean the place up, but never seemed to find the time. His house and his life . . . were in shambles.

He looked around his home. *Just because I'm living alone does not mean I need to live like a pig. Today's the day,* he told himself. If he was going to rejoin the human race as he had promised his son, he had to start now. *Let's clean up!* He grabbed a large black contractor's trash bag from the garage and started shoving piles of trash inside, soon filling it. He reached for another one. Then another. He soon had a pile of six trash bags outside before taking a break, grabbing a beer and a leftover half-eaten pizza from the fridge. He popped the pizza in the oven and set it at 350 degrees. He filled another three black plastic trash bags. It was then he noticed the message light flashing on his ancient answering machine, informing him he had two new messages, and pressed the button.

"Hey, bro, this is Ryan. Don't forget to come on over Sunday afternoon. Mary Katherine wants to talk with the three of us—together. If you speak to Eian, remind him as well. Hope you had a good trip to the Keys. See ya. Bye for now."

The second message was from his son, Bobby. "Hi, Dad, I really enjoyed the week. Don't forget to telephone that Callahan woman on Monday. I'll call you tomorrow night to see how your conversation went. Love ya." He pulled the card from his pocket and thumbed the name and number. *Tomorrow. I'll call her tomorrow.*

The phone rang; it was Ryan. "Where the hell are you? Mary Katherine was already here; she was looking for you and Eian."

"I just got in from Key West. Now I'm cleaning up the place a bit."

"Well, you better get your ass over here, pronto. And yes, I have plenty of beer. See ya soon, brother. Bye."

He grabbed his beer in one hand and the cooler filled with the fish fillets in the other and was out the door. It was not a long drive, but it was worlds away. Ryan lived facing the ocean in the high-rent district just outside Boca Raton. His house was a big white beach house with a pool, but Ryan said it always felt so empty now with Gracie gone.

When he pulled into Ryan's driveway, he noticed Eian's SUV parked in front of the garage. The courtyard was large enough to hold ten cars.

Hail, hail, the gang's all here! Robert grinned, thinking of his two younger brothers waiting for him inside.

He walked down the terrazzo sidewalk lined with pink-and-purple bougainvillea vines, with their blossoming flowers dripping from the white stucco walls that surrounded the courtyard. The fragrant bouquet was welcoming. The scent reminded him of sweet honeysuckle. Mum and Da had had them at home when the brothers were growing up in Georgia. He did not bother to ring the doorbell. This was family; this was home, especially after everything the three of them had been through.

Ryan's furnishings were very modern, mainly glass and chrome, and white leather furniture. One of the top decorators from a chic Boca Raton boutique had decorated it. The house was monochromatic, all in white, except for one huge painting hanging over the fireplace, done in subtle blues and bright reds. Gracie had painted it in one of her many creative moments.

"Hey, bros, the good-looking one is here," Robert announced, opening the front door.

"Yeah, well, the smart one is already here," joked Ryan.

"Hey, let's not forget the famous one, the one all the ladies love," chimed in Eian.

Robert set the cooler down on the tiled floor of the kitchen.

"What'cha got in there?" asked Eian.

"Cobia fillets, fresh caught. Bobby and I just caught them yesterday. Want me to grill up some? Ryan, what about you? You said you got beer?" he asked in rapid succession as he opened the huge subzero refrigerator.

"Yeah, I'll have a beer and some of that fish," said Eian. "I'm starvin'."

"Yeah, well, homelessness will do that to you. Besides, you're always hungry," said Ryan in jest.

"What do you mean, homeless? What happened to you?" asked Robert as he continued to search the fridge for beer.

Ryan chimed in, "Robert, get this. Laura came by and evicted him. Nice in-laws, huh? So Eian is staying with me for a couple of days until he can find someplace else to live or work it out through their attorneys. Can you believe that, his only daughter evicting him?" Ryan started to laugh and soon could not stop himself.

"Stepdaughter, please," Eian interjected, his face turning red, showing his annoyance, before he too began to laugh.

Robert was amused as he imagined his tall, famous, baseball-playing brother being thrown out of his own home.

"She evicted you . . . from your own home? I'll be damned," Robert said, laughing at the turn of events.

"That's true family love," joked Ryan, still smiling.

"Ryan, where the hell is the goddamn beer?" Bob asked.

"Robbie, look in the beer chiller on the side of the dishwasher, there, next to the wine cooler."

"Got it! For Christ's sake, college boy, you have separate refrigerators for food, beer, and wine? God, some people live really well."

"Don't start on me, brother."

"I'm just saying that some people live very well and—"

"Hey, can you two cut it out?" interrupted Eian. "I'm hungry. Robert, are those fish steaks done yet?"

"I'm on my way, now that I've found the goddamn beer!" he shouted. "Beer fridge," he said, muttering under his breath. "What'll they think of next?"

"What'd you say?" asked Ryan.

"Nothin'. Do you want some fish or not?"

"Yeah, I guess so. Hey, Bob, do me a favor and don't grill those in the house. Take them outside and cook them on the barbecue grill. I don't want the house to smell like fish for weeks." Ryan never grilled or cooked fish in the house—too messy, too smelly.

More muttering about a beer fridge came from Robert as he slid open the door and made his way to the outside grill.

"Put the baseball game on, will you, Ryan? Use the big screen," Eian said. He switched the channels back and forth, trying to watch two games at one time, until Robert came back into the kitchen. The constant brotherly banter between the two continued for the next fifteen minutes until they heard movement from the outside deck.

"Fish steaks are done! Grab some plates and clear a space on the table. We need knives and forks. Let's go! Who's winning?"

"The Yankees!"

"No!"

"Hey, guys, what do you say we eat in the dining room?" Ryan chimed in nervously as he buzzed around them, envisioning spilled beer and fish stains on his expensive Italian white leather sofa or worse, his expensive Persian rug. "Hmm? Okay? What do you say? We'll be more comfortable in there, and it'll be easier to clean up and . . . ," Ryan said, but his pleas went unnoticed.

"Nah, this is okay, Ryan. Don't worry about us. We'll be fine. We're good." They both looked at the TV screen, shouting. "Come on, hit the ball!" Eian and Robert yelled at the batter on the huge screen. "Damn!"

They watched the rest of the game and then switched to an intense soccer match, the proud Scottish Aberdeen team playing against its fiercest rival, Manchester United. Neither team scored for the first half, until Aberdeen scored one goal at the whistle.

"Ryan, don't you have any Scottish milk here at all?" asked Robert, searching the kitchen for a bottle of Scotch.

"Check his whiskey fridge," yelled Eian in his tongue-in-cheek way.

"Funny," Ryan replied, "I don't think I have any whiskey, Robbie. If I do, it'll be in the liquor cabinet in my office. Bottom shelf."

While the rest of the house was filled with modern furniture, glass, chrome, and Italian leather, Ryan's office had their father's old polished cherry desk and worn leather executive chair. A picture of the five of them at the lake sat prominently on his desk. Da was still alive. Mum was smiling. Good times.

A few minutes later, Robert came in and said, "Here we go," holding a bottle of prime Scotch whiskey in his hand, high over his head. "Now we can have a true party." They trooped into the kitchen for ice and glasses.

Soon the whiskey bottle was half-empty on the kitchen table, and they were having a grand time simply being together, joking, laughing, just as when they were younger.

Finally Eian shouted to his brothers, "Hey, let's go out on the town and have a really good time. I know a place where they have dancing girls, lots of booze, and we can enjoy ourselves. What do you say, guys? Huh? Make a night of it and we can maybe even . . . ?" He turned to look at his brothers, who were standing in front of him staring at something behind him.

He turned to see what they were staring at and why they had not answered him. It was Graw.

"Ah . . . hiya, Mary Katherine," Eian muttered. "We were just talking about you. Come on in, Graw. We've been waiting for you to get here, right, guys?"

"Yes, I'm sure you have," she said, giving them all the evil eye. "I need to talk to you, all of you. Out there," she ordered. The three tall brothers towered over the tiny redhead as they shuffled back into the living room and took their seats to listen to what she had to say. She picked up the remote and clicked the TV off.

"Okay. I'll be brief. Thanks for coming today." She sounded as if she were giving a business presentation. "I just have a couple of things to go over with you and then you can go about your business, but no dancing girls, understand? All right? Besides, you boys are too drunk to drive anywhere."

"Oh, Mary Katherine, we were just joking. We were going to—" started her uncle Eian.

"Give me a break, and don't you 'Mary Katherine' me. I'm no dummy," she lectured them, wagging her finger.

The three brothers were sitting on the long leather sofa in the living room facing her. The scene was reminiscent of a schoolteacher in front of her classroom, rather than a young woman about to lecture the elders of her family.

"Listen to me," she started solemnly. "These past two years have not been good years for the Macgregor clan. We lost our best . . . our dearest." Her voice began to tremble.

"Over the past two years we have lost Mommy, Auntie Alice, and Aunt Tess. We miss 'em all." The mere mention of the names of the missing hushed the room. She stopped for a moment before resuming.

"Uncle Eian has done his very best to get out and meet people and make new friends, and get on with his life. Now we just need to have some of those women work in a job that allows them to keep their clothes on." The ice was broken as the three brothers laughed and kidded the celebrity in the family. They began to joke among themselves.

"Okay, okay, now listen up. Hey, guys, quiet, please." The room became still.

"Uncle Robert, we all miss Aunt Tess so very much. I know you started out with group counseling, but that seems to have tapered off. I want you to rededicate yourself to attending one of those sessions or one of those new social programs and get out and meet some people. Talk to them and listen to what they have to say. They have experienced the same kind of loss that you have. I think it will really help you. And that's what Tess would've wanted you to do. Okay?"

"Yeah, okay. Funny you should mention that, Graw," he said, as he pulled the business card from his shirt pocket. "I just got the name of someone who coordinates different programs locally. I plan to call her first thing tomorrow."

"Good," and her eyes narrowed, giving him the *look*. "Make sure you do. I'll be checking back to see how it went." Then she turned to her father. "And Daddy, almost two years ago we lost Mommy, and I know it hasn't been easy on you. It hasn't been easy for me either, losing Mommy, starting a new job, and looking in on you. We'll never stop grieving. I've always dreamed of Mommy being there for my wedding. Helping me put on my wedding dress, my makeup, and just being there for me." The strong-willed Scottish woman stopped, wiped a tear from the corner of her eye, and looked at all of them. Today she was the true head of the household. *A glass of Scottish milk would go down good,* she thought to herself. This was tougher than she had thought it would be. She pressed on.

"We miss them all and always will, but we know that each and every one of them would have wanted us to get on with our lives, and that's what we are going to do, starting now. I have some things that I am going to need all of you to do for me. I'm getting married in two weeks, and you all promised me months ago you would learn to dance so you could dance with me at my wedding." She looked at each of them and gave them all the evil stare. "And that hasn't happened. So . . . I've bought dance lessons for each and every one of you." She could hear them grumble.

"I can dance, Graw," said Robert. "You know that. Hell, I been dancing since I was little up at the Scottish-American Club down the road in Lake Worth. The three of us just went two weeks ago to the Scottish Highlands Club and wore our dress kilts and all."

"Uncle Robert, that's Scottish swing. That's not dancing."

"I dance a bit too," said Eian.

"Yeah, I know, a little bit of this and a little bit of that. You probably dance the best of the clan, except for Daddy—and he hasn't danced in years."

"I'm not taking any lessons, nor dancing with another woman. I only danced with your mother, nobody else. Never have and never will," said her belligerent father.

"You will now! You'll take lessons and you'll dance or . . . ," she said with her hands on her hips, glaring at her father. "I have bought all three of you dance lessons starting this Tuesday night. I set the first one up for five p.m.—sharp! You only need to learn a few dance patterns for the wedding, and don't worry, I'll lead. You will all go together on Tuesday and then arrange your next classes with the dance instructor. Her name is Alexi Cassini. Here's her card. She's a champion professional dancer and dance instructor from Argentina, and I told her not to take any guff from any of you." She let her gaze settle on each one to tell them she meant business.

"She has also been instructed that if you don't show up, or if you give her any problems"—she turned to look each of them in the eye—"she's to call me, and I will personally take care of it. Do you understand?" She stood looking at them. She was serious.

"Yeah, yeah, yeah," they grumbled.

"My dream was to dance the foxtrot with my two uncles and"—she turned to her father, pointing at him—"I want to dance the traditional *Tatusiu Waltz*, Daddy's waltz, with my father. It has always been my dream. So don't screw around with my dreams—do you hear me? All of you." She spoke it like a command.

"What's this Tatusiu waltz?" Eian asked Ryan.

"It's a father-and-daughter first dance," he whispered. "Polish tradition. Remember, Gracie was Polish?"

"Yeah, yeah, yeah," they rumbled again.

"And finally, guys, can you please—" Her cell phone rang, and they jumped from their seats. "Hold on, I'm not finished yet. Keep your seats."

She looked at the caller ID, and a smile lit her face. "Hiya, Mickey!" She turned away to talk to her fiancé.

"Hey, girl. How's it going with the gang there?"

"Oh, just some grumbling and such, but they took it well. I'll be leaving here soon. Call me at home, all right? Love ya."

"Love ya too, bye."

Turning back to them on the sofa, she said, "Where was I?"

"Wait a minute, when do we get to know this Mickey of yours better?" asked Robert. "We only met him that one time at the Thanksgiving party. Is he a ghost or something?"

"No, he's not. He just travels a lot for business."

Theirs had been a whirlwind courtship. He had swept her off her feet and proposed six weeks later. She had hired a wedding planner to help with all the details, and now the date was fast approaching.

"Well, I'm having dinner this Thursday with him and Daddy. Next week he'll meet all three of you at Duke's Tuxedo Shop on Linton for a tuxedo fitting. The four of you can go out to dinner together afterward. Just don't give him a hard time, okay?" She softened her tone and said to the trio, "Oh, and one last thing . . . I want you all to bring dates to my wedding."

"What?" they all howled in unison.

"You heard me, and . . . this is not a request. It's time for the three of you to rejoin the human race again. And by the way, clean this place up. It's a mess. You have beer bottles, whiskey glasses, and pizza boxes everywhere."

"Pizza! Oh my God!" shouted Robert as he sprang to his feet. "I gotta go. I forgot, I left a pizza in the oven."

She hollered at him as he ran for the door, "Don't forget, Uncle Bob, Tuesday is your first dance class. Don't be late."

His tires squealed loudly down the driveway as he sped away, hoping it was not too late. He drove as fast as he could toward home.

As he approached his street, racing down Boynton Beach Boulevard, he saw the flames rising above the tree line from three blocks away. He turned onto the gravel road leading to his house. It was blocked by fire trucks, police cars, and an ambulance, with their red, blue, and yellow lights flashing in his driveway. He could only stand there and watch his house be consumed by the flames as they blazed high in the sky.

Hours later he realized the house was a total loss as he walked through it searching for anything that had been spared. The tall Scotsman's shoulders drooped as he walked amid the still-smoldering rubble. Everything he had had was gone. The only things he had left were his memories. Gone. Now he would even have to find a place to stay. What was he going to do?

When he turned around, he saw his two brothers there, standing beside him. They all joined together, wrapping their arms around each other.

"Everything will be okay. We can rebuild it, Bob, better than before. You'll see," said Eian.

"Grab your things, you're staying with me," said Ryan.

Robert turned to have one last look at the smoldering ruins. His home was gone, but not his memories. Time to move on.

Chapter Six

Michael Thompson, Mickey to his friends, listened to her voice on voice mail before ending his call. No answer. Her cell-phone message box was full. Where was she? He tried again and finally left a message on her machine at home. "Graw, are you there? Call me when you get this message. Love ya." *She must be out and about,* he thought to himself.

Mickey loved her and trusted her, even though they had known each other for only a little over six months. He did not normally give of his emotions so freely, but he had been in love with her from the moment they met. He believed in fate, and as fate would have it, he was in love with a Macgregor. Head over heels in love.

They had met at a charity dance event his company was sponsoring for the House of Ruth. They clicked immediately—like a match and gunpowder. At first they fought every other day, then made up at night. They both were headstrong and iron-willed. Friends said it would last only a week, but they endured.

He had never felt this way about anyone else before and had asked her to marry him six weeks later. Much to his surprise, she had accepted. How he loved that fiery redhead. Yelling at him at the top of her lungs one minute, and wrapping her arms around him, kissing him, the next.

He stood in his penthouse office, high above the city of Boca Raton. He looked at his reflection in the tall window and instinctively touched the wavy white streak in his hair for good luck. He would need it for his meeting today.

As a kid Mickey had lackluster grades in school. His teachers told his father he was not very motivated about anything except soccer. He would practice his kicking at least two hours every night after school. His goal was to kick a soccer ball through a swinging tire to score a point. He always imagined it was the winning point. He kept trying.

One Sunday night his father drove him to a nearby practice field. His dad was good that way—taking him to practice, games, and tryouts for the new kids' league. Mickey wanted to make the team so bad he was willing to practice day and night. The skies were overcast that day and threatening rain. His dad watched and waited while sitting under a nearby tree.

That gray day Mickey had spent the last hour trying to perfect his technique, but to no avail. It began to thunder and lightning, and soon began to rain. It was getting late. One more kick, he promised his father, and then they could leave.

"Just one more, Dad," Mickey pleaded.

"All right, just one more, but hurry; I don't like the looks of that sky."

He was determined to hit his target, and he raised his foot and kicked the ball. It sailed right for the center of the swinging tire, but right before it did, he was struck. A crack of lightning at his feet sent him hurtling through the air, and he landed against a tree with a broken leg and two fractured ribs. He never saw the point being scored.

When he woke two days later in the hospital, he remembered nothing of the event, but life had changed for young Mickey. His father, a single parent, had died from the lightning strike. A wealthy Scottish family Mickey had worked for—cutting grass, shoveling snow, and washing their cars—adopted him. They lived near his home just outside Boston and had grown fond of him.

He had worked in the family's real estate business, Boston Real Estate Advisors, since high school. They started him at the bottom, working for minimum wage as a janitor during the summer, and he worked his way up. The family was known to be tough but fair in business dealings, and over the years, the company and the family prospered as a result.

The accident and the loss of his father changed him: he became more aggressive after the incident and went from a carefree, happy-go-lucky kid to a very intensely dedicated young man. The lightning also changed his appearance, giving him a distinctive white streak in his ink-black hair that extended from his forehead to the back of his head. When he was angry, his dark eyes flashed an intense red, cobra-like warning to those foolish enough to cross this tall, muscular man. Very few people ever did.

Mickey dialed her number again. No answer. *Sunday? Where is she?* he thought to himself as he watched a black-and-gold helicopter flash by his office window, heading for the rooftop heliport of the building. The side of the copter was emblazoned with a large initial *R* painted in bright gold. He was here. The one and only Fabian Rumpe.

Mickey's office was the corner suite on the top floor of the Boston Real Estate Advisors office building. The office was carpeted in white plush Berber wool, and original modern artwork adorned the walls. The floor-to-ceiling windows behind Mickey's broad oak desk provided a splendid view of downtown Boca Raton to the west and the Atlantic Ocean to the east. The view was magnificent, and many times calming, but not that day.

He heard the engine of the helicopter cease. Mickey was ready for him.

Minutes later, when the door opened, the flamboyant presence of the famed Fabian Rumpe filled the lavish office. He walked in with his arms spread wide and a smile on his face the size of Manhattan. The pompous developer was a study in false bravado and joked with an uneasy laugh—always at the expense of others. Mickey did not care for him much.

"Fabian, good to see you again. Have a seat and make yourself comfortable," Mickey said in the most gracious voice he could muster. "Can I get you anything to drink?"

"Scotch, or I think you call it mother's milk." He laughed hard, almost coughing, as if he was making fun of Mickey's heritage. Mickey let it slide.

"If you don't mind, I'll join you," Mickey said, handing him a glass of the finest premium Scotch available anywhere. His extended Scottish family had connections in Inverness, who sent him two cases of their finest private-label Scotch every year for his birthday.

He surveyed Rumpe sitting before him and almost laughed. He was tall, with a strawberry-blond pompadour hairstyle that was fifteen years out of date. His custom-made suit was oversize to hide his growing heft. The jacket was buttoned in the center to disguise his ever-present girdle, which was squeezing him tight. He looked very uncomfortable.

Mickey thought of him as a buffoon, but knew he was not to be taken lightly. He was shrewd and still a considerable force in real estate. It did not pay to make enemies in this business. Mickey knew that, but he had work to do. *Be firm, but tread lightly.*

"Not bad stuff," Rumpe chortled, raising his glass. "I'll have to send you some of mine. I get it directly from my own discount distillers in Miami. My stuff is the greatest." He gulped down his glass of fine sipping whiskey.

Must not have been too bad. He drank the whole thing. Easy now. I don't like this man, never did. He's a bully, but this is business.

The developer coughed, then said, "Mickey, let me get right to the point. I know you're planning to build a big hotel resort complex on the ocean, near Gulf Stream. I will consider letting you use my name as the headliner on the marquee in exchange for a twenty percent cut of the gross. You know my name will bring customers in by the droves. It will tell them instantly that it's quality and pack 'em in." Rumpe smiled that silly smirk of his. His forehead began to bead with tiny drops of sweat that ran down onto his shirt collar.

Rumpe picked up the empty glass and promptly set it down again after not receiving an offer of a refill.

"Well, it's certainly something to consider, Fabian, along with the other proposals we have received."

"Others? Like who? I was told we were the only ones you're considering. Did I waste my time coming down from New York to this malaria hellhole?"

"All I am saying is we're considering all of our options, but I will also tell you that no one is demanding a twenty percent cut of the gross and with no skin in the game. That's a little excessive."

"But look what you get for it. I can . . ."

I've had enough of his bragging. Time someone cut him down to size. Enough.

"Like what, Fabian? How much money are you willing to pump into the construction costs? Our total costs will be well over six hundred million dollars. Can I count you in for twenty percent of that? Your share would only be a little over a hundred and twenty million. Cash. Can I sign you up? How about it?"

"This is bull. I thought you'd be reasonable about this. You're still the same stubborn punk, and you'll never change." He shifted gears with a veiled threat: "You know I have many friends in the construction business, the banks and . . . in the unions; you might just need those friends one day, my friend. Your last chance, my Irish prince."

"I'm Scottish," Mickey said, standing. "If you are going to make an ethnic slur, Fabian, at least get it right. I think we've concluded our business here."

"Are you dismissing me, you little jerk? Do you know who you're talking to?"

Mickey turned, and his eyes flashed red for the briefest moment; he had heard enough and was not going to take it anymore, at least not from the likes of Rumpe. "Yeah, I'm looking at a guy who's living off his past building projects and trying to suck the lifeblood of the business that sent him to the top. You have a reputation for not treating your employees well, or your staff, or your suppliers. Most of them are suing you just to get paid. So yes, I can understand why you would want this piece of business. To save your ass." Mickey took a deep breath before continuing.

"And I expect the next thing out of your mouth would be a demand for an advance against the earnings that, quite frankly, I don't think you ever do anything to earn." He paused and said, his voice calmed, "Fabian, I saw you as a favor to my father, but I run the company's operations independently here in Florida. I think I can handle this deal well enough without you."

The New Yorker looked at the tall Scotsman and said, "Well, I guess there's nothing else to talk about." He stood and turned to leave after shaking his hand. "Hey, Mickey, how's that hot little redhead of yours? Wow, what a body on her. She's a real hottie! If you ever break it off with her, and she wants the taste of a real man, give her my number. I'd like a shot at that myself."

Mickey turned to look away, not wanting Rumpe to see his anger. His eyes flamed red, hotter than white fire, at the lusty mention of his fiancée, especially from some lowlife like Rumpe. His hands closed tight into fists. *Easy now. Just get him out of here.*

"Thank you for coming today, Mr. Rumpe. Have a good day." Mickey turned to walk him to the door. "I think you should leave— now, before you make me angry."

"You'll regret this, friend."

"I'm not your friend, Rumpe."

Careful, Mickey. This had not turned out the way he expected. What would his father say?

Chapter Seven

The four-story glass-and-chrome Callahan Building sat in the heart of Boca Raton's premier business district, under the shady umbrella of two huge ancient mahogany trees. On Sunday only the security guard stationed in the white-marble-tiled lobby was working, and he greeted Diane Callahan warmly as she came inside.

"Mornin', ma'am," he said with a familiar smile.

"Morning, Seymour. I saw her Mercedes in her parking spot, so I must assume she's upstairs?"

"Yes, ma'am, been here for hours." He leaned forward to whisper to her, "She's been doing that a lot here lately, ma'am."

"I know. Thanks, Seymour. How's Mary and the kids?"

"She's just fine, ma'am, thank you. Can you believe it, the eldest is graduating from high school?"

"Little Henry? Graduating from high school. Oh, sweet mother of God. Where does the time go?"

"Somethin' else, isn't it? You turn around and you wonder where the years went. You know what I mean, Miss Diane?"

"Sure do. You take care now." She pressed the elevator button and stepped inside to make the short journey to the fourth floor. When she alighted, she looked around. It always felt strange coming in on a Sunday—so quiet. There were no ringing phones, no hustle and bustle of employees, no clients visiting, and lots of empty desks and darkened conference rooms. She walked to her mother's corner office, which was right next to hers, and saw the light on there.

"Mother?" she shouted as she neared her office and then saw her sitting at her desk, poring over statistical reports. "I should have known I'd find you here."

Coleen Callahan looked up from the spreadsheets on her desk and peered over her glasses at her daughter before returning to her work. "I won't be long," she muttered while she waited for the onslaught of questions that was sure to come.

"So this is where you've been hiding when I call you and you don't answer your phone."

"I've got a big presentation and meeting tomorrow. I want to be on my game."

"Mom, we need to talk," Diane said as she laid her purse on the sofa and settled into one of the black leather chairs facing her desk. "You brought me into Dad's business four years ago with the promise that you would slow down and ease out of the day-to-day stuff, before turning it over to me. You're working more hours now than ever before. Right?"

Her mother slumped back in her chair. "Yes," she sighed.

"And another thing, we talked about you selling the house; it's way too big just for you. I don't see any of that happening. Maybe I should just go back to work at Philby's."

"Diane, honey, I know . . ."

"Don't 'Diane, honey' me. I know all your tricks . . . and your secrets."

Her mother looked away, and her glance caught the family photo of her and her deceased husband, along with a freckled little girl playing in the sand at the beach. The three of them. It was a happy photo. He was healthy. She winced as she tried to hold back the tears. "I just miss him so much," she whispered. "I know I should be ready to move on, but . . . I just can't. We had something special, something most other couples never achieve. I miss him so much."

"I know it's been five years since we lost Dad, but look what you've accomplished in that time. You built this tiny commercial real estate company into the second largest in the state. Now you have conglomerates that wouldn't even talk to you years ago, knocking on our door wanting to buy the company."

Coleen looked at her daughter, her business partner, and said firmly, "It's not for sale."

She had a reputation for being a tough but fair negotiator, one who was loved by her employees. On her desk sat two engraved walnut plaques. One read,

LEAVE YOUR EXCUSES AT THE DOOR.
WE'LL FIND A SOLUTION TOGETHER.

The second one proudly proclaimed,

COLEEN CALLAHAN
CEO: THE CALLAHAN CORPORATION

"I think Dad would be proud of the new Callahan Corporation and the way you've grown it. However, I think he would also say . . . it's time for things to change, to move on. Maybe even find someone else to help fill your life and your time."

Her head snapped toward her only daughter. "Never! There will never be anyone to take your father's place. Now just go on . . . I'll be done here shortly. Leave me be."

"I didn't mean that he would take Daddy's place; it's just that everyone needs somebody to talk to, to be with, to warm up to, and share a life with, that's all I meant, Mom."

"I know, dear heart, but every time I think about dating or going out with someone, I just . . ."

"I know. It hurts." Diane stood and hugged her. "I love you. Come on, time to leave."

"You go on, dear. Just a little bit more. I'll be fine. This is a perfect time for me to get some work done. I'll see you at dinner."

"Mom, you're playing in the club's mixed-doubles tennis championship later on today. Or did you forget about that?"

"Oh . . . no, I didn't forget. Of course not. I'm sure Perry will be calling me soon to remind me. Just what I need, another trophy. This is the last year I'm playing in that damn thing, I swear."

"Yeah, that's what you said last year and the year before. The truth is, you enjoy the competitive contest, and you love to win. That's what drives you. Well, now maybe it's time for you to slow down, like you promised."

"I'll think about it. I've had my turn at winning in tennis. Maybe you should go out for it next year . . . with Perry. Although he would never, ever say anything, I think he's kind of sweet on you."

"Mother, my divorce just became final, so the last thing I need now is another husband, and besides, he's an employee, remember?"

"No, Diane, he's a partner," she said sternly. "Senior vice president of insurance sales and operations here at Callahan, not just an employee. Don't forget that."

"I won't forget, Mother. How can I? You're constantly reminding me."

Coleen started to respond, but instead turned back to the computer and stared at the screen filled with rows and columns of numbers, then gazed out the huge glass windows beyond her desk. "Maybe you're right; I could use a change of scenery. But you're one to talk; you live the business twenty-four-seven."

Words were on her daughter's lips, a sharp response, but instead she thought better of it and said, "Well? Are we leaving?"

"Let me just finish this last . . ." She was interrupted by the sound of a ringing phone and reached to answer it. "Coleen Callahan. Can I help you?" Her face lit up with a smile. "Hi, Perry. No, no, of course not. I didn't forget. I just stopped by the office to pick up some performance reports for our meeting tomorrow. As a matter of fact, I was just getting ready to leave and change clothes." She covered the mouthpiece and whispered, "He is so nice and pleasant all the time. So polite. How does he succeed in sales?"

"In spite of himself," her daughter whispered in return while making a face. Diane picked up her purse and her mother's briefcase, dangling it in front of her, motioning that it was time to leave.

Perry Winston had been the young owner of a smaller but very successful agency that Coleen had bought two years earlier. Part of the sales agreement was that after the merger, he would be not only in charge of operations but also part owner of the combined larger company—as a partner.

Coleen nodded. "Okay, then, I'll see you for lunch." Then she paused to listen to what he was saying before she responded, "I don't know if Diane will be there for lunch, but I am sure she'll come to cheer us on to victory. See you soon. Bye."

Coleen turned off her computer and said, "Come on, let's go. It's too nice a day to be stuck inside."

Her daughter smiled.

"Join me for lunch?" Her mother asked with her trademark grin.

"Mother. You're incorrigible."

Chapter Eight

"Miss Macgregor, I really want to thank you for coming in on a Sunday to meet with me."

Mary Kate smiled and nodded for the woman to proceed. Even though she was new to the firm, she had been involved with pro bono abuse and divorce cases before and knew how these cases turned out—badly.

The woman swallowed. "Well, I'm not sure where to begin. And I'm a little nervous; I've never been to a lawyer before."

"I promise, I don't bite." She smiled, trying to make the nervous woman a little more comfortable. "Start wherever you want, or try starting at the beginning. And please call me Mary Kate."

The woman smiled and set her coffee cup on the glass cocktail table. "Of course. My name is Calley Terrell. I've known Phil, my husband, my whole life. We dated through high school and college, and when all of my other friends got married, we just followed along with them. Things were going great until they closed the office location where he worked and he lost his job. He tried, but couldn't find a new job, even though he looked everywhere." Mary Kate offered her a tissue.

"He tried the Internet, family connections, old bosses, and the newspapers, and even called all of his old friends." She dabbed her eyes with the tissue.

"Take your time. Would you like some more coffee?"

"No, thank you."

"What does Phil do?" she asked, looking over the information sheet her new client had completed and handed her.

"He was a salesman, working over the road for a glass company, and he was real good at it. After they closed the office here, the company wanted us to move back to the New Jersey home office, but we just love it here in Florida and hated the winters back home. My mom begged me to come back to Parsippany and move in with them. Just until we got settled, but Phil had too much pride to do that, said he wasn't going to take any handouts from anybody. Well, then I got pregnant, and he took a job with a builder to pay the bills and a night job with a car dealer. He had a misunderstanding with his boss and got fired . . . he started drinking and then taking drugs. He was a different man, not the man I married." She paused to stifle a tear and hold back her emotions.

"At first he just drank on the weekends, and then he began to drink nights, when he came home from the dealership. Soon it was nonstop. He had an accident with our car and borrowed one from the dealer to use; he told me it was a 'loaner.' The police came to our house and arrested him. The dealership didn't press charges, but only on the condition he quit his job." She stopped and looked away, putting her hand to her mouth.

"Then it began. He didn't mean it, really, he didn't. He was drunk and depressed when he first hit me. He apologized and felt bad, bought me flowers, but then a few days later he had a couple of drinks and got mad when the television broke—then he hit me again. I went to go to the other room, and he grabbed me and . . . broke my arm. I was in pretty bad shape for a while, and three weeks later . . . I lost the baby."

Mary Kate moved to sit with her on the sofa and put an arm around her to comfort her. "That will never happen again," she whispered to the distraught woman sobbing next to her.

They talked for more than an hour in the young attorney's office. Her newest client poured out her heart about her dreams and aspirations—now all gone as she struggled in her abusive relationship. Calley had clearly been trying to be brave and hold back the tears, but soon a steady stream began to roll down her cheeks. "I don't know what I'm going to do."

"Calley, listen to me . . . ," Mary Kate said, handing her another tissue.

The young woman paused for a moment, making a valiant effort to stop crying. "I don't even know how I'm going to pay you. Or where I'm going to stay or . . ."

Mary Kate looked at her and said in a comforting voice, "There's no charge for this service. Our firm believes in giving back to the community. But first things first. Where are you staying?"

"Home . . . he doesn't know I'm here."

"Hmm. Do you have any friends you can stay with for a few days until we get the paperwork processed?"

"My girlfriend Heather and her family live down the street from us, but she is out of town until Wednesday. Her husband took her and the kids to the theme parks in Orlando."

"Well, you can stay with me if you like, with me and my cat."

"Oh, that would be great, except I'm hyperallergic to cats."

"Okay, here's what we're going to do. Wait here." She walked back to her desk and opened a lower drawer. Pulling out a large legal folder, she retrieved the cash envelope and withdrew some money, then handed it to her newest client. "Here, this should help out for the next few days until your friend gets home."

"Miss Macgregor . . . Mary Kate, I can't take your money."

"I insist, please. That's what this is here for, just in situations to help people like you get back on their feet. Use it for whatever you need to get situated, check in to a hotel, or buy an airline ticket and visit with family. I would strongly urge you not to go back home until we get things sorted out. My limited experience with situations like this show it can sometimes be very dangerous. Okay?"

Calley sobbed before whispering, "Okay, but I was thinking if I could find a temporary hotel room, or maybe if I could just talk to Phil with somebody there in the room with me, then maybe we . . ."

"Calley, that's taking a big chance. But we'll see. Okay? First we get you situated in a hotel. Try the Delray Dunes about six blocks from here. Ask for Robin. If she's not there, tell them your name is 'Julie Rush,' then mention my name, and they'll take good care of you. It's a very small place, modest but clean. Go there and we'll talk soon. Do you have transportation?"

"Yeah, a neighbor lent me her truck to use for a few days."

"Good. Get something to eat, take a long hot shower, have a glass of wine, and get a good night's sleep. We'll talk tomorrow." She handed her a business card. "It will all work out, okay?"

"Sure, Mary Kate. Thanks for everything." She walked onto the elevator, and Mary Kate watched her face disappear behind the closing doors. She had an eerie feeling as she watched the elevator doors close on the frightened woman. Calley's timid wave gave Mary Kate shivers down her spine. *Could this be the last time I see her? Alive?*

She had spent the whole morning doing paperwork, and in a rare Sunday meeting with the firm's senior law partners. Then she had met with her uncles and father, and last, with Calley. Four hours later, she was done for the day, and her Sunday was almost gone. It had been a long day.

When she left the deserted high-rise office building, she walked down the stairs since the elevator was off after hours. It was dark until the motion detectors switched on the lights, and she finally opened the door to the garage and went to her car. Then she made herself comfortable, turned on her music, and was ready to head home.

Graw removed her suit jacket, laid it carefully on the car seat next to her, and unbuttoned the top two buttons of her blouse. She pressed the release lever on the dashboard of her red sports car and the convertible top dropped quickly into the rear compartment.

She shook her hair in the warm evening air and was off. She still had paperwork to review at home and then countless wedding details, all of which demanded her attention. At a stoplight she could feel eyes wandering over her body. Looking up, she caught sight of a truck driver ogling her long, lean, athletic legs, now revealed by her skirt, which was hiked high up her thighs. That was the only problem with a convertible, she mused. She hit the gas, and the pounding engine surged as she pulled away from the stoplight in her powerful red machine, leaving him in the dust. *Creep.*

Looking at her bulging briefcase sitting on the passenger seat, she figured she had at least three hours' worth of work left to do that evening. But she didn't mind; she loved her job.

She had graduated at the top of her class in her Ivy League law school, and she had fielded many job offers nationwide before she finally took a position with the respected Delray Beach law firm of Block & Sawyer. It was run by one of the most respected attorneys in South Florida, Irwin "Sonny" Block. She knew she could make more money in New York, but she wanted to stay in Florida, near her family. Then her mom died, and she wanted to be close by her dad. He seemed so lost.

The law firm was involved in divorce and corporate law; it was tough, and the firm was relentless in pursuit of justice on its clients' behalf. Graw fit right in with the rest of the firm. Clients loved the firm and referred their friends. The business grew by word of mouth when clients told others about the good work it did and, more important, that it could be trusted. Threats and unsigned notes came with the territory.

"Don't worry about the threats, but don't ignore them either," said the senior partner, Sonny, on her first day of work.

Graw pulled into the garage at her apartment complex and took the elevator up to the fourth floor. She threw her briefcase into her darkened home office, kicked off her shoes, and untucked her blouse from her skirt.

God, it's good to be home. Now she had to look over all her texts and e-mails about the wedding, the rehearsal dinner, and the hundreds of other details that needed to be handled. She still didn't know if Mickey's parents were coming to the wedding. *Is there something else going on? Could it be they don't approve? How could that be?* Yet try as she might, she had never met his parents. *Strange, very strange.* She needed to talk to Mickey; there was not much time left.

Chapter Nine

Early Monday morning Robert Macgregor sat slumped over his desk in his office at the secondhand shop as his employees began to show up for work. Word had spread quickly about the fire and the total destruction of his home, and genuine offers of help had poured in.

"Good morning, Mac," said Madge, his eighty-one-year-old front-desk person, who had worked for him for the last twelve years. "I was so sorry to hear about the fire at your place. Were you able to salvage anything, anything at all?"

"No, nothing . . . other than my wedding album. That's the only thing left. Fate, I guess, had a hand in that. Tess had put it in a steel container under the bed, and it wasn't incinerated like everything else. Quirky, if you ask me. But thanks for asking," he said, managing a weak smile.

"You let me know if there is anything I can do to help. Do you need a place to stay? Some clothes? How about a good meal? Join us for dinner tonight?"

"Thanks, but I'm staying at Ryan's house along with my brother Eian for the time being. I had some of my clothes already at my brother's place, and they should work until I get back on my feet. I'm going to look through our clothes rack we have here and see if we have anything I can use. I'm sure that . . ."

"Ahh . . . umm . . . ," Madge started to object.

He looked at her, looking at his clothes. She never approved of the clothes he wore, so he changed the subject. "I may take you up on the meal offer, though. My brother mainly eats out at restaurants, and I'll be either broke or fatter than a pig ready for butchering if I do that every night."

Her face brightened. "Sure, anytime, Mac. Just let me know."

"Thanks, Madge, I really appreciate it."

He spent the entire morning on the phone with the insurance company and the insurance adjustors, trying to sort things out, when the phone rang. It was Bobby.

"Hey, Bobby, how are you? How's Patti?"

"We're okay, Dad; we're just worried about you. Howya doing?"

"Okay, I guess. The insurance company is going to give me some money for clothes and a hotel, but it's not a lot of money since I didn't have it insured for a lot. That old place had a lot of sentimental value. Ryan wants me to stay with him until I find a new place. He wouldn't hear of it any other way. Shouldn't take long for me to find a place."

"Hey, Dad, he's your brother. Want to come over tonight for dinner? Patti said she would take you clothes shopping, if you like."

"Thanks, Bobby, I may just do that. Let me get back to you." *I have plenty of clothes here at the store. Why go shopping and spend hard-earned money for new clothes?* Then he remembered what Ryan had said to him as he left for work that morning: "Stay here as long as you want, but just buy some new clothes."

"Okay, Dad. I'll talk to you later."

"Oh, Bobby, I called that lady at the counseling program and left her a message. Her secretary called me back, and I scheduled a meeting with her tomorrow."

"You did? With everything else you have going on in your life? You're something else. Love ya. Gotta go, Dad."

Customers began to dribble into Robert's eclectic secondhand store just off West Atlantic Avenue, in downtown Delray Beach. Whatever you needed, you could find it at the Frugal Scotsman. The store was jammed full of items, including stoves, tools, books, barbecue grills, guitars, pots, pans, and racks of clothing for men, women, and children. Three kayaks hung from the rafters, along with tents and bicycles. The aisles were so full you could walk down them only sideways. Around two o'clock the crowd began to thin.

"Mr. Macgregor," a voice rang out over the store's loudspeaker, "you have a phone call, line one."

He walked past his secretary with an inquisitive look on his face and asked, "Who is it?"

"Coleen Callahan, line one," she said with a smirk, since the company had only one phone line. *We only need one line. I can only talk on one phone at a time,* Robert would always say.

He picked up the phone as he settled into his desk chair. "Ms. Callahan? Hi, this is Robert Macgregor."

"Hello."

"Thanks so much for returning my call. I don't really know where to start."

"Well, I see we are scheduled to meet tomorrow. How did you get my name?"

"I was given your name by my daughter-in-law, Patti Macgregor. Her uncle had been in one of your groups. She seemed to think you might be able to help me. You see . . . I lost my wife two years ago . . . to cancer. I've been to counseling groups before and stopped. They just didn't seem to help."

"Mr. Macgregor, as a volunteer, I hear that a lot in my role with this program. Most of the people we have in our groups have been through other meetings and not found them to be helpful, until they come to us." Her voice sounded so pleasant, even captivating. "We are different in what we do and how we do it. We first meet with you and then talk about your interests, your background, as well as your loved one, and what you would like to get out of our program. We also offer bereavement sessions, which you may find helpful; however, we prefer to stress activities to get you out meeting other people in the same situation that you are in. How does that sound, Mr. Macgregor?"

"It all sounds good, except the 'Mr. Macgregor' part. Please call me Robert."

"Okay . . . Robert. I'm a volunteer and usually do my volunteer work out of my business office. The program has a real small budget. I would like to have you come in and sit with me for an initial meeting and evaluation here at my office. It should take no more than thirty or forty minutes."

"Sure."

"I know my administrative assistant set a meeting for us at ten o'clock, but could we do it later tomorrow afternoon, say four o'clock?"

"Can we make it earlier than four? I have a dance lesson at five o'clock."

"You dance?"

"Ah . . . yes, of course. Doesn't everyone?"

"Wonderful. Okay, how about two o'clock tomorrow?"

"That works great. I do have one question for you, though."

"Yes . . . ?"

"I remember . . . years ago, I went to school at Saint Mary's with a Coleen McGrath. Your voice sounds vaguely familiar. That doesn't happen to be you, does it?"

"Yes, it is. My legal name is Coleen McGrath Callahan. You said your first name was Robert? Robert Macgregor? And you went to Saint Mary's?"

"Yes. Do you remember me?"

"No, I'm sorry. I can't say that I do." A twinge of guilt went through her body. "But it was a very big class with a lot of students. I only went there for three years before my parents moved and I transferred to a different school."

"Oh well, I guess I'll see you tomorrow, two o'clock. Bye for now."

Coleen hung up the phone but continued to look at it in a strange sort of way, daydreaming back to her school days.

Robert Macgregor? *Wow!* She had lied; of course she remembered him—she remembered him so very well. Tall, dark hair, broad shoulders, with an easy smile and a mischievous twinkle in his eyes. He drove the girls wild at school. She had the biggest crush on him all through school but never had the nerve to approach him. Good girls just didn't do that back then. He asked her out to the movies a few times; she was always shy around him. He was so persistent and kept asking until she finally started going out with him.

She smiled as she thought about what she was going to wear the next day for their meeting. Yes, it was going to be a very special day. *And he dances! I wonder how much he's changed? Time will tell,* she thought, as she hummed an old tune and left her office.

As Robert hung up the phone, he could not get her out of his mind. How would she look after all these years? Would she remember him? She had said she was widowed. Was she . . .

"Hi, Pop!"

He looked up to see his irreverent and very pregnant daughter-in-law standing before his desk. Patti looked as if she was going to have the baby right there in his office as she asked, "You ready?" Then she plopped down heavily into a nearby chair.

"For what?" he asked.

"Clothes shopping. Didn't Bobby tell you?"

"Well, he mentioned something about you wanting to take me shopping, but, Patti, I have so many clothes right here at the store. And I can just use them if . . ."

"Nope. No fights and no arguments. Get your car keys; we're going to the mall. Now."

He looked at the old and worn clothes he had gotten from his brother's house, and his gaze went from the picture on his desk of him and Tess at the cabin fishing, to the telephone. He recalled his conversation with Coleen. "Okay, let's go."

Patti was shocked, as she had fully expected to have a long, drawn-out discussion with him about spending money on clothes, then they would negotiate which stores, which clothes, and an overall budget, and after two hours he would finally agree to go. She had never expected that he would capitulate so easily.

He walked from his desk and helped her from her chair. Then he hugged her and whispered, "Thanks, Patti. I love you as one of my own."

Her eyes began to fill with tears from her father-in-law's sudden display of affection; then she looked at him. "I love you too, Pop, but you're still going shopping with me." She kissed his cheek and put her arm in his and said, "Come on, let's go before we both break down in tears."

Chapter Ten

Monday morning Ryan Macgregor arrived early at his office, hoping to speak with his partner, Doctor Mary Gladings. He noticed that her car was not in her assigned parking spot as he guided his SUV into the space next to hers, marked "Dr. Macgregor." She had asked him to cover for her while she was on an extended cruise with her husband and family, just in case any of her patients needed to speak with someone in an emergency. He himself usually did limited talk therapy but was going to be lecturing at a convention about the benefits of mixed therapy and medications. Talking to patients would be good practice for him.

He waited in the car for a few minutes, hoping to see her, but then remembered that she was leaving that day and would not be in the office for at least a week. He would talk to her when she returned. Maybe he would take some time off when she was back in the office. It had been years since he had had any vacation. *Or maybe next year,* he thought.

He entered through the private rear door to his office and set his briefcase next to his desk as he perused his calendar of patients. *Busy day,* he thought. A patient just about every forty-five minutes, then an hour for lunch at one o'clock and then busy again until three p.m. He took a deep breath and flipped the switch. A green light went on in the waiting room to alert June, his longtime assistant, that he was in his office and ready to see patients. A few minutes later she knocked on his door and nudged it open, holding a mug of coffee in one hand and two chocolate chip cookies on a plate in the other.

"Good morning, June. How many times do I have to tell you, you don't have to bring me coffee . . ." He looked at the homemade cookies and finished by saying, "But I do appreciate you bringing me these homemade cookies. Thank you."

"Happy to oblige, Dr. Macgregor." She laid a napkin on his desk and set the plate of delicious morsels on top, next to his steaming cup of coffee. "There you go. Let me know when you're ready for your first patient. They are already outside waiting." She walked to the door and paused before turning. "And Dr. Macgregor, I added a patient at ten a.m., one of Dr. Gladings's. His file is on your desk. You said it was okay if one of hers called in and had to see someone. I hope you don't mind?"

He looked up from his newspaper and cookies and said, "It's all right. Who is it?"

She hesitated before she said, "Jeffrey Long. He was very insistent. I'm sorry. Did I do something wrong?"

He started to say something but thought better of it. She had only been following his instructions. "No, it's fine, June, really."

Ryan was not ready for someone like him today; he had seen him once before when Mary was out of town for a wedding and had ordered a special blood test done on him. He constantly babbled about such nonsense going on in his life. During his last visit, Long had spoken incessantly about his refrigerator's needing a replacement part and how the manufacturer did not make the part anymore since his refrigerator was nearly fifteen years old. He talked in a monotone, on and on. But that's what Ryan was there for, to listen to people drone on and on and . . .

The door opened, and in walked his first patient. His day was about to begin.

The morning seemed to crawl by as he thought about Mary Kate's wedding preparations, the endless stream of invoices, the continual details, the dresses, the bridesmaids' phone calls referred to him, the number of contractors and consultants they both had to deal with. "I thought that's why we hired a wedding planner," he once told his daughter, to her inevitable response: "Oh, Daddy."

He had finished his notes on his first two appointments when June buzzed him. "Dr. Macgregor, Mr. Long is here to see you."

"Give me just a minute, please, and then you can send him in." He wanted to review his file again before seeing him.

"Yes, sir."

He opened the file and saw that the results of the blood test had ruled out other conditions and confirmed his suspicions: the diagnosis was dysthymia, resulting in mild to sometimes severe depression. Strange, there was no note of any medication for it. He read the file and finally saw a note at the bottom of the last page: "Patient refuses to take any and all medications." *That explains it.*

He buzzed her a few minutes later, saying, "Okay, June, you can send him in."

"Good morning, Doc. Thanks for squeezing me in today," Jeffrey Long said. He took his place on the sofa and rearranged the pillows to his liking. He next stood and closed the blinds half an inch; he said the light bothered his eyes. He looked as if he had not slept, bathed, or changed his clothes in ages. He was wearing a soiled tan T-shirt and rumpled trousers. He managed a weak smile and said as he sat down. "Mornin', Doc."

"Morning, Jeffrey. How've you been?" Ryan asked, as he sat in his usual chair behind him.

"Good. I finally bought a new refrigerator. I was afraid that my last one would give out and leave me stranded without a . . ." He continued.

Why won't he take any medication? Especially since it has been shown in studies to help others like him? His mind drifted. Ryan began to doodle on his notepad. *Mary Kate's tenth birthday party. Cake was in the fridge. Everybody was there, except for Mum and Da. I miss them. Why are we having so many people at the rehearsal dinner? You rehearse, you eat, and . . .*

"The refrigerator was first to go, then the microwave. Everybody says things start to go bad after ten years. Next it'll be the goddamn . . ." He heard Jeffrey mumble in the distance.

If only Gracie were here. She would know what to do. She always knew what to do. What would she think of Mary Katherine's future husband? She would embrace him and tell me to do the same. Right. I guess he's all right, but everything about the wedding is just so rushed. What's the rush? These young folks, sometimes I just don't know how . . .

". . . then my wife got so mad . . . that was just before she died . . . she asked me to . . . I needed someone to talk to . . . the pain . . ." Jeffrey's voice went in and out of Ryan's consciousness, but one word stuck in Ryan's subconscious vocabulary: *died.* It was a painful word for him.

Ryan looked up to observe Jeff still lying on the sofa, almost serene, with his arms folded on his chest. He shifted in his seat and wrote Gracie's name everywhere on the notepad, surrounded by a heart and with his name penciled underneath. It was only then he heard something strange . . . silence. Jeff had stopped talking. Then Ryan heard a loud metallic click. When he looked up from his notepad and turned his attention to his patient, he was staring down the barrel of a gun, a very large black gun—pointed directly at him.

"Do I have your attention now, Doc? Huh? What do you say?"

"Yes . . . ," he managed to stammer, his eyes never leaving the black hole of the gun barrel facing him and following his every move. "Yes, you do. You have my full attention."

"Good. Now why don't you put down your notepad and sit over here where I can keep my eyes on you," Jeff said, motioning him with the gun to a chair at the foot of the sofa. "Then we can talk more comfy-like. Okay?"

"Sure, Jeff, but you don't need a gun. Why don't you put it on the table, and then we can talk as long as you want. Okay?"

"No . . . I kinda like holding it. I like the power it has over people. Gets their attention. Come on now, move over here," he said again, pointing to the large brown leather chair.

Ryan stood and found that his knees nearly crumpled beneath him as he made his way slowly to his desk and reached for the phone.

"Over here, Doc!" Jeff shouted, insistently pointing at the chair.

"I was going to tell my assistant to clear my calendar for this morning so we can talk as long as you want. This way we won't be disturbed. Okay?"

"Okay, but use the intercom so I can hear her as well, and don't try any funny business."

His hand was shaking as his finger went toward the intercom button. Then he saw the gun pointed at him, and it sent a shiver down his spine.

"Easy now, Doc. Real easy," Jeff whispered behind him.

Chapter Eleven

"June?" Dr. Macgregor said through the intercom.

A few moments later, her voice came over the speaker, "Yes, sir?"

"I'm going to need a little bit longer with Mr. Long this morning than I originally anticipated." He looked over and smiled at Jeff, who sat back on the sofa and seemed to relax, as he uncocked the gun and returned the hammer to its resting position. "So I want you to cancel all my morning appointments, please. All of them."

"Cancel? Did you say cancel, Dr. Macgregor?"

"Yes. Cancel. Thank you, June. Oh, and reschedule Billy for tomorrow afternoon."

"Uhhh . . . okay."

"That'll be all. Thanks, June." He stood, his legs now able to fully support him as he walked to the chair at the foot of the sofa and sat down.

"Good job, Doc," Jeff said as he leaned back on the sofa with the handgun resting on his stomach. "Now where was I?" He stopped, his eyes narrowed as if watching prey. "Were you listening at all, Doc? Huh?"

"Yes, I was, Jeff, but let's go back to your wife. Tell me about her. And you can put the gun down. You have my full attention. It makes me nervous. You don't need it."

Jeff looked at the gun before he started. "My Dottie? She was the best," he began, and set the revolver on the chrome-and-glass table between them. It clattered loudly as it hit the glass. "She kept me sane and out of trouble. I never wanted to do anything crazy-like because of her." He paused, nearly in tears. "All anybody wants to do is to give me drugs. They say it's supposed to help, but it just gives me terrible nightmares, over and over . . . reliving the day she died." He stopped talking for a moment.

"And now—she's gone. Gone from my life forever. I wake up every morning thinking of her. Damn!" he shouted. Ryan nodded in agreement, which only seemed to anger his already-agitated patient. "What the hell do you know? About loss? You got it all. Fancy clothes, nice office, I bet you got a new car—yeah, Doc, you got it all." He picked up the gun from the table and began waving it around.

Ryan's hands began to shake as his gaze met the raging eyes of the broken man sitting before him. "No, I don't. It may just look that way, Jeff, but without my Gracie, life is not worth living. I miss her terribly, but you tell yourself every day that you have to go on living."

"You lost your wife?" Jeff said, looking visibly shaken. "I didn't know . . . really. Nobody ever told me that she died."

"Yeah, close to two years ago. She was riding her bike along the beach road, on A1A, and somebody hit her and kept going." His voice drifted off. "She held on for a few hours at the hospital, but she had too many internal injuries to survive."

"Did they catch the guy? The guy who did it?" Jeff asked, leaning toward the doctor, the gun drooping in his hands, toward the floor.

"Yeah, they thought so, but they couldn't make it stick. His wife and best friend came through with an alibi for him. I would have done anything to save her." He stopped for a moment, his voice cracking.

"And I miss her so much that sometimes I wish it had been me that had died because without her I just don't want to go on living if . . ."

The sound of car doors slamming drew his attention to the window. Jeff was on his feet in an instant and peeked through the small wooden blinds covering the windows. Police.

"You almost had me there, Doc," he said in the voice of one betrayed, "but you had to send for the police, now didn't you? Get on your knees! Kneel down! Now! Put your hands behind your head. Move!" he commanded, waving the gun in Ryan's direction.

The scared doctor knelt down as he was told, facing his desk, and soon felt the hardened steel of the pistol barrel against the back of his head. He heard the now-familiar sound of the hammer's being cocked, the gun ready to fire. He knew he was going to die.

"So you want to see your wife, is that it? You want to join her? Right? I can arrange that for you, Doc, if that's what you really want. Is it? Is it, Doc? Huh?"

He did not know what to say. He had always thought he wanted to join his Gracie, and now all he had to do was say yes, or nod his head, and he would be with her. As he always said to himself, she was only a breath away. *But what about Mary Kate? Robert? Bobby? Eian? And . . .*

"No. No, I don't want to die a needless death like she did."

Jeff pressed the gun barrel harder against the back of his head. "Why not, Doc? What you got to live for? Tell me, Doc; tell the world. What do you have to live for?"

Ryan stopped to think before saying, "I want to see my daughter get married. I want to hold my grandkids in my arms, and I want to spoil them and see them walk down the aisle and get married too. I want to travel, to see the Acropolis in Athens, the pyramids in Egypt, the Colosseum in Rome, and the mountains of Scotland. I would love to see the green fields of . . ." He heard a noise behind him but kept going as if he was praying for his life, placing his hands together in front of him.

He slumped over but kept talking, almost praying, hoping that something he would say could save his life. He thought back to growing up with his brothers, his mom and dad, family picnics . . . the best. Good times. It all flashed through his mind.

"I want to see both of my brothers happy and help them leave their pain behind. I want them to both find somebody to love. And hell, maybe I want to love again, I want to find somebody to hold in my arms and . . ." The office door came crashing in, splintering, and soon his office was filled with uniformed police officers. They stood over him, watching as he still knelt on the old multicolored Moroccan prayer rug Grace had given him years ago. Finally one reached out a hand to help him stand up.

"Did you get him?" he asked in a shaky voice before he noticed his office's rear door was ajar.

"He must have left through the rear exit there. But we're still searching the building for him. Don't worry, we'll find him, he can't be too far away," said one of the younger officers as he leaned over and picked up a hand-scribbled message from the chair. "He left a note, Dr. Macgregor: 'See you soon doc.'"

Ryan's legs began to shake again.

Chapter Twelve

The two jovial voices came out loud over the airwaves. "Well, that's it for us, South Florida. Thanks for joining us on *The Sports Show*. I'm Terry Walker . . ."

". . . And I'm Eian Macgregor, signing off. We'll be back here tomorrow to talk sports on *The Sports Show* on WFLX. See you then." The red-and-white "ON THE AIR" light went dark, and they both took off their headphones and grinned. They had been working together for the past three years and now were both glad their workday was over.

"Good show, buddy boy," said Walker, a former pro-football quarterback.

"Yeah," Eian chimed in quietly.

"Hey, Mac, everything all right with you?"

"Just one of those days, you know?"

"Yeah, man, got plenty of those myself. What's goin' on?"

"Well, to start with, I got evicted from my own house—by my stepdaughter."

"Laura?"

"The one and only. So I had to move in with my brother Ryan at his beach house."

"You and him living together? He's the meticulous one, right?"

"Yep. Then my brother Bob's house burned down, so he's living there as well."

"Oh my God, all three of the Macgregor brothers living under one roof?"

"Yeah, and . . ." He grew silent. "Tomorrow marks the anniversary of Alice's death. So let's just say it hasn't been a good couple of days."

He missed her more than ever, lonely for her smile, her touch, her laugh. She had always made him laugh with her practical jokes, then she had amazed him by learning to speak both German and Greek at home, but in the end . . . she had made him cry when she couldn't remember what lipstick was used for or even what it was called. She was always his rock, his confidante, even when she no longer knew who he was. It was not easy, but he always remembered the promise he had made to her so many years before . . . "in sickness and in health, till death do us part." He had always been big on commitments. Goddamn, he missed her.

His radio-booth-mate coughed and brought him back to reality.

"And on top of that, I have to be fitted for a damn tux again for my niece's wedding."

"So?"

"Man, I look terrible in a tux. I'm so tall I look like a damn oversize penguin. And she wants us all to take dance lessons . . . and get a date for the wedding. Can you believe that? I think I'm going to call her and tell her exactly what I think of the whole idea."

"Wait, you're going to call Mary Kate Macgregor and give her a piece of your mind?"

"Yeah."

Terry leaned back in his chair, put his hands behind his head, and grinned. "Man, this I gotta see."

"Well," Eian stammered, "I don't have time right now, but she's on my list to talk to, got it?"

"Got it," Terry said, laughing. "Hey, you wanna get lunch?"

"Sure. That'd be good. Oh no, can't do it. I got an autograph session set up by the station later on this afternoon with some young kids. So I can't go missing for an afternoon. Maybe tomorrow?"

"Yeah, man, have your gal call my gal and we'll compare calendars." They both laughed as they went to their desks on opposite sides of the tiny cubicle they shared. He missed having a regular office. *Office? Damn,* he thought. *Rose.*

"Oh, gotta go. I got an appointment today for the reopening of my office. I finally get my office space back. And my sofa."

"Let me know what you think of your decorator. I may want to do something with my Miami office."

"Rose? Oh, she's good. She listens, takes lots of notes, and comes in under budget. I just can't wait to see it and finally get some working space again," Eian said, looking around the cramped, shared cubicle, which was no larger than a clothes closet.

"Is she good-looking?"

"Rose? Gee, man, I don't know. But, yeah, I guess she's rather attractive . . . I just never thought of her in that way."

"What do you mean?"

"She was married to my best friend, Tony Gilardo, for some twenty years. The four of us did everything together until he died and we drifted apart. Then Alice was diagnosed with . . ." He stopped for a minute before saying, "She's a good friend, and the wife of my best friend."

"You mean the widow of your best friend. Either way, let me know what you think of how your office turned out. Gotta go. I'm starving. See ya tomorrow."

Eian pulled his phone from his pocket and dialed her number.

Two rings. "Hello? Eian?" he heard her say in her pleasant way.

"Yeah. Hi, Rose. I just finished my radio show. I can be there in twenty minutes, if it's all done."

"Sure, but make it forty-five minutes. We're just about done here. I want it to be perfect for you," she said.

"Okay, see you then."

"See ya."

He saw a head poke into his cubicle opening.

"Hey, come on in."

The young twentysomething in red sneakers, with a thick head of unruly black hair and a scraggly beard, walked inside. "Have you fired up your computer yet today, Mr. Macgregor?" he asked.

"No. Should I?"

"Yeah, you should, I fixed it. Remember you said you were having a problem with your computer slowing up or freezing?"

"Yeah."

"Well, while you were doing your show this morning, I came in and fixed it."

"Yeah?" Eian spun around in his chair and turned it on. The screen came up with his computer games there waiting for him, at his beck and call. He clicked the keyboard and—voilà! It worked. "Hey, man, this is great. Good job." He kept typing.

"Anytime, Mr. Macgregor," the young man said with a grin and turned to leave.

"Hey, Joey? Got a question for you."

"Fire away."

"You know, I'm kinda new to all this computer and search engine stuff."

"Yeah, most ancient guys your age are the same way. Why?"

He let the reference to his age and computer savvy slide.

"Well, what if I wanted to find somebody's phone number? Say, an old acquaintance, you know, out of state, from times long ago?"

Joey smiled his knowing smile and said, "Slide out from your chair and let me sit at your keyboard and see what I can do. What's her name?"

"Paula Pragna. At least that was her name when I knew her." Just the mention of her name gave him goose bumps. They had been high school and college sweethearts . . . and a little bit more. But over the years they had lost contact. The last he had heard, she was living in Europe somewhere, with some prince or something.

"Birth date?"

"Fourth of July. That's a date that's kind of hard to forget."

"Paula Pragna, with a matching birth date, lives in Santa Monica, California. You want her phone number?"

Eian was stunned and could only try to act nonchalant as he nodded in agreement.

"Well, you want her number?"

He swallowed and whispered, "Yeah, sure. I guess."

The young man printed out the information and handed it to him. "Anything else?

"No, I'm good. Thanks, for everything."

The aging baseball star's eyes were transfixed on her name and phone number. It was just that easy, amazing. Before he sat down at his desk, he stood and looked around the office, then dialed her number. It rang once, twice, and he was about to hang up, but it was too late . . . someone answered the phone.

"Hello? Paula?"

"Eian. Is that you?"

"Yes."

"It's been a long time," her sweet voice said, as if it were yesterday they had last talked. She had been waiting years for him to call.

Chapter Thirteen

"Paula, it's so good to hear your voice again. How long has it been?"

"Time just flies, and faster and faster every year. Let's just say it's been years since we talked last." She laughed. "How the hell are you? I watched your World Series performance. A no-hitter! That must have really helped your career. I was so impressed and happy for you. I wanted to call you to congratulate you, but . . . I didn't want to stir up any hornet's nest at home." She talked in her usual rapid-fire manner.

"I understand."

"What else have you been up to? I saw you retired from baseball but kind of lost touch."

"I have my own sports marketing company and do a sports radio show here in Florida. Sign lots of autographs, manage a couple players as an agent, attend sports openings, and throw out the first pitch around the country. It's a good gig, boring sometimes, but pays well."

"I'm impressed. I read in the newspapers about your divorce a long time back. Sounded messy. Did you ever remarry?"

"Yes. A few years after my divorce I met a really sweet gal and we were married." He stopped for a moment before continuing. "Her name was Alice. She died recently from complications from Alzheimer's."

"Eian, I am so sorry to hear that. My condolences."

"Thank you. You know, I almost called you years ago, after my first marriage ended, but . . ." He paused, not really knowing what to say. "What about you? Married?"

"A few times," she laughed. "But you know how that goes." The phone went silent. "I would love to see you again, Eian. Unfortunately, I never get to the East Coast. Do you ever travel to California?"

"Occasionally. Hey . . . as a matter of fact, I'm supposed to go to Los Angeles for a few days next week. The professional baseball team there is opening a new training facility and asked me to come there for a ceremonial baseball pitch for one of my old coaches. They'll pay for everything—air, hotel, rental car, food—the works."

"No need for a hotel room or any of that stuff. You can stay with me, at the beach house. It would be like old times. Remember?"

He nearly blushed, thinking back to those days. *Why not?* "Sure, why not? It's set for Tuesday."

"Let me give you my cell-phone number. I'm rarely at home. You're lucky you caught me."

They exchanged phone numbers, and as he was about to say good-bye, she said, "I'm so glad you called me. I was just thinking about you the other day. I've missed you, I've missed us. Call me soon. Bye."

He hung up the phone and felt elated. His life was beginning to turn around. He glanced at his watch and grabbed his jacket. He didn't want to be late for his meeting with Rose. *Rose?* A feeling deep in his stomach began to gnaw at him, and he didn't understand what it was. Time to go, but for some reason he could not shake the feeling inside him.

Chapter Fourteen

After Eian left the office, he made the quick drive on I-95 until he saw the Boca Raton turnoff onto Glades Road. It was a perfect South Florida kind of day, sunny and bright, a chamber-of-commerce kind of day. Hardly any traffic. *Maybe I should just go to the beach and take some time off.* He pulled into his parking lot and parked his big SUV in the spot marked:

RESERVED
CEO
MACGREGOR SPORTS MARKETING

He smiled that boyish Scottish grin. He liked that; it had a nice ring to it.

Rose met him at the elevator, excited as a schoolgirl. "Close your eyes," she said, then grabbed his hand and led him into the elevator. The elevator still felt sluggish and noisy, but some things never change. However, he also noticed something new: the sweet scent of honeysuckle perfume, and the warmth of her hand. The honeysuckle took him back to his youth, growing up and playing baseball in open fields ringed with neighbors' backyard fences covered with honeysuckle. Good memories.

"Keep your eyes closed," she told him. "And no peeking."

The elevator came to an abrupt stop, and the doors slowly opened. She led him down the familiar hallway, then stopped and grabbed him by the shoulders. "Okay, now you can open your eyes."

Before him stood new glass-and-chrome double doors, which had replaced the old wooden one with its rusty doorknob. The new front doors were prominently stenciled with MACGREGOR SPORTS MARKETING—WORLD HEADQUARTERS. He turned to her in amazement, speechless.

She smiled a coy smile. "I threw in the World Headquarters line just to add some cachet. Like it?"

"I love it!" He was so impressed and excited, he hugged her tight and kissed her for good luck. "Rose, this is so awesome."

She swallowed hard, then recovered by saying, "You ain't seen nothing yet. Come on inside and see your new offices."

His longtime assistant stood to greet him. "Looks great, doesn't it, boss?"

"You bet. Oh my God, this is awesome."

Posters of him during his playing years adorned the walls, along with pictures of him shaking hands with many of the players he currently managed. The old dingy coffee room was now a modern meeting room with a large cherry conference table and six black leather executive chairs. Colorful baseball pictures and posters hung from every wall. He nodded his approval.

"Now to your office." She took him by the hand and led him to the corner office and motioned for him to open the tall, imposing walnut door. Once inside he was speechless. His desk was in the corner. Rose had replaced the dark, dingy commercial-grade flooring with a soft and subtly patterned white wool Berber carpet. In a glass case in the corner was his baseball glove and one of the baseballs he had used to throw his monumental no-hitter against the Yankees. The final strikeout to win the game. Other memorabilia lined the walls, as well as pictures of him with some of baseball's greatest players. Rose had made it really feel like home. She knew him well.

"Rose, I can't believe it. Look at this place. You're great. And under budget, wow!"

"Well . . . almost under budget, but close. Only one thing . . . I used your old storage closet back there for filing cabinets to hold all the records, files, and receipts. I had a lot of surplus baseball equipment left over. New stuff that you had in boxes, like bats, gloves, jerseys, and baseballs—stuff like that. There's no more room. Maybe you can sell it online or donate some of it?"

"Sure."

She spun around his new office and smiled. "You like it?"

"Rose, I absolutely love it," he told her as he sat in his new high-back executive chair. "Tell you what . . . let me take you out to dinner to celebrate."

"Sure," she said with a broad grin. "How about tomorrow night?"

"Okay . . . sure. No, wait, I can't do tomorrow. Ryan's daughter, Mary Kate, bought dance lessons for me and my brothers, and the first one is scheduled for tomorrow night."

"Dance lessons?"

"Yeah. She's getting married in two weeks. So she said she wants to dance with her father and uncles and bought us some dance lessons."

"Oh," she exclaimed. "Hey, I got a good idea," she chirped. "You can't just take a dance lesson and not practice. Why don't we do dinner at Germaine's on Yamato? You remember the place. They have a band and serve dinner and have a huge dance floor. We can practice all your dance moves and celebrate your new office at the same time."

"Germaine's? Is that the place the four of us used to go to years ago? The one on Dixie Highway, in Boca?"

"The one and only. What do you say?"

He took in a deep breath and said, "Lots of memories there. With Alice. Tony."

She looked at him and put her hand on his shoulder, whispering, "Come on, it'll be fun."

"Sure, why not? You want me to pick you up, or . . . ?"

"I have a client to meet with earlier, so why don't I just meet you there? Say, seven? Okay?"

"Sounds great. I thought maybe we could—"

He was interrupted by a voice over an intercom saying, "Excuse me, boss, but you have a call on line one. Mike Humphreys, calling from Los Angeles."

"I must speak with him. I'm supposed to go to Los Angeles next week to meet with him. I think I need to talk to . . ."

"Go ahead and take your call. I'll see you Wednesday." She kissed him good-bye, once lightly on the cheek.

"See you then," he said as he picked up the phone and plunged into his office routine.

In the privacy of the elevator, she looked down at her hands; they were shaking. *Hang on, girl; remember this is Eian, dear old Eian. Your best friend. Tony's best friend. Yeah. My best friend.*

Chapter Fifteen

Ryan met with his brothers that night, and as they sat around the deck overlooking his pool and watched the waves crash on the shoreline, he told them what had happened that day in the office. They could see he was still shaken up from the experience.

"I saw you on television. You looked pretty shaken up, bro," Eian said quietly.

"I was. I just knelt there, shaking, with a gun to my head. It's true what they say. Your whole life flashes before your eyes. But thinking about it, everything I thought about was family. I saw Mum and Da laughing. I saw us growing up as kids, playing ball, I saw my wedding, and I saw Mary Katherine being born—everything."

"Damn!" said Eian. "That's scary."

"Have they caught him yet?" Robert asked.

"No, but all this really makes you think about the things in your life." He paused and looked at both of them. "When you think you only have two minutes to live, it makes you decide what's important."

Robert finally spoke. "Yeah, we may fuss and fight, but I don't know what I'd do if I ever lost you or Eian. I just don't know, but everybody has been telling us to get on with things. The fire at the house got me to thinking about how I live my life. At least for me, I think it may be a wake-up call, that it's time to get on with living."

His brothers nodded in agreement.

"I need a drink," Robert said, rising quickly and heading for the liquor cabinet. "The good stuff."

Robert returned with three glasses of Scotch whiskey and toasted, "To the Macgregor brothers."

"Long live Scotland," they all chimed in.

They sat in silence, each lost in his own world, his own thoughts, and his own resolutions.

Chapter Sixteen

Tuesday afternoon Robert parked his old pickup truck in the parking lot and, after looking in the mirror, brushed his unruly hair away from his face once again. As he sat in the truck waiting, he glanced down at his transformation—his new shoes, trousers, belt, and shirt. He had to admit that Patti did have excellent taste—expensive, but good. After taking a deep breath, he made his way into the lobby of the Callahan Building for his first meeting with the social coordinator. The tall chrome-and-glass building behind a grassy knoll was in stark contrast to his squat one-story shop, which was set back in the corner of a shopping center.

"Robert Macgregor to see Coleen Callahan," he said to the security guard at the desk.

Looking up, the genial uniformed guard smiled and pointed to a clipboard. "Driver's license, please. Then just sign in."

Robert retrieved his license from his old brown leather wallet and handed it to him.

"I'll call her office and someone will be right down to escort you," the guard said as he handed Robert an ID badge marked VISITOR. "Just have a seat, please," he said, motioning him to the leather sofas in the waiting area.

The waiting area had glass-and-chrome tables filled with newspapers and real estate magazines, but his mind still pondered the conversation he had had the night before with his youngest brother. *Ryan could have been killed, murdered right in his own office. My own brother. Life is short, too short. Ryan was shaken, retelling the story. But the real question is—could that crazy guy come back? Will he try to . . .*

"Mr. Macgregor?"

"Yes," he said, looking up at the young man standing before him in a dark suit and tie.

"Good afternoon, sir. Will you please follow me?"

"Sure."

"Ms. Callahan's office is on the top floor, the executive floor." As they exited the elevator, they walked past employees in large meeting rooms seated around long wooden conference tables. Other employees were busy on the phones in cubicles and in larger offices with windows bringing in the bright Florida sunlight. The phones were ringing non-stop, making the whole scene seem almost surreal. The closer he got to her office, the darker and thicker the carpet felt beneath his feet. Soon they were standing before a woman with short dark-brown hair, wearing small round glasses and dressed in well-tailored clothes. *This is not the Coleen I remember. Must be a different Coleen. There must be a million Coleens in the world,* he thought to himself.

His escort stopped and turned to him. "Here you go. Nice to meet you, Mr. Macgregor. This is Margaret, Ms. Callahan's executive assistant, whom I believe you spoke with on the phone. You're in good hands."

"Thank you, Tony," she said as he departed, then smiled a kind and comfortable smile, the kind that comes from being good at one's job and from one's boss's knowing it. "Good morning, Mr. Macgregor. So nice to meet you. I'm Margie. We talked on the phone yesterday."

"Ah yes, please call me Robert. My friends call me Mac."

"Sure, Mr. Macgregor . . . I mean Robert. I expect Ms. Callahan back soon. Why don't you have a seat in her office and make yourself comfortable. Can I get you some coffee? Soda? Tea? Sparkling water?"

"No, I'm fine, thank you," he said as he glanced at his watch. He was nervous, and he did not know why.

"She won't be long. She's never late. Please have a seat."

He glanced around her corner office and could not help but notice a large silver tennis trophy in the center of her dark cherry desk. He read the multiple civic citations on the wall, along with plaques honoring her and the company's charitable programs. A dozen or so birthday cards littered her desk and credenza. He glanced at the inscription on one:

Mom—
Happy birthday—you get better every year.
Diane

His eyes searched for a photo, any photo. Then he found it. A small photo of a woman wearing a hard hat, standing in the center of a group of men at a ground-breaking ceremony. She was carrying a silver shovel and was about to kick off the start of a new building. He leaned in to get a closer look. He squinted. *Could it be? Could that be . . .*

"Great day, but a terrible photo," he heard a female voice say from behind him. "That was the ground-breaking ceremony for this building."

He turned to face her as she extended her hand. "Hiya, Mac. It's been a long time," she said in a whisper. "I wasn't sure if that was you on the phone when we talked."

He was speechless, standing there, slowly shaking her hand. "It's good to see you," he finally said.

"Yes," she said, slowly removing her hand from his.

He didn't know what to say, what to do. He stood there with his mouth partially open, staring. It had been so many years since he had seen her last. She looked the same in his eyes. Beautiful. He was awestruck, as if he were meeting a rock star backstage.

"I'll leave you two be," said Margaret, coughing, slowly closing the door behind her as she exited the room. They were so intent on each other, they never noticed her departure.

"Sit down, Mac, before you fall down," Coleen said, pointing to a nearby sofa. "You look like you've seen a ghost."

"No, just somebody I haven't seen in . . . in . . ."

"In a very long time, but at our age we don't have to count the years anymore, now do we?"

"You're right. You look the same." He immediately felt at ease. "Oh, and happy birthday," he said, pointing to the birthday cards on her desk.

She laughed. "You always did know how to sweet-talk the ladies."

"Not all of them, just some."

She felt her face flush and, to change the subject, asked, "So tell me, how long have you been a widower?"

"Going on two years. She was a ten-year survivor, and we thought we had it licked . . . but instead it came back with a vengeance. It was everywhere in her body. Damn insidious disease. She only lasted less than six months after she was diagnosed the second time." His voice was breaking.

Coleen looked down. "It's been almost five years for me. One day he was fine, and the next day he was gone . . . or at least it seemed that way. Thank God I have my daughter, Diane. She's been great; I don't know how I would have survived without her. In addition, I have the business, and I do a lot of volunteer work, like the counseling programs. I like it all; it keeps me busy. Do you have any kids?"

"Just one, my son, Bobby. He's just like his dad. A boneheaded Scotsman, but I don't know what I would have done without him and his wife, Patti. She's been a great help. As a matter of fact, she's the one who gave me your card and pushed me to call you. I'm glad she did."

She squirmed in her seat and put her hand to her face. "Well, then," she said with a start and a slight cough. "Why don't we begin?" She went to her file cabinet and pulled out a folder. He admired her athletic figure as she walked across the room. Her high heels accentuated the athletic curves in her legs, and her skirt clung softly to her. *Whew, she's more beautiful than I ever remembered.*

"I couldn't help but notice the tennis trophy on your desk. Looks new."

She laughed. "It is. It's from this past weekend. Kind of a tradition. My partner and I have won it every year at our country club. However, this is my last year to play and compete. Let somebody else have a chance to win it," she laughed. "Three years in a row is enough for me."

Coleen sat down next to him, and he could smell the heavenly scent of perfumed soap, sweet heather. *Nothing better than the smell of a fresh bar of scented soap, other than maybe the strong aroma of bacon frying in the pan on a Sunday morning,* he thought to himself.

She opened the file on her lap and crossed her legs as she thumbed through the materials. "There are two groups for your age category. Both are very active and run by professionals. They have such things as the traditional bereavement circles, but we also feel it's helpful to get participants meeting and socializing with people who share the same issues, loss of a loved one. They even employ speed-dating sessions to encourage folks to meet other attendees, as well as dancing sessions."

She put a sheet of paper on a clipboard and began by asking him some questions. "What do you miss the most about your spouse? I'm sorry, what was her name?"

"Tess," he whispered. "I miss her laugh. Her sense of humor. Her kindness to others, even to perfect strangers. Her touch. Her practical jokes. Her being able to complete the *Times* crossword puzzles in less than an hour. Damn, it takes me three hours to get halfway through it."

"What do you like to do when you're not working?" She stopped writing and asked, "What do you do for a living, by the way?"

"I own the Frugal Scotsman; it's a secondhand store on West Atlantic Avenue in Delray. I love to spend time at the store, even though now I pretty much only work there part-time. My son Bobby runs it now, but I like to help out, to fix stuff. I'm pretty handy with tools and can fix just about anything. I also like to fish, hunt, target shoot, and skeet shoot. I do woodworking, and dabble in electrical and carpentry work. I love to watch sports, especially baseball, football, soccer, tennis, golf—anything where there is competition."

"What about music? What music do you like?"

"Country-western, rock and roll, and some rap."

"What about the theater?"

"No, not really," he joked.

"Opera?"

"Ugh."

"Ballet?"

"Nope. Never been." He suddenly got the feeling that he had just failed some unknown test and that Coleen was the prize.

"I guess you don't like dancing either?"

"Well, yes, I do."

Her face brightened.

"Remember, I mentioned that I have some brush-up dance lessons to take for my niece's wedding."

"Right, I remember you said that yesterday."

"But I also belong to the Scottish Highlanders. It's a traditional Scottish clan meeting group where everyone wears their tartan colors, their kilts, the bagpipes, you know—the works. Just the other night was formal night. I wore my formal brogues, my dress sporran held with a silver chain, my sash, white shirt, tie, kilt with my kilt hose, and my tartan waistcoat topped off with my Highland bonnet. Everything. Me and my brothers attended. Ah, it was grand," he said, his voice betraying the influence of his father's heavy Scottish brogue.

She had to laugh. "Now that I would like to see."

"Well, you just missed our annual formal shindig. Food, music, dancing. You would have seen these knobby knees in a tartan kilt dancing the Scottish swing dance."

"I would have paid money to see that performance." She laughed. He always could make her laugh.

"I've so missed your laugh." *Go on Bob, do it,* he thought to himself. He took in a deep breath and blurted out, "Come to dinner with me."

"Are you asking me out on a date, Robert Macgregor?" she replied coyly.

His face screwed up in a comical expression. "Aye, I guess I am. Come to dinner with me?" He leaned in close to her.

She backed away, stopped laughing, and placed her hand on his chest. "No, Robert, that would not be wise. I'm sorry if I led you on."

He sat back with a questioning look on his face. "What's wrong with a nice dinner with an old friend, some wine, and some companionship?"

"I haven't dated in years, not since Hal passed away," she said with a serious look on her face. "But if you're looking for a date, then I suggest you call this number and ask for Jeremy Clearwater." She held out Jeremy's business card. "He runs one of the social groups and also the bereavement group where you can sit and talk out your issues with other widowers. He also runs some other programs that I was telling you about, and they are always looking for eligible bachelors." She smiled. "They're having a round-robin speed-dating program tomorrow. I think you would enjoy it. Tell you what, call me afterward if you decide to go, and let me know how it went." She wrote her home phone number on the back of the business card, then took a quick glance at her watch. "I'm afraid I must be going. I have a staff meeting to attend." She stood and held out her hand. "It was so good to see you again, Robert. Good luck."

As he rode down in the elevator he wondered, *Was it something I said or did? Or didn't say? Or didn't do?* This was all so new to him and so unexpected. *I guess I'll never know, but if she thinks she has seen the last of me, then she has never seen a Scottish Highland hound on the trail of a mate. Patience.* He looked at the business card she had given him and thought to himself, *Why not? What do I have to lose?*

When he reached his truck, he called Jeremy.

Chapter Seventeen

Slightly after five p.m., the three Macgregor brothers walked into the Cassini dance studio. It was a huge ballroom with high ceilings, and tables scattered around the outside of the dance floor. The dance hall was filled with instructors and students practicing. Each group was dancing different dances to diverse music, but all of it made a beautiful sound together.

Their instructor was there waiting for them. She was dressed in a leotard dance outfit and was looking at her watch, impatiently tapping her foot. She was tall, with dark hair and penetrating eyes. A gold pendant hung from her neck and was draped just above her chest. She was built like a dancer: tall and firm, with the form-fitting dance outfit she was wearing accentuating her curves. Her long black hair was tied tight into a bun high above her head, and her dark-brown eyes sparkled as they approached her.

"Good evening, gentlemen. My name is Alexi Cassini. My mother was French and my father was from Argentina, and they were both world-champion dancers. I have won three Grand Sport International Dance Championships in Latin, Smooth, and Ballroom, both here and overseas. They are the most prestigious awards anyone can attain in dancing. So, having said that, I'm your instructor for these dance sessions. We have a lot of work to do."

Eian coughed to make himself noticed.

She glanced in his direction and turned away, taking in a deep breath, looking annoyed. "Gentlemen, I take my work here very seriously, and I would appreciate your full attention and cooperation . . . and I would also ask that for all of your future lessons that you arrive on time, if not fifteen minutes early. So we can start on time. I have specific directions from Ms. Macgregor to teach you to dance some specific steps for her wedding, and I do not plan to let her down."

"She sounds like Mary Kate," Eian chuckled to a disinterested Ryan.

"Who here has danced before?"

They all reluctantly raised their hands.

"Good. I only have you for a few sessions, so we must be very diligent in our lessons. I see we are going to be learning different dances, the foxtrot and the waltz. I'm going to put you into two different groups. Which of you are Eian . . . and Robert?"

The two brothers raised their hands.

"Follow me, please. You are going to be taught the foxtrot by one of my associates, Trudy Gonzales." She motioned for another woman to join them and then introduced her to the two brothers before returning her attention to Ryan.

"So you're Ryan Macgregor, the father of the bride?"

"Yes."

"Your daughter wants me to teach you the waltz?"

"Yes."

"You have danced before?"

"Yes, frequently, when my wife was alive."

"The waltz?"

"Yes."

"So, Ryan, this is more of a refresher for you, correct?"

"Yes."

She liked him from the very first moment—his quiet, shy, but confident manner. "You don't talk much, do you?"

He didn't say anything at first, then slowly raised his gaze, and their eyes met. "It's just that . . . in twenty years I've never danced with anyone other than my wife. It's going to feel a little awkward."

She stood there looking at him, uncomfortable, not sure if she should embrace him to try to take away the pain he was feeling . . . or try to make him laugh.

"I understand. But let's at least try . . . for your daughter's sake. We'll take it slow. I promise. Just one step at a time." She turned on the music, "The Last Waltz." *Maybe not a good choice,* she thought as it began to play.

She apologized, watching him. "I'm sorry. Maybe this is not the right song to play, considering everything."

"It's fine," he said in a low voice.

She watched him closely. *What the hell is going on here?* she asked herself. *Strange.* She had not felt this way in a long time.

"Ready?" They began to glide across the dance floor as she whispered the count to keep him in step, "One-two-three, one-two-three, one-two-three, one-two-three. Very good. Now turn me, slowly." He spun her out smoothly, then back again to her original spot. "Good." He held her at a distance from him all the while they danced.

"Don't be afraid of me . . . I won't bite, I promise. And I won't break," she said.

He smiled at her attempt to put him at ease.

"Let's try again. Firm hold, my hand in yours. Now put your right hand on my shoulder blade. Very good. Remember now, walk softly on your toes, with a slight rise and fall of your body, and then begin slowly to turn." She could feel him as he touched her and held her. His grip was gentle but firm. He began to relax; he had always enjoyed dancing with Grace.

He began to move to the rhythm of the music, and as he got more comfortable, he slowly pulled her closer to him. He was a firm leader, directing her with his hand on her back. She liked this; it was something she could never teach anyone. It was instinctive, and he did it very well. That night the two of them danced as one, close together; he held her in his arms, and he forgot about the world surrounding them. He spun her out in front of him and pulled her back to him.

As he pulled her closer, she began to feel something turning in her soul. A yearning. She was a professional, and he was her student. She pulled away and swallowed deeply. "Good, very good. It's obvious you've done this before," she said, nearly out of breath. She walked to the table and took a long drink of water.

"Okay, now where were we? Waltz? Right?" she asked.

"Yes."

He watched her. She was beautiful and so talented. She was like an angel in his arms, so light, like his Gracie.

"Let's try a different move, called the butterfly. We dance just like before, and then we open up parallel to each other, shoulder to shoulder. I step to one side of you and we open up, looking just like a butterfly. Then we repeat it from side to side. Can you do that?"

"Yes." He was not normally so lacking words, but around her he just could not get them out of his mouth. "Okay." *Wow, two words together. Pretty soon I'll be able to say a whole sentence to her. Great, Ryan. Put a beautiful lady in your arms and you become all tongue-tied.* Then he saw a wedding ring on her finger.

"Good job," she said as they did five butterflies in a row.

Walking back to where they had started, he asked, "Does your husband also teach dancing?"

"No," she said abruptly, and then she softened, adding, "He died in an auto accident four years ago."

"My Gracie died the same way, auto accident, hit-and-run—eighteen months ago." He paused, then asked, "And you never remarried?"

"No," she said and then, changing the subject, she added, "Now we're going to end our lesson with a dip. It's customary, at the end of the father-and-daughter dance routine, to end with a dip move. Let me show you."

She pulled him close, holding on tight, and they danced a box step before she spun close. He held her tight as they dipped. His face was only inches from hers, and their lips were nearly touching. They both swallowed hard. Inches away, he could not take his eyes off her. *What the hell is going on here? Does she want me to kiss her? No, idiot, she's a dance instructor, and she just showed you a dance move. Get over it. You're not sixteen anymore, far from it. Maybe she wants me to . . .* He continued to hold her in his arms in that dip position. His lips moved closer to hers, and he closed his eyes.

"Okay, lover boy, dance lesson's over," he heard Eian say behind them.

They stood and he said a self-conscious good-bye. As they reached the door, she said, "Oh, Mr. Macgregor . . . Ryan, when did you want to schedule your next lesson?"

"I'll call you and let you know if I need another one."

"Okay," she said, her disappointment obvious in her voice, before she made her way back to her office, closing the door behind her.

"What the hell was that all about?" asked Eian as they walked to the parking lot.

"What?"

"You know what. Here you have a gorgeous woman in your arms, ready to ravish her, she asks you to call her, but instead you say, 'I'll have to think about it.'"

"I didn't say that . . . did I?"

"Just about. I think it was more like, 'I'll call you and let you know if I need another lesson.' Are you nuts?" asked Robert. "You must be nuts, because, man, she's beautiful."

"No. It's just . . . all of a sudden when we finished our lesson and I was there . . . holding her . . . so close, I felt . . . guilty." He paused and took in a deep breath. "Like I was cheating on Gracie or something," he whispered.

Robert leaned over to him to say, "Bro, Gracie's gone, and she would want you to get on with your life. Trust me. Just like you would want her to move on."

"I don't know and . . . I don't care. But I think I'm finished with my dance lessons," Ryan said matter-of-factly.

"Yeah?" Eian said in disbelief. "And you're going to tell Mary Kate that? 'Oh, I'm done with dance lessons, my dear.' Really?"

"I'll tell her . . . later."

As they reached their cars, Robert said, "I must tell you that Alexi is a beautiful woman, and I think she may just have an eye for you. However, if you're not interested, I'm sure there are plenty of other guys out there who would be, if you know what I mean."

"Well, she'll just have to—" he began, but Robert interrupted him.

"Ryan, your only daughter is getting married and has asked you to do one thing—learn some dance steps to be able to dance the waltz with her on her wedding day. That's the least you can do for her."

"I'm not sure if . . ."

Robert's voice rose as he continued, ignoring his brother's comments, "Yes, you'll finish your lessons, that I am sure of. Aye?" As the elder in the clan, he turned his dark gaze toward his younger brother.

"I don't care. I think I'll . . ." Ryan's voice trailed off. It sounded hollow because deep down inside he really did care. Feelings that he had thought were gone had now risen to the surface in just the short time he had held Alexi in his arms and danced around the floor holding her. He had felt so alive dancing with her. He kept thinking about her and could not get her out of his mind. Her easy laugh, her engaging smile—he had not felt this way since . . . Grace. *What the hell am I going to do now? Go home and have a drink with my brothers. Yeah. I'll figure it out tomorrow.*

Chapter Eighteen

"Gloria, I don't know any more information than you do. I'm sorry, but we still have to have a place setting for Mickey's mom and dad. Mickey said his parents may have to go out of the country on business, but they're trying to rearrange things since we decided to get married so quickly."

Mary Kate's wedding planner interjected, "Has Mickey spoken with them? Or have you?"

"Mickey speaks to him all the time. He works for his dad at the company, remember?"

"What about after your announcement?"

"They called once to congratulate us after our engagement announcement, but I have not heard from them since then. His mom's very nice, but his dad is hard to figure out. It's kind of strange. Just leave a seat for both of them and we'll figure out something." On Sunday Mickey had promised he would have an answer for her by Monday. Today was Wednesday. He had promised, but still no answer.

She glanced at her watch; she had been on the phone for more than forty-five minutes again. She didn't have this kind of time to spare at work for her wedding details.

A knock at the door caused her to look up. It was Alison.

"Come on, Mary Kate, we're going to be late for the meeting," said her close friend and bridesmaid, who was helping her pack up her things for the weekly Wednesday meeting with the senior partners.

She rushed her wedding planner off the phone. "Gloria, I gotta go. Call me tonight if you need me."

Her coworker looked at her while grabbing her files. "Come on, MK, hurry. We don't want to be late." The two of them nearly ran down the hallway, entering the conference room precisely at nine a.m. "Sorry, Mr. Block, sir."

From the look on his face, she could tell he was agitated. Tall, distinguished, impeccably dressed, with perfectly groomed white hair, Irwin "Sonny" Block had a reputation for honesty, trustworthiness, and hard work in South Florida. In fact, he was one of the most esteemed attorneys in the region.

"Ladies . . . ," he began while he stood, looking even taller than his actual six foot five. "Grab some coffee and a bagel before we begin." He was good to his staff, to all of them. He had been the first attorney in Florida to hire female attorneys, and treated all staff equally, both men and women. The female attorneys with the firm affectionately called him Poppa behind closed doors but never to his face. They could tell him or ask him anything.

Mary Kate sat down quickly and opened her portfolio on the conference table. There were eight male and six female attorneys, and they all worked long and hard hours. They were expected to carry a full workload and still perform public service for the community. For their reward they were well paid and highly recruited. There were more alumni of the Block & Sawyer law firm on the Florida courts than of any other law firm in the state of Florida. It was a good firm to work for—actually, the best.

"Who wants to start?" asked Sonny to start the meeting.

Each attorney presented their casework for input from the other attorneys, and the status of any pro bono work they were involved in for the firm. One by one they briefed their fellow associates, so should anyone need to fill in, they would be familiar with the case.

Mary Kate made a note at the top of her legal pad. Calley Terrell? She had never heard back from her. Was she okay? Was she still staying at the hotel? Calley was supposed to call her.

When it was her turn, she briefed the group on the status of her cases and her pro bono work. Regarding Calley she gave a brief explanation, and moved on to her next case.

As they filed out of the conference room, Sonny asked her to stay behind so they could talk. "Mary Kate, I know you have a wedding to plan and there's a lot of pressure on you. But please don't forget there are many people out there who are depending on the work you do here. Like Calley Terrell, for instance. I strongly suggest you check into where she is. Is she all right, and what are the next steps? Did she go back home to him? Just because it's pro bono work doesn't mean that we take it any less serious. Do you get my point?"

"Yes, sir."

"That'll be all. Back to work . . . and Ms. Macgregor . . . next time, if you're not fifteen minutes early for a conference—you're late. It's disrespectful to everyone in the meeting. Their time is valuable too." No lectures. No yelling. No screaming. No admonishments, just the facts. He turned and walked toward his office. Not another word was ever said. Tough but fair. Out of respect to him, she made a mental note never to be late for one of his meetings again.

Once back at her office, she called the Delray Dunes and spoke to the manager, Robin.

"Hey, Robin, this is Kate Macgregor. Howya doin'?"

"Good, Ms. Macgregor. I want to thank you again for getting me this job. It's been a lifesaver, in more ways than one."

"No problem. I'm just calling to check in on one of my new clients I sent over to you, Calley Terrell?"

"You know, that's funny, she called about getting a room here until she got situated somewhere, but she never showed up. I was just about ready to call you about her. Anything wrong?"

"I'm not sure. Tell you what, call me if she checks in or if you hear from her, and ask her to call me." The concern was now obvious in her voice. She called Calley's cell-phone number. No answer. Then she called some of the friends Calley had listed on her contact sheet, but nobody else had seen her. A chill went down her back as she recalled the fear in Calley's voice when she mentioned the name of her husband, Phil. She did not feel good about this.

She glanced at her watch, then tried to call Mickey, but got his voice mail. When she finally looked up from the piles of paperwork on her desk, she saw it was nearly nine p.m. and the office was deserted. *Give it a break, girl. Time to go home.*

Mary Kate grabbed her briefcase and thought about soaking in a warm bath with a glass of chilled chardonnay once she was home. Just the thing after a long day at work, but she still had many phone calls to make tonight.

She pressed the button for the elevator. Damn—it wasn't working again, off for the evening. She took the stairs, and the motion detector slowly turned on the blinking fluorescent lights to help guide her way. It was only three flights down. At each landing the light came on to greet her. *Where's Calley? Why hasn't she called me? Does she have my home number? Why hasn't she called me to let me know what's happening?* She had calls to make, then a nice hot bath and a glass of chardonnay. *Yes.* All these thoughts ran through her head as she made her way down the steps. The bottom landing light did not go on as she slowed her descent into the darkness, feeling her way along the wall and the railing.

A hand grabbed her in the dark, and she felt the cold steel of a knife blade pressed against the right side of her throat as the other hand grabbed her around her waist. She was about to scream, but a man's gruff voice said, "Shut up and don't scream, you hear me?" She was petrified.

"Y-y-you lawyers are all th-th-the same," he stammered. His breath was foul; it reeked of stale cigarettes and booze. His clothes smelled of gasoline and diesel fuel. "I'm only going to tell you this o-o-once—you stay away from mmmy Calley. Just st-st-stay away, you hear me? Don't be filling her head with some strange notion that she can l-l-leave me. She'll never leave me, at least not alive."

His hand shifted from her waist and moved up to grab her and hold her tighter. "Nice," he said cruelly as his hand searched her body. "Real nice. Come here, girlie-girl." He removed the knife from her neck and began to turn her around to face him while his other hand kept exploring. She turned to face him in the dark, not seeing his face but only his outline in the shadows.

Mary Kate remained calm and then struck back with a vengeance, shoving his nose upward with the heel of her hand, then kneeing him in the groin. Surprised, he screamed in a high-pitched pained voice, cursing her.

She pushed open the exit door and ran. She ran as she had never run before and thanked her father for those self-defense courses she had taken. She kept running, and when she reached her car, her hand was shaking so violently she could not put the key in the ignition. *Calm down, girl. You're all right.* Finally it worked, and she stepped on the gas pedal and raced home, calling 911 from the car as her hand shook with a nervous tremor. *Calm down, girl,* she told herself. She had to report what had happened to her and then she had to find Calley. He was gone—*but what about Calley?*

When she returned to her apartment, the police met her there and took her report. Mickey called, and when she told him what had happened, she could hear the anger in his voice. He said he was on his way. She was comforted by the thought of him and felt safer. Then the phone rang again. It was Sonny.

"Are you okay?" he asked her in a concerned way. "The night watchman found your briefcase in the stairwell and called me." It was past ten o'clock. "Is everything all right?" he asked with genuine worry in his voice.

After she told him what had happened, he said, "Maybe you should go to the hospital or call your family physician?"

"No, I'll be okay."

"Do you want Doris to come over? It's no problem, really. We would both feel better if she did. Please?" Doris had worked as a nurse for many years before becoming his personal assistant.

"No, my fiancé is on his way. And I called 911 and just met with the police. But thanks, Sonny. Thanks for caring."

"Call me if you need anything, anything at all."

She lay there on her bed, the room silent. Gone were the thoughts of a warm bath and a cool glass of chardonnay. Instead, she retreated into a darkened corner and stripped off her clothes to rid herself of the lingering gasoline smell. She sat shivering, naked, with a blanket wrapped around her, and waited for Mickey. But the longer she sat in the dark, the angrier she became. Angry with herself—how could she have let her guard down? Angry he had gotten away with it, degrading her, violating her privacy. Fury rose inside her. That would never happen again—never.

She stood and dropped the blanket to the floor. She grabbed the clothes she had worn that day and frantically began to shred them with a pair of scissors. Piece by piece she sliced and cut, feeling liberated with every slash. Soon a pile of rags lay at her feet. Then she began to plan. *Tomorrow is the first day of a new life.* Calley had come to her for help; she trusted her. Tomorrow she would find Calley.

Chapter Nineteen

He sat at his desk, intently watching the phone as he waited for his next patient to arrive.

"Dr. Macgregor?" June asked.

Startled, Ryan looked up at her.

"That phone won't dial itself, you know?" She had known him long enough to tell he was preoccupied.

He was quiet at first. "I know."

"And it won't ring just because you want it to." She looked at him and turned to walk away. She was glad he was alive; he was a good person and a good boss. Anything could have happened—that crazy patient could have killed him and . . . killed her. She shuddered just thinking about it.

He continued to look at the phone on his desk. *I'm going to call her. Right now. Yes, that's what I'm going to do.* He went to grab the receiver just as the phone rang.

June reached across his desk to answer it. "Good morning. Dr. Macgregor's office." She nodded her head as she listened. Then a small smile crept across her face. "Hold on just a minute, please; let me check to see if he's available." She put the call on hold. "Ms. Alexi Cassini on the phone for you. Do you want to take the call?" she asked with a wry grin on her face.

He coughed as he sat up in his chair, moving his head from side to side to help himself relax and to loosen his neck muscles as he prepared to take the call. "Yes, I'll speak with her. Of course." He picked up the phone but waited to press the button to speak to her.

June stood and watched before she finally turned away, saying, "Men. Umphh."

"Hi," he said quietly into the phone as the door closed behind her.

"Hi back." An awkward moment of silence ensued.

Then he said, "Hey, listen, about last night, I was a little off yesterday. Must have been something I ate or . . ."

"It's okay. I understand, but you still have dance lessons left on your package, and I was thinking, that is, if you want to, we could do it later tonight or tomorrow, depending on your schedule."

"Tonight works fine for me. If that's okay."

"Sure," she said with a bouncy cheer. "See you about . . . eight?" Her laugh was like Gracie's lighthearted way.

"Perfect. See you then." He hung up the phone, but something was troubling him. His memories of Gracie were slipping away and being replaced by thoughts of dancing, dining, smiling . . . and Alexi. *Where is all of this going?*

Later Ryan drove to the dance studio and found her waiting for him when he arrived. Other instructors were scattered about the room, practicing with their students.

"Hey. Sorry about last night. Like I said, it must have been something I ate or . . ."

"It's okay," she said sweetly. "Don't give it another thought. We all have days like that . . . it's fine, really. Follow me."

She started her music in the private lesson room and walked back to him. "You just missed your brothers. They came in for their lesson."

"Yes, I couldn't make it with them; I had a late-afternoon patient I had to see."

She smiled her sweet smile. "You did very well with your lesson, especially the waltz. Let's just practice a little more. Okay?"

"Sure." The music began as he took her in his arms. He looked at her. Tonight was different; she was different. Her hair lay gracefully on her shoulders and was not pinned tightly above her head, as it had been during their last lesson. Gone was the gym leotard, replaced by a chic beaded top and tailored skirt, the kind Gracie always wore.

Taking Alexi in his arms, he detected the slightest hint of perfume as they began their dance. It was Grace's favorite. He closed his eyes, listened to the music, and could not help himself. He dreamed he was dancing with his Gracie. She felt perfect in his arms—so soft, warm, and tender. The rise and fall of the dance came naturally, his shoulders perfectly squared as he spun, rotated, and danced to the music. He opened his eyes, then led Alexi back across the room in a butterfly movement, alternating sides until finally the song was over.

When they were finished, she stepped back and looked at him, impressed. "That was wonderful." She just stood there looking at him. He had surprised even himself.

"You were dancing with your wife just now, weren't you?"

He hesitated for a moment before saying, "I'm sorry. Yes, I guess I was. It felt so natural."

"I could tell, but that's good. I dance with my husband all the time," she said quietly, touching her chest. "You know, you remind me of . . ." She paused for a moment before changing the subject. "Let's try it one more time, then we can add some other moves."

It was all coming back to him as he remembered the dance steps from years gone by. It was more like dancing than a lesson.

They sat for a break and soon discovered they had been practicing for over an hour and that the studio was empty except for the reception-ist reading a magazine at her desk.

Alexi dabbed her face with a towel, leaned back in the chair, and looked at him. "I can understand how uncomfortable it can be to dance with someone new. Or be with someone new. I only danced with my husband until he passed away."

"Gracie and I took lessons for years, and we danced once or twice a week. I loved to dance with her. To hold her in my arms . . . was magical." He realized he was rambling. "How long has it been since your husband passed away?"

"Four years. We were in Argentina at a dance competition. Juan stopped at a stoplight in Buenos Aires, and when he went to kiss me, a truck came up behind us. He hit us at full speed. The next thing I knew, I woke up in the hospital. I found out later the truck had lost its brakes and slammed into us. I was hospitalized for weeks. My husband died a few days after the accident. I still miss him terribly, but I realize he would want me to get on with my life. It still took me over a year before I could even practice dance with anyone else."

Alexi looked over at him with a sweet smile on her face. "My brother owns this studio. He invited me to come here, to dance and to teach. So three years later, here I am." She stopped and looked at him. "You know, you have his laugh. My Juan Carlos. You shouldn't be afraid to show it. It's a wonderful gift. It tells the whole world you're happy."

Alexi stretched out her legs, then crossed them, causing her skirt to rise slightly. She had beautiful legs, long and athletic. His eyes lingered on them. She was intoxicating. He took a deep breath as he sat looking at her.

She caught his gaze, swallowed once, and asked, "Once more around the dance floor?"

"Sure."

"I think you have the waltz down pretty well. Would you like to brush up on any other dance? Maybe the rumba? The one they call the dance of love?" she laughed.

"Yes, that's exactly what I was thinking. A nice slow rumba to end the evening, and help wind down."

They danced together while she slowly brought her head close to his, dancing the slow Latin classic. When they separated for a spin or turn, she came back to him, each time closer. When the music was over, he spun her out and she returned to his arms, her face this time mere inches from his. He moved to her, wanting to kiss her. *Heaven help me,* he thought as they both closed their eyes and . . .

"Excuse me, Ms. Cassini?" came a voice over the intercom from the front desk. "It's after closing time, and if you don't mind, I have a bus to catch for home. Can you lock up for the night?"

With the moment broken, they both looked toward the receptionist, and she waved good night.

"I have one more lesson left with you. I thought perhaps, maybe . . . ," he began.

"Saturday night?" she said, finishing his sentence.

"Yes, yes, exactly what I was thinking. What time?"

"Later. Say nine o'clock."

"That works fine. See you then. Good night."

He could not wait to see her again. To dance with her, to hold her in his arms, and . . .

Chapter Twenty

The Boynton Beach Town Hall Center was filled with people. So many women, all very well dressed, sipping tea and coffee, eating doughnuts and bagels. The room was abuzz with chatter. Robert felt uncomfortable wearing the new tie that Patti had bought for him. He was tempted to remove it, but when he spoke to her that morning, she had told him, "Whatever you do, don't take your tie off until you're done and back in your truck." He heeded her advice.

A friendly male face in the crowd waved at him. "Hi, I'm Jeremy. You must be . . ."

"Robert, or just Bob Macgregor."

"Good to meet you, 'just Bob.' Is this your first time doing a senior speed-dating session?"

"Yes, I'm afraid it is."

"Piece of cake. Here's how it works. You take a seat across from one of the ladies, and you get three minutes to talk to her. A buzzer will sound, and you thank the woman for her time and move to the next seat. The tables are set up in a circle so you just keep going until you're back at the seat where you first sat down. If the lady likes you, she will give you a bio card with some information about her—her background, her interests, her photo, and contact information. And she'll invite you to call or e-mail her." Jeremy could tell that Bob was overwhelmed.

"At the end of the session, there'll be coffee and cake, and you'll have the opportunity to mingle with the ladies and to talk with them again. Just remember to be yourself and be respectful. And don't be disappointed if you don't get any cards, this being your first session and all. I made up some bio cards for you to hand out to the ladies that you like, which lists the information you sent me." A bell rang to alert all the participants to take a seat.

"Good luck, Bob. You'll do just fine. Listen for the buzzer."

Bob grabbed an empty chair and smiled at the woman across from him. The buzzer went off, and the room was suddenly filled with voices.

She had a very pleasant smile. Bob liked that about her. "Hi, I'm Matrice. I'm a snowbird and flew down here from Maine. I usually stay here in Florida for the winter, and I like to attend as many of these dating sessions as possible. Then go back to Maine in the summer. So tell me, are you divorced, widowed, or what?"

"My wife died of cancer almost two years ago."

"I'm so sorry to hear that. My Claude died six years ago, and I've been looking for somebody for about that long. Are you handy around the house?"

"Very handy. Why?"

"Well, my other home, the summer place, is kind of remote, in the mountains of Maine, and it needs a lot of work. So I thought I would kill two birds with one stone, so to speak, if you know what I mean?"

Bob smiled at her. "Can I make a suggestion?"

"Sure," she said and her expression perked up.

"Talk to some of the handymen advertising up there, and bring them in to do some work for you. I am sure there are many single repair people in Maine who are also looking for potential mates. You could even invite them in for dinner if you like."

"Wow, that's a great idea. Two birds with one stone. Here's my card and bio if you think you may be interested in the job. I would really like to—" *Buzzzzzz.*

He shook her hand and moved to the next seat.

"Hi, I'm Betty. I live here in Boca full-time. Have you been to many of these? I come here and to the one in Delray all of the time, but I just haven't had any luck yet. You must be new; I've never seen you before." The words came tumbling out so fast Bob could not keep up with her.

"I'm Bob. This is my first—"

She kept talking, and Bob was afraid she was going to pass out. "What's your name again?"

"Robert. I mean Bob, Bob Macgregor."

"Irish, huh. I once dated an Irishman in New York. Great guy, but—" *Buzzzzzz.*

"Nice to meet you, Betty."

She handed him a card with her bio. "Call me. We can talk."

He smiled and moved on to the next chair. "Hi, I'm . . ."

That day he met more than thirty-six women and accumulated thirty-two cards, including the one from Matrice. Afterward, when it was calmer, he poured himself some coffee and mingled with the group. They were by far the nicest, most considerate women he had met in a long, long time. Although a few were forceful, he talked with all of them. He laughed and was glad he had taken the time to come to the event. Robert arranged to call three of them. He also had a list of twelve others he needed advice about, so he phoned Patti when he got to his truck to ask her guidance.

She could not stop laughing as he told her of his adventures, and he started to laugh as he thought about the conversations. He loved Patti's ways and how she made him laugh, just as his Tess always had.

They talked for a half hour, but when he started to ask her advice about the next steps for some of the women he had met, she stopped him. "Whoa, wait a minute, Dad. I suggest you call your old friend Coleen. You told me she wanted to hear all about your adventures. Talk to her about it. I'm sure she can give you some good advice, much better than I can." She paused. "I just don't feel comfortable talking about your love life, if you know what I mean?"

"Oh yeah, sure. You're right," he chuckled and hung up. *Well, Coleen did say to call her, to let her know how it went.*

Later that evening he decided to call her. Bob was nervous about rejection when he picked up the phone and dialed her number. The phone rang twice, and he lost his nerve. He was about to hang up when he heard her sweet voice, say, "Hello?"

"Hi, it's Robert."

"Hiya, Mac."

"I haven't caught you at a bad time, have I?"

"No, I was just sitting here relaxing with a good book. What's up?" He could hear her getting comfortable, with the sounds of rustling pillows and a book closing in the background.

"Well, I went to the senior speed-dating session today."

"You did?" she nearly shouted.

Robert could not tell if she was surprised, excited, or somewhat disappointed. "Yeah. It was fun. I met some very nice ladies there. And I got over thirty bio information cards."

Really? she thought, upset with herself. This is not what she had thought would happen. What did she think? Wait . . . did she care? Yes, she reluctantly admitted to herself—she did care.

"Wow! Tell me about them, and don't leave anything out." She tried to sound enthused.

They talked for an over an hour as Bob gave her a play-by-play of the dates he remembered.

"They were all very nice. I made arrangements to call some of them and go out."

"Good for you." *What?* she thought. *Coleen, what did you think was going to happen—he's a single, good-looking guy. And you turned him down when he asked you out.* She swallowed hard.

He paused; he wished he were sitting there next to her talking and sharing a glass of wine with her. He coughed. "I know it's late, and I don't want to keep you. But maybe we could do dinner one night, and I can tell you about the rest of them. Maybe you could give me some advice."

Something held her back. She did not want to go down that path. "No, Bob, I don't think that's such a good idea."

"Can I ask you why not?"

She paused. "Bobby, you're an adorably handsome guy, almost sexy—but it would never work out."

"Why not?"

She took in a deep breath. "Because we're cut from different cloths. I like the ballet, the opera, the theater, classical music, and you like hunting, boating, fishing, country music, and camping. It wouldn't work. I'm sorry, Mac, I have to go. Good-bye." She was nearly in tears when she hung up the phone. *Damn him. Why me? Why now? I only wanted to be left alone. Why did he have to come back into my life? Why can't he just leave me be?* She sat and watched the tall and serene grandfather clock in the corner, waiting for it to strike its melodious chimes, and she thought to herself, *I wonder when he'll call me next?*

Chapter Twenty-One

Germaine's lot was full that night, and after searching and finally finding a parking spot, Eian and Robert walked inside. As they waited in line to pay their cover charge and be seated, Robert whispered to his brother, "Look at all the single women here. They're all so beautiful."

"Yes, I remember that a lot of singles and couples come here," Eian said, his eyes searching the room for Rose. Then he spotted her at a table near the dance floor and waved. "There she is."

Robert smiled, and then leaned in to whisper to Eian, "Hey, I don't want to be an odd man out, if you know what I mean? If you two guys want to . . . be alone or . . . ? I don't want to butt in, you know?"

Eian's brow creased with a frown. "Rose? Hey, man, we're just friends. Old friends. It'll be fine. Don't worry about it."

As the line moved forward, Robert reminded him, "Well, as I recall, years ago you were the one who introduced Rose to Tony. Right?"

"Right. So what's your point?"

He could tell Robert was getting uncomfortable. "Well, I always thought she was kinda sweet on you, that's all," he blurted out.

"Bob, we're just friends, and besides—"

He was interrupted by Rose as she came up to them. "Hi, Eian! I'm really glad you could make it tonight. Lots of opportunity to practice your new dance steps."

"Yeah, I see," Eian responded, looking around the room. "I hope you don't mind, but I brought my brother with me. He needs the practice more than I do, but I also thought this was a great place for him to meet some people."

She was silent at first but then said, "Sure. Why not? The more the merrier. Right?"

Turning to his brother, he said, "See, I told you Rose wouldn't mind. This is going to be some night," Eian said, looking out over the dance floor.

"Yeah, some night," she said with a meager smile. "I'll meet you back at our table. See ya."

The three of them had dinner, wine, coffee, and dessert, and then the band began to play. She stood and reached for Eian's hand. "Come on, let's dance. Practice. That's what we're here for, remember?"

Germaine's was on the top floor of Boca Raton's "bridge hotel," overlooking the Intracoastal Waterway on one side and the Atlantic Ocean on the other. From the fifteenth floor, the view stretched for miles beyond the glass walls. In the center of the room was a large parquet dance floor in front of a three-piece Latin band. They played music to dance rumbas, cha-chas, bachatas, salsa, swing, waltzes, hustles, and a host of others. Bob sat and watched until more dancers were on the floor.

Rose and Eian returned to the dinner table after dancing. "Wow, that was fun," said Eian. "I remembered all the steps we learned. And did them perfectly, brother." He smiled at Robert.

Rose joined in, taking a sip from her wineglass. "Well, I don't know about that. You still need a lot of work, trust me. But we have all night."

The next dance was a rumba, and she said to Eian as they danced, "You're supposed to hold me closer for this one, remember?"

"Like this?" he whispered, slowly pulling her close.

"Yes, like that." Try as she might, she could not stop the feelings that were building inside her. They moved closer to each other during the slow dance and next began to move gently about the floor. Eian and Rose were lost in their own thoughts.

When they finally sat down to take a break, she touched his arm and asked, "Can you get me a glass of ice water, please? I'm dying in here. It's getting very warm."

"Sure, Rose. Bob, you want anything?

"No, I think I'm going to ask that woman over there to dance."

"Oh yeah? Which one?" asked Rose.

He nodded in the direction of three women sitting together on the other side of the room. "The one in the pink top. She has been watching me all night. Wish me luck."

"Be a gentleman," Rose said under her breath.

"Thanks," he said with a smile after taking a big gulp from his glass of wine.

Soon everyone was on their feet dancing . . . including Rose.

When she returned to the table, Eian gave her the glass of ice water and asked nonchalantly, "Who was that?"

"Who?"

"The guy you were just dancing with."

"Barry? He's a friend. I met him here a couple of weeks ago." She saw the look on Eian's face. "I come here all the time with my girl-friends, just to dance and have a good time. But you're the first man I've come here with, like a date . . . since Tony." She took his hand in hers, held it, and let it linger for a few moments, while they made eye contact. She smiled and was about to say something when Robert returned.

"Nice place. Thanks for letting me crash your party. Sorry."

Rose smiled. "Bobby, it's fine, really. I'm glad you're having a good time." Her voice and intentions were genuine.

The bandleader then called for all single men and single women to form two circles around the dance floor, and directed the circles to turn in opposite directions. The band began to play. When the trumpeter finished blasting his horn, the circles stopped moving, and the dancers took the hand of whoever was across from them, and then they danced with each other. This was repeated for five different songs. Bob loved it.

It was a wonderful evening of dining, dancing, and being together with old friends and family. Rose and Eian danced every slow dance as if they were the only ones on the dance floor. Traveling in slow, small circles, holding each other tight. Something was happening to both of them. Soon the call came from the bandleader that it was the last dance, another slow one. It had been a wonderful evening.

"Rose, I had a great time," Eian said as he walked her to her car. "Let's do this again, just you and me."

"I would love to," she said enthusiastically. "They have music and dancing here every night of the week except Monday."

"I'll call you tomorrow and we'll set something up."

"Promise?"

"I promise."

She kissed him on the cheek, and her fingertip traced the contours of his chin. "Talk to you tomorrow."

The two brothers drove home in silence, both lost in their own thoughts. When Robert pulled into the driveway, he waited in the car by himself. "Eian, why don't you go on inside. I'll join you in a couple of minutes. I just want to make a quick phone call."

Eian smiled, leaning into the car to look at his older brother. "You can call from inside if you want. It's starting to rain."

"I'll be okay. I won't be long."

Then Eian smiled and asked, "Coleen?"

He nodded. "Yeah."

"Okay, see ya inside. Good luck."

"Thanks."

He dialed her number, and his face grew into a smile when he heard her voice say, "Hello? Bob?"

"Yeah, it's me. It's not too late to call, is it?"

"No, it's fine. I couldn't sleep anyway. I usually don't have a problem falling asleep, but here, lately . . . just don't know. What's up?"

"Just thought I'd call and tell you about my evening."

"Oh. Was tonight dance night?"

He smiled, glad that she had remembered. "Yeah, yesterday were lessons, and tonight I was practicing my dancing at Germaine's. It was fun."

"More fun than the speed dating?"

"Oh yes, definitely. I had a great meal and good company."

"You went with your brother Eian, right?"

"Yeah, him and an old friend of his, Rose Gilardo. She was married to his best friend, Tony, who died a couple of years ago. They go way back."

"Just the three of you went, then?" she asked, trying not to sound too inquisitive.

"Yep. I danced all night." He went on to tell her about the dance circles and everyone he had danced with, including the woman dressed in pink.

"Hmmm, sounds interesting. Did she let you take her home?" She sounded different.

"No, it was just dinner and dancing." Then he added playfully, "Hey, you had your chance. I asked you to join us, but you blew it, my dear. Great food, music, and dancing. Everything you could possibly want."

She laughed. Their conversation seemed so natural, so familiar. "It sounds like fun."

"They have it every night—dinner, music, and dancing. You want to join me tomorrow night?"

Her laughing stopped. There was silence on the phone, and a light rain began to fall on the car windshield. Silence.

"I'm sorry. I shouldn't have pressed you," he said apologetically.

"It's all right."

"How about just dinner? You and me? Wherever you want. You choose."

"No, Bob. I don't think so. I would really like to . . . I just don't think it's such a good idea. Okay?" As much as she wanted to see him again, she just could not . . .

"I understand." There was that awkward silence again as they both looked for something to say. Finally Bob asked her, "But on a different subject, I wanted to mention something to you. One of my customers came into the store today and gave me two box-seat tickets to the Friday show at the Kravis Center for Puccini's *Madama Butterfly*." He had taken great pains to learn the correct pronunciation of the opera. He heard her gasp, and he knew he had her. He waited for it all to sink in before continuing, "I hate to throw them away. So I thought of you, thinking maybe you . . . and a friend, could use them? And at no charge, a gift from one friend to another. I just hate to see them go to waste."

"*Madama Butterfly*? Wow, it's my favorite."

"Great, I'll just drop the tickets by your office or the house, wherever you prefer." There was silence on the other end of the line for what seemed like centuries. *Don't say a word, Robert. Don't . . . don't.* He could almost hear the wheels spinning inside her head, then she finally asked, "Are you busy Friday night? Would you like to go . . . with me? To see the opera? *Madama Butterfly*."

He hated the theater but was willing to learn to like it. Hell, if he could learn to eat brussels sprouts, he could learn to love anything. "Well, if you like, I'd be happy to accompany you. Sure, why not? It would be fun."

"But only on the condition that you let me buy you dinner . . . to thank you for the tickets."

"No, the tickets were a gift from a customer. No charge. How about I pick you up, say . . . six o'clock?"

"Perfect. See you then. And Bob . . . thanks a lot. That was very sweet of you to think of me."

He ended the call, grinning, and opened the car door. The rain was coming down harder, but he didn't care. He danced around in a circle and jumped for joy, clicking his heels in the process. Around and around he danced, singing an old Scottish drinking song. From the open front door, Ryan and Eian stood watching their crazy older brother.

Eian shouted, "Come out of the rain, bro! You'll get sick."

When he finally stopped his rain dance and came inside, they both asked, "What's this all about?"

"I just spent two hundred bucks on theater tickets," he said as he passed by them on his way to find a towel and dry off. "Best two hundred dollars I've ever spent! I'm taking Coleen to the opera! Can you believe it?"

They looked at each other. It was too late, they both thought—he was already crazy in the head.

Robert was happy and not afraid to show it. He was going to the opera . . . with Coleen! He knew he was crazy. He hated spending money, and he hated the opera. Yes, he hated it, but there was something else, something more. He realized he was falling in love with her.

Chapter Twenty-Two

Mickey Thompson had just finished a three-hour meeting with his top executives and was on his way back to his office as he discreetly checked his cell phone—no message from Mary Kate. At his office he heard his executive assistant, Bashir, say, pointing to the phone, "Sir, it's for you."

"Who is it?" he asked as he made his way to his desk.

The patient Bashir waited behind him at a respectful distance. He lowered his head but did not say anything. Bashir was from Nepal and had a long history with the family. It was his job to serve and protect Mickey, his young charge. He had saved his life one night from a wandering cobra in their tent outside Kathmandu and now was his lifelong aide and protector.

Mickey waited.

"Line four," he finally told him.

He knew immediately who it was. His father.

"Hold all my calls, unless it's my fiancée."

He drew in a deep breath, ready for the firestorm. "Morning, Angus."

"Don't you goddamn 'Good morning' me, you ingrate. Why is it that I have to hear about your disastrous meeting with Rumpe from his goddamn interview with the New York tabloids?"

Mickey could tell he was furious, but his father had always told him that Florida was his operation to run as he saw fit, and that was exactly what he intended to do.

"What the hell were you thinking?" his father shouted.

"I was thinking that we don't need Rumpe's name to make this project a success."

"Are you daft, boy?"

"Father, he brings nothing to the table, not even money."

"Well, my boy, the big banks like him; they make money from him."

"And they lose money with him when he goes bankrupt. Everybody loses with him. All he was offering was his name, and demanding a twenty percent cut off the top line for that privilege. Nothing else. Father, I met with him out of respect because you asked me to see him. If you want someone else to run the operations down here in Florida, then so be it." There was silence on the line between the two hardheaded men.

"No, son, I don't want to replace you . . . yet." He stopped talking, then said, "Kill you, yes, but replace my golden-haired protégé—no. But after you sign the contract to begin this project, I want you to take some time off. Not a lot of time, mind you, just some time to clear your head. You've been working way too hard, and I think it's starting to addle your brain."

"Like father, like son. I'll take some time off after the wedding. Not right away, but . . ." Silence. "Are you coming to the wedding?" he ventured to ask his father one more time.

Once again, silence. "No. I need to be in Australia to negotiate a big deal there."

"Angus, anybody can do that for you."

"Then maybe I should have you go there and take care of it for me?"

"That's not what I meant. I would like you and Mother to come our wedding. It would mean the world to me and to Mary Kate to have you there."

"She's a goddamn Macgregor, and I'll not be—"

Mickey's blood boiled to hear those words. "That's my future wife you're talking about, Angus. I'll mind you to keep a civil tongue in your mouth when talking about her."

"Damn them. See, they bring out the worst in me."

"Like me?"

The conversation degenerated into its usual pattern, as it had ever since Angus had learned about the upcoming wedding.

"Like our children will be, your grandchildren?"

"She's pregnant?" he screamed. "Is that what the rush is for you to get married?"

"No, sir, she's not pregnant. But where does this vendetta, this hatred, stop? And when?" Frustrated, he said, "I'm sorry, I must go. Good-bye, Father." He hung up the phone. He felt bad and angry at the same time. He loved his father, but his wedding had become a sore point between the two of them. And he had heard nothing from his mother.

As if by instinct, Bashir appeared through the door, slowly opening it before quietly closing it behind him.

Mickey looked up and already knew what he was going to say.

"He's your father; always remember that," whispered the diminutive man from Nepal, standing by the door, as always, on guard.

Mickey looked up to correct him. "Adopted father."

Bashir remained calm but determined when he spoke. "Young one, when your father died, Angus chose you when no one else would. Nobody! He chose to be your father, your family, and beyond that—to honor your parents . . . he let you keep your family name. Angus Campbell gave you a great honor. Never forget that."

Bashir was direct and to the point, as usual. Always the teacher.

"You're right." He was ashamed. He picked up the phone and dialed his father.

"Angus? This is Mickey."

"I know who the hell this is. What do you want now?"

"I forgot to tell you something . . . I love you, Dad. That's all. Good-bye." He knew then, in his heart, what he had to do.

He hung up the phone and did not hear his father reply, "I love you too, son." But Angus still wasn't coming to the wedding. Never! The bride's family were Macgregors, and that would never change. The Campbell and Macgregor clans had been at war with one another for more than four hundred years. *Of all the lasses in the world, why . . . why in God's good name did he choose a Macgregor to marry? Damn him, damn him to hell, and damn that cursed woman.*

Chapter Twenty-Three

"Angus, what did Mickey want on the phone?" asked his wife, Claret Campbell.

He mumbled something from the other room as he walked away.

She raised her voice. "Angus Macleod Campbell, don't you walk away from me when I'm talking to you, and don't you dare mumble to me. What did my son want on the phone? I heard you two shouting. What's wrong?"

He never liked to argue with his wife.

She shouted again, "Angus!"

He returned to the room, his face still red with anger. He tried to bluster his way out of the conversation. "Ah, woman, if you really must know . . . he's wantin' to know if we're comin' to his wedding. Aye, there, now you know. Are you satisfied?"

She set aside her knitting and asked, "And why would he be asking that now? Of course we're going to our son's wedding." There was no response from her husband of forty-four years.

Her shrewd eyes narrowed, focusing all her attention on him. "You mailed back that invitation RSVP that I gave you . . . now didn't you?" she asked. Her lips tightened.

"Well . . . I had something important come up at the office at the same time as the wedding. A deal in Australia that's very good for the company. Worth a lot of money. So . . ."

"Angus Campbell," she shouted, now on her feet, wagging her finger at him, so close her face was nearly touching his, "you pick up that phone and you call your son and you tell him once and for all that we're coming to the wedding. And you do it now."

His chest puffed, his face crimson as he bellowed in return, "Nay, woman. I'll not be attending no Macgregor's wedding. And that's the end of this talk."

"Is that what this is all about? Some old Scottish feud that's five hundred years old? Is that it?"

He looked down. "Aye."

She picked up her knitting tools, tucked them under her arm, and, before she left, slowly turned to face him. "Angus, you have always been one headstrong, bullheaded Scotsman. But this . . . this is beyond that. This is mean, and I don't understand it—you're not a mean man. Not the Angus Campbell I married." She whispered, "I'm ashamed of you, Angus Campbell, for the first time in my life. Ashamed to call myself a Campbell."

She came closer to him, then touched his cheek. "Dear heart, marriage is tough enough for two people to live and work their way through life. It is something you must work at, each and every day, day after day. You're only making it tougher for our son to find the happiness he deserves." She sighed and, with a sense of resignation, said, "If you don't want to go to your son's wedding and risk not seeing your only grandchildren, then so be it. I can't force you. But I'm going . . . either with you or without you. Good night."

For the first time in their marriage, they went to bed angry at each other, with issues still unresolved. She wouldn't let him see her tears, no, never. But she ached for a resolution. She loved each of them and wanted both to be happy. *Damn stubborn Scotsmen. Both of them.*

Chapter Twenty-Four

Eian had called twice to make sure the grass on his Delray vacant lot had been cut and trimmed and the trash removed. The property manager had assured him that it was taken care of, but Eian had received a notice from the city that it would take legal action if the grass and trash situations were not addressed. What a pain. He decided to drive by on his way home, just to make sure everything was done. The lot was much more convenient to drive to from Ryan's house than from where he had been living before.

He drove to Delray, turned onto Clinton, and saw for himself that the lot had indeed been cut, weeded, and cleaned up. He made a mental note to make sure the management company kept it that way. He sat in the car watching some neighborhood kids play baseball on the now-cleared lot and thought back to when he and his brothers had done the exact same thing so many years earlier at home. Those had been fun times. Great times. No, those had been the best times of his life. Hanging out with his brothers, playing baseball just for the fun of it. Before college, before the big leagues, before making the big money, just playing baseball for the sheer fun of playing, and throwing a baseball.

Eian decided to watch the boys awhile and got out of his car. He watched them throw, catch, hit the ball, and field the hits.

"Great catch!" he shouted without thinking, causing the group of boys to look in his direction. He clapped, and they smiled but kept on playing, stealing short glances in his direction. Finally, the tallest one in the group conferred with the catcher and set his bat down on an old piece of cardboard that served as home base to approach him.

"You're Eian Macgregor, aren't you, sir?"

"Yep, guilty as charged. Watching you guys play ball just now brought back memories of when my brothers and I were kids and we used to play in a small field down the street from our house. We had some great times."

"Really?"

"You bet. You guys keep playing this way and you'll make it to the big leagues when you get older and get out of college."

"Hummph. College is for idiots," said the tall one, now surrounded by the eight other boys.

"Oh, you think so?"

"Yes . . . sir."

"Well, let me tell you, college is the best place to get not only a top-notch education but also some of the best baseball practice in the world." They looked at him as if he were speaking a foreign language.

"Come on, you guys know that the pro scouts come to all the big schools searching for talent, and if they like what they see, they'll ask you to try out. Then one day that phone call comes, just when you least expect it. Somebody says on the other end of the line, 'Hey, kid, we got a spot for you. Be here tomorrow.' If you do well, they'll put you into their AA league to get you ready for the big leagues. And you're off. But it all starts right here, on that little patch of ground." He pointed to the makeshift baseball field behind them as he walked toward the car. "Practice, practice, and more practice. Remember that," he said as he opened the car door.

"That's it? That's all the advice you can give to us, is to practice?" said their leader, sounding disappointed.

He started to lecture the headstrong kid, but instead he took off his suit jacket and threw it inside the car and, pointing to him, said, "Grab the boxes from the trunk of the car and let's pass 'em around to everybody. Then let's play some baseball."

They all yelled in delight.

He passed out the gloves, bats, and balls from the boxes in his office so that they all had a baseball glove and a ball. Some of it was too large for the smaller ones, but they did not seem to mind. They had a baseball glove—a major-league glove!

He stayed for two hours, working with them, showing them the right way to hold the bat and throw the ball. He showed them how to catch a fly ball or a line drive. He showed them where to position themselves on the field. He hit them some short pop-up balls and a couple of line drives, and had them make throws to the first baseman, then to the catcher at home plate.

They were not bad, he thought to himself, as their impromptu game was soon halted due to darkness.

"You guys are pretty good," he said as they all gathered around him in a small circle.

"Mr. Macgregor, I'm Miguel Hernandez," the tall one began, "and I want to apologize for spouting off to you earlier. I'm sorry. I was out of line. I think I'm speaking for all the guys: it was really super of you to do this for us today, and we all really appreciate everything you did. I'm just sorry it had to end." He stuck out his hand to shake Eian's.

"You're welcome, Miguel. I'm sorry too. This was fun. Have a good night." They slowly started putting the gloves and balls back into the boxes. Eian watched them. "Hey, guys, keep the gear. Use it and enjoy it." He stopped and looked at them. "Tell you what: I'll be here Saturday morning at eight a.m. for anyone who wants to come back and practice."

Miguel smiled a huge grin, tucking his newfound glove into his jeans, and said, "Really? Anyone? We have some other friends who usually play with us, but they couldn't come today. Is it okay if they join us Saturday?"

"Sure, why not?"

"There's only one problem. We usually get chased off this field by the property manager. The owner of this property doesn't like us playing here."

"Really? Don't worry about it. I'll take care of it."

"But, Mr. Macgregor . . ."

"Miguel, I own the property," he said with a knowing grin. "Go home so your mom won't worry about you."

Driving home that night to his brother's house, he had a good feeling. He wanted to play some baseball with his brothers, just like the good old days. He felt good. Yes, he felt very good.

Chapter Twenty-Five

Mary Kate called Robin again at the Delray Dunes hotel to see if Calley had checked in to the hotel or called. Nothing. The police had told her they had been to Calley's house many times, but she had again refused to file charges against her husband. Mary Kate was determined to file her own charges against him for assaulting her in the stairway. He could not go around attacking people as he had, she said to herself, rubbing her still-sore ribs.

Finally, Mary Kate, against the direct wishes of not only her father but also Mickey and her boss, decided she would drive by the home address that Calley had given her. There was no answer from her cell phone. She just wanted to see where she lived, that's all, she told herself. *See what?* What if she saw him? Or her?

The address was located in an older, working-class section of the city of West Palm Beach, in an area that had seen better days. Abandoned cars and old tires littered the landscape of the homes, which were set back from the street. Wayward weeds and tall grasses sprouted from the sidewalks and the fences. Most homes had what looked like old colored bedsheets hanging in front of the windows. Children's toys littered the uncut front lawns.

She drove past an elderly woman sitting on her front stoop, with a beer bottle in one hand and a cigarette in the other. Then she spied the blue-and-gray house with one shutter dangling from its screws. That was it, 6820 Maxilla Street. There were no cars or trucks in the driveway. She parked her car just past the house and turned around to observe the small home. No activity. She remembered Calley had said Phil worked irregular hours. She tried to call her one more time, again no answer. Was she home? Alone? She did not want to meet up with him again. Just thinking of that night and remembering the harsh odor of gasoline and diesel fuel, and his hands groping her, made her sick to her stomach.

Mary Kate pushed open the car door and searched her purse for her newly acquired can of pepper spray; however, the cold steel can provided little comfort. *It's now or never, girl.* She pushed the rusty metal gate, and it swung wide open. She looked around the littered front yard.

Steady, girl, she thought to herself, climbing the old wooden steps to the front porch. It creaked under her feet, and she stopped and listened. No sounds. She knocked softly on the front door. Then harder and louder, gaining courage. Still nothing. She knocked again, repeating to herself furiously, *I am an agent of the court. Any attempt to hinder me in my official duties can be cause for arrest. Back away! Cease and desist.* She felt the reassuring metal of the spray can at the bottom of her purse. She was ready but received no response.

Nobody home? No movement. No sounds. No answer at the door or on the phone. It didn't feel right to her. *Where's Calley?* No one home. She would call the cops again and have them do another welfare check on her, to make sure she was okay.

She saw a neighbor across the street sweeping her front sidewalk. *Could that be her friend? What was her name again? What the hell did she say her name was? Damn. Heather? Yes, that was it. Heather.* She began walking toward the gate when she heard a noise behind her and turned and saw the window drape open slightly. A face appeared inside. "Calley!" she screamed.

As she approached the front door, she could see her battered face, bruised eyes, and sad expression. "Oh my God, Calley," she nearly wept when suddenly she saw something out of the corner of her eye racing toward her. Big. Brown. Fast. Pit bull!

It was upon her in a flash and then leaped high in the air at her. She moved at the last moment, and its jaws snapped emptily as it landed past her. She ran toward the gate, fast, faster. She could hear him panting just behind her. Gaining. At the last moment, she swung her briefcase at the charging pit bull, knocking him off his feet. It all happened so quickly she did not even have time to think about her can of pepper spray. She just wanted to be away, safe, as she quickly closed the gate behind her.

She could hardly breathe; she was panting hard just like the beast who had just chased her. His teeth, inches away, were gnawing at the fence as he tried to get to her and finish her. Globs of goo dribbled down his jaw as he snarled at her, mere feet from her face.

When she finally looked up at the window, she saw Calley standing there again, and he was standing beside her. He was laughing as he slowly closed the curtain. Then they were both gone.

Mary Kate was going to need help. Lots of help. And the police could not help because Calley would not press charges. The precinct where she filed her charges did not give her much hope. She had nowhere to turn. She went back to her car, and as much as she hated to admit it, she knew what she had to do. No, she had promised herself she would never talk to him again—never. But now she had no choice. She needed his help. *Why now? Why after all this time?* She would have to call Max for help.

Chapter Twenty-Six

Delray police detective Max Haines was not in a good mood. Somebody in the property division had lost key evidence in a case he was working on. Two kilograms of heroin were missing, and he wanted them back. His case would be thrown out of court, and the scum he had spent six months investigating and building a case against would walk out of jail a free man if he didn't find it. He was not going to lose this one. Somebody was going to pay for this mistake, and it sure wasn't going to be him. His team had caught the man with drugs in the car Max had been following for two days. The narcotics disappeared a week later from the property room.

"Just some paperwork snafu, that's all," is what Jerry Malin, the property-desk sergeant, kept telling him.

"I don't give a damn," he whispered forcefully to him. "Just find it, because if this guy walks," he growled, leaning into the metal mesh separating him and the sergeant, "then I'm not going to be a very happy person. And you don't want me unhappy, now do you, Sergeant? So call me when you find it."

The desk cop had heard about Haines's fiery temper, his short fuse, and about the last cop who had gotten on the wrong side of him.

"I'll check it out personally, Lieutenant. There are a couple of other places we can check, that we may have overlooked when my guys searched earlier. But no promises."

"Find it, you hear me? Now. I'm going back to my office. You call me when it surfaces. Got it?"

"Yes, sir, right away," he said as he got off his chair inside the mesh cage of the property room.

"I'm going to kill somebody," Max muttered and cursed under his breath as he stormed out of the basement and made his way to his office, slamming the door behind him. His office had a desk, a chair, assorted boxes, and piles of paperwork strewn about everywhere. There were piles on the floor and on the sofa, and more stacked by the door. A narrow pathway led through them from his door to his desk. His boss sent clerks to help clean it up and file everything, but he just chased them away. He didn't have time for all that nonsense.

"Hell, I know where everything is. Just leave it be." He was the most productive cop in the precinct, so his system clearly worked—in some perverse sort of way.

Ten minutes went by. Then twenty. The phone on his desk rang. He reached for it. "Haines here."

"Lieutenant, this is Malin, down in the property room."

"Yeah? What ya got?"

"Just wanted to let you know we found one of the property boxes tagged from that night. It's half-empty. It only had his personal effects in it. But we see another evidence box on the top shelf, and the guys are pulling it down now. I'll call you right back and let you know if your heroin is in it."

"Okay, but be quick about it."

"Yes, sir."

Two minutes later the phone rang again. "You better goddamn well have some good news for me, Malin." Silence. "Malin?"

"Max?" she whispered in disbelief.

The sweetness of her voice took him back to times past; he would never forget her voice.

"Mary Kate?"

"Yeah. It's been a long time."

He fell back into his chair in disbelief at the sound of her voice, moving the phone from one hand to the other. "Eighteen months, but who's counting? How are you?"

"I'm good. How you been?"

"The same. The life of a cop never changes. Remember?"

"Yeah." There was an awkward silence between them. "I know you must be busy, but I need some help and advice. Can you meet me for a cup of coffee?"

"Sure. Where?"

"Dada . . . the Delray coffee shop . . . on Swinton—two o'clock?"

"Okay. See you there."

"Thanks, Max."

Max arrived early at the little offbeat bistro just off Atlantic Avenue, shrouded under the canopy of a huge banyan tree. A large flock of wild green parrots flew by, squawking as they flew their quick, erratic patterns overhead. He was sitting at an outside table sipping his second cup of Columbian coffee when he saw her round the corner, approaching the white picket fence that surrounded the popular funky café. He set the cup down and just watched her, taking in the visual feast unfolding before him. Maybe this was not such a good idea. *Don't let her know, Max,* he told himself. *Damn.*

The last time they had seen each other it had ended in a yelling match with her leaving. He had been assigned to a routine hit-and-run case involving her mother. He spent hours interviewing potential witnesses, canvasing body shops for repair damage that matched the bike, and walking the neighborhood where it had happened. He called her regularly to keep her updated. His persistence finally paid off, and when he told her what he had done, and that the guy responsible was in jail, she hugged and kissed him. She was in tears.

He didn't want his regular phone calls to her to end; he wanted to see her again. Against his better judgment and departmental policy, he asked her to dinner. They had some wine, a nice Italian dinner at Luna Rosa, more wine, and some dessert while they talked for hours. He took her home, and they had coffee and after-dinner drinks and . . . later she said she was the happiest she had been in a very long time.

Two weeks later, when Max had to release the driver because his wife and best friend had provided a solid alibi, Mary Kate was furious and came storming back into the precinct. She yelled, she screamed, and finally she stomped out his office. Now here he was, almost two years later, sitting and watching her walk back into his life.

She waved a subtle hello as she walked into the outside courtyard. "Hi, Max," she said, kissing him softly on the cheek before sitting down.

"Hey, Mary Kate. It's good to see you."

"You too," she said and ordered a coffee from a nearby waiter.

"I can't stay long," he said. "I have to be in court to testify at a hearing."

"Me neither." There was an awkward moment of silence; then they both began to speak at the same time. "Max, I wanted to say I am so sorry . . ."

"Mary Kate, I wanted to tell you . . ."

They both laughed and Max said, "Sorry, you go ahead. You called this meeting."

"Max, first I want to apologize for the way I acted when we last saw each other. You were just doing your job and following the law. And I was acting very emotional."

"Mary Kate, you had just lost your mother, and then the guy who did it was caught and then released. You were angry at the world, and

I was just the one who took the brunt of it. You were on some roller coaster at the time. I understand completely."

"I'm sorry, Max, truly I am."

"No problem," he said as she looked up at him. "You said on the phone you needed my help and advice."

"Yes. I'm now working as an attorney at Block & Sawyer and doing some pro bono work with a woman who came to my office."

"Yeah, I'm familiar with the firm. Great reputation in town."

"Thanks. My client had been abused by her husband, and she wanted to leave him and then file for divorce. She was supposed to check in at a hotel I recommended. It's a safe-harbor place we use sometimes to get women in her situation out of the home and somewhere safe. Well, she never showed up. I think she went home to gather up some things, and he was there waiting for her. Or they reconciled, or maybe he . . ." She paused to sip her coffee. The whole situation seemed surreal to her, sitting under the shade of the huge ancient banyan trees, with him, after all this time, and . . . she knew that if anyone could help, it would be Max.

"I went to her house and knocked on the door, and there was no answer."

"What? You went there . . . alone? You should never do that. It's too dangerous."

"You're right. As I look back at it, I don't know what I was thinking. I should have let the cops handle it. A few days before that I was accosted by someone in the stairwell at work. He held a knife to my throat. He said her name, but I never saw his face. I think it was him, her husband."

"Did you call the police? 911?"

"Yeah, I did. They took a report, questioned him, and held him for a day or so, but had to let him go due to insufficient evidence."

"What? Who is this guy?" asked Max, now visibly agitated.

"Calm down, Max. He warned me to stay away from his wife."

Max muttered something under his breath she did not hear. He looked at her. "Even more reason not to go there. You should've called me sooner," he said, his anger rising.

"I thought I could help, I thought I could handle it. Looking back, I should have taken her to the motel myself, and then I know she would be safe. I suggested to the police and our building security to maybe check the surveillance cameras at the building where I work and maybe . . ."

"Unfortunately, beat cops don't have the time to do that. Security should do it but . . . I can pull them and look to see if he was loitering about the parking lot or near your building, or see his car in the parking lot. Then I can bring him in for questioning. We can do a voice lineup . . ."

"Right. That's at least enough to hold him on an assault charge so we can get Calley to someplace safe."

"Mary Kate, don't blame yourself. It's not your fault, and it happens all the time. Women think they can talk rationally to their abuser, but . . . ," he said, leaning toward her, taking her hand in his to comfort her. "She first had to feel she was in danger, and most women don't want to admit it. I can't tell you how many women continue to return to an abusive situation repeatedly. Until something violent . . . or deadly happens. Then it's too late."

"You're right. I should've known better."

"What's this guy's name?"

"Phil Terrell. They live on Marilla Street in Delray. Be careful; I know he has a knife and . . . a pit bull, and God knows what else. So be careful. I just want her out of there, and in a safe place. She also told me he's using drugs."

"Okay. That's all good information to have."

"Also, the last time I saw her, she looked in pretty bad shape, and I called the local precinct to have them go and check on her. It hasn't happened yet."

"No promises, but let me take it from here. I need you to promise me that you'll stay away from her house," he said, still holding her hand.

"I promise. Thanks, Max. I really appreciate it. It was good seeing you again," she said, slowly sliding her hand from his. She stood and hugged him with a smile, then turned to walk to her car and saw him standing there with a hurt look in his eyes. He had witnessed the entire scene. It was her Mickey. His eyes told the story of his pain. He turned and left, crossing the street to his car. She called to him, running to try to catch up with him, but it was too late as she saw him drive away. Gone.

Chapter Twenty-Seven

"I don't want to be disturbed . . . by anyone. Do you hear me?"

"Yes, sir," said Bashir as Mickey rushed past his desk outside his office. "Oh, by the way, sir, these tickets came for you from the travel agent today."

"What are they?" he asked, turning and pausing with his hand on the doorknob.

"For your trip."

He took the tickets, mumbling to himself, "What trip?" Then he looked at the paperwork. Travel arrangements from Angus—for his trip to Australia. *Damn him.* He set the tickets on his desk.

He sat down in his chair and looked out over the scene of South Florida and the waves of the Atlantic Ocean below. A group of pelicans flew in formation, in no rush at all. Drivers drove by in convertibles, taking advantage of the gorgeous weather. South Florida was such a beautiful place. He loved it. It would be a good place to raise a family and settle down. *Nice beach day,* he thought. Usually on a day like today, he would call Mary Kate and they would slink away to the beach, grab some champagne and cheese, and just watch the waves roll in and roll out—but not today. *Mary Kate.* He could not get her out of his mind. *I trusted her. But now? What the hell is going on?*

His phone rang. He ignored it. It rang again.

He finally picked it up. "I said I didn't want to be disturbed!" he shouted, and hung up.

There was a knock on the door, and it began to swing open. It was not like Bashir to ignore his requests. Now he was mad. "What the hell do I have to do to get some privacy around here? Is what I want . . ."

The door fully opened and there she stood . . . Mary Kate.

Seeing her with tears in her eyes, he was without words. *Take the pain away, goddamn it.* He never wanted to hurt her. Never.

Mary Kate stood there; she was afraid she had hurt him. She had to go to him, tell him what was going on. "Hi," she whispered quietly as the door closed behind her. "Can we talk? I really want to explain . . ."

The fury returned as he recalled the scene. "There's no need to explain. I saw what I saw. You, hugging some other man . . . behind my back. I think that about says it all."

"No, it doesn't. And if we are going to make it in our marriage, then we need to be able to communicate with each other and . . . trust each other."

Her words calmed him.

"The man you saw me with today was a Delray Beach police lieutenant by the name of Max Haines." She sat down in the chair in front of his desk. "He was the officer in charge of the investigation into my mother's death. He found the man, and I was so happy. We dated a few times. He wanted it to go further, but I didn't and broke it off."

"And now you're back to hugging him in public?" he blurted out.

"I needed his help with getting Calley away from her husband. He was abusing her, and Max is the only one able to help me. I think she's being held against her will at her home. I saw her, and she looked pretty bad. That's why I went to see him today . . . for coffee. That's it. End of story. All right?"

She stood and started to walk to the door.

"Mary Kate. Wait." He went to her and slowly put his arms around her. "I was wrong, dead wrong. I love you. And it breaks my heart to see you in tears. I should have waited and talked to you—right then and there. I'm sorry. It won't happen again." He gave her a funny face, then said, "Wait a minute. You're the one caught hugging some strange guy, some old flame who has the hots for you, and I'm the one who's apologizing? Something's wrong with this picture."

She smiled and kissed him on the cheek. "That's the way it's supposed to be, my dear," she said, grabbing her purse from the chair. "And, oh, don't forget we're having dinner tonight with my father at the Ke'e Grill in Boca. Pick me up at six thirty?"

"Okay. See you then."

And with that she was gone.

He sat down in his chair and toyed with the travel documents in his hand. He pressed the button for the intercom. "Bashir, can you get my father on the phone for me, please? Thank you." He knew what he had to do, and now was the time to do it. He knew the worst was yet to come.

Thirty minutes later he was driving home to shower and get ready to have dinner with Mary Kate and her father. *What a day,* he thought to himself.

Chapter Twenty-Eight

As they drove to the restaurant, Mary Kate spent the whole time on the phone with the wedding planner discussing the entrées for the wedding, the color of the flowers, the color of the favors, the place mats, the dresses, and the corsages. She also talked about the music the band was going to be playing and in what order. She told Mickey about the ring bearers and who would be performing the church service. It was being held at the Chapel-by-the-Sea on the island of Palm Beach. Very exclusive. Very expensive.

Mickey had something to tell her, something important. He had to tell her and tried, but he knew that now was not the time. It would have to wait until after dinner.

He smiled as Mary Kate read off list after list of things that needed to be attended to for the wedding, but he could not take his eyes off her. She looked ravishing in her crisp linen pants and soft silk blouse, slightly unbuttoned at the top. He could see the lace pattern of her bra through the sheer material. She caught him stealing glances at her while they drove to dinner.

"What?" she asked with a demure smile.

"You look wonderful tonight," he said.

"Thank you," she said as she placed her hand on his leg, absent-mindedly massaging it as she continued with her list.

His attention was now diverted elsewhere. He was glad when they pulled into the parking lot and parked the car. He kissed her, once, twice, then a third time. "I love you," he said.

She kissed him again as his hand slipped down to her waist.

"Come on, lover boy, I know how this ends, and my father is waiting for us. And besides, I'm starving. Later." They walked hand in hand to the restaurant.

Ke'e Grill in Boca Raton was a casually elegant restaurant, the finest in Palm Beach County. The decor, with its South Pacific theme—over-size stuffed swordfish hanging on the walls and informal tiki tables—made for an intimate evening with some of the best food in South Florida. The bar was cozy and, with its accommodating bartenders, made for a comfortable place for the inevitable wait for a table at this popular bistro.

Still holding his hand, she saw her father sitting at one of the coveted window tables and waved to him.

"Hey, there they are, the lovebirds," said her father as they approached. He kissed his daughter on the cheek and shook Mickey's hand.

"Good to see you again, Dr. Macgregor."

"Hey, Mickey, call me Ryan, okay? We're family now . . . or close enough. Just one more week until the big event." He wore a huge grin on his face.

They ordered cocktails and toasted to good health after the waiter brought their drinks to the table.

She looked at her father and asked, "How are the dance lessons going, Dad?"

"Alexi is a very nice person and a good dance instructor."

"And very attractive at that," interjected Mickey.

"Mickey," Mary Kate said, elbowing him in the ribs, "behave. Dad, have you found a date yet? For the wedding?" she asked as she sipped her martini.

"Not yet."

"Father. I've only asked two things of you: one was to brush up on your dancing, and the other was—"

"I was going to ask Alexi . . . the dance instructor," he interrupted.

"Oh?" Mary Kate responded, sounding surprised.

"You don't approve?"

"No, to the contrary, I wholeheartedly approve. Have you asked her yet?"

"No, not yet. I'm a little rusty at this. It's been a long time." He stopped, looking perplexed. "But what if she says no?"

"She won't be able to say anything unless you ask her, Dad. Go ahead, ask her. My guess is you'll be pleasantly surprised."

The young waiter dressed in a white polo shirt came by and took their dinner orders. By this time the restaurant was full; a crowd of patrons waited patiently at the bar.

Ryan smiled and turned his attention to his future son-in-law. "What exactly is it that you do again, Mickey?"

"I am in the commercial real estate development business. The firm I work for is called Boston Real Estate Advisors, although now more than sixty percent of our business is located here in the southeast—and growing rapidly. This area also provides more than eighty percent of the firm's profits."

"Wow," said Ryan.

"And Mickey runs it from right here in Boca Raton," Mary Kate interjected proudly.

He smiled before continuing. "We're totally turnkey—buying the land, planning, developing, and renting the properties. Rather unusual hybrid business approach, but it works."

"Public or privately held business?"

"Private. It's a family business. I work for my father . . . or rather, my adoptive father."

She cleared her throat and after sipping her drink asked, "Have you heard back from your folks yet, Mickey? Are they coming? To the wedding?" she whispered, not wanting to put him on the defensive.

He had planned to wait until later to tell her everything, but now he had no choice; he did not want to lie to her or her father. He took in a deep breath. "Well, my mother called me tonight just before I left my condo to pick you up and . . . she told me she was coming."

Mary Kate's eyes and face brightened with a huge smile as she leaned over to hug him. "That's fantastic. For a while there, I didn't know if they were going to come. It's going to be great to have your mom and dad here for our . . ."

"Just my mother." He paused before saying, "Not my father."

The joy left her face. "What do you mean? Your father's not coming to our wedding?"

"No. He's not coming." He knew a storm was brewing.

Her father interceded. "Perhaps it would better if the two of you discussed this later, privately. Among yourselves."

"Thank you, sir, but this does involve you, and I would welcome any advice you may have. Please?"

"Okay. What's going on?"

"My father has been using an Australian business trip as an excuse not to attend my wedding."

"Why on earth would he not want to attend your wedding? I don't understand. Did you have a fight with him? Is it something we did? Or didn't do?"

Mickey raised his hand to the waiter to order another round of cocktails. "This sounds like a two-martini discussion." The drinks arrived quickly along with their dinner, and he resumed his explanation. "My father is an old-time Scotsman. Tradition is everything to him. He is the grand leader of the Highlanders Scottish Lodge in Boston. It is the oldest Scottish fraternal club of its kind."

"Yes, we're very familiar with the organization. My brother, Robert, is the grand pooh-bah, so to speak, at a Scottish lodge here in Delray."

"Well, when he heard . . ." Mickey stopped short, not really wanting to go on.

Ryan could tell by the look on his face that he was struggling. "Go ahead, Mickey, spit it out."

"Well, when he heard that Mary Kate and I were getting married, he blew his top."

"Why?"

"Because she's a . . . Macgregor and . . . our family are Campbells. I never gave it a second thought. It's ridiculous, and it never bothered me, but it sure bothered him. He says he still believes in the Macgregor-versus-Campbell feud that's been going on for the last four hundred years. Therefore, he has refused to attend our wedding next week. I don't know what to do. But my mother is coming, and now she's angry with him and not talking to him. Hell, maybe we should just elope and just say the hell with it."

Mary Kate looked at him with a subtle grin. "Nice try, Mickey, but you're not getting off that easy. We'll figure out something."

"There's more."

"What happened?" she asked.

"Well, he's a hardheaded Scotsman. His latest trick was to try to send me to Australia for two weeks to handle a business deal he's been working on."

"What? When?"

"Tomorrow."

She looked at him in horror. "Mickey, our wedding is next week. What are we going to do?"

"Already taken care of." He paused again. This was not how he had envisioned telling her. *I should have told her earlier, alone, in the car. She has a right to know. Suck it up and spit it out.* "Red, I quit my job today. So . . . I'm now in the ranks of the unemployed. Do you still love me?"

"Hmmm, do you need an answer right away?" she joked, then hugged him. "Of course I love you; I always will." He kissed her once, then again, until her father coughed to clear his throat.

The table was silent until Graw asked, "But Mickey, surely there must be something more to it than some old Scottish feud?"

Mickey paused for a minute. "There is. Growing up I played with Angus Campbell's son, Bryce Campbell. We were the best of friends— no, he was my best friend—until . . ." He could not go on.

"What happened?" Graw whispered, clutching his arm tight.

"Well, one Halloween night we were supposed to out together, but I was grounded and had to stay at home. He went with a couple other guys from school and pulled a prank on some neighbor's front porch, knocking out the porch light. Well, the man thought someone was trying to break into his house and came to the door and shot Bryce with a gun. Killed him. He was arrested, but Bryce was gone. My best friend gone in an instant, all because of some dumb prank. We were as close as brothers."

"What does his death have to do with him and the Macgregors?" she asked.

"The man who shot and killed their son was named . . . Macgregor."

"So he holds all Macgregors accountable for this senseless act?" asked Ryan.

"Yes, sir. I know it seems convoluted, but that's my father. He needed desperately to blame somebody or something for this tragedy. Sometimes I think he even blames me for not being with him that night and keeping him from harm's way."

"And you quit your job because of it?" she asked.

"Yes, I could not see any other way out of the situation. It would just get worse and worse unless he changed or I went to work somewhere else. Something had to change. He certainly won't."

The waiter took their dessert orders, and they sat glumly in their seats.

Mickey tried to cheer them up by saying, "Hey, everybody, I knew what I was doing. I'm a big boy. My father will come around eventually; he usually does when my mother is involved. But I thought to myself, maybe it's time for me to do something else at another firm. I don't think it will take me long to find another job. I already made a couple of phone calls and have two job opportunities lined up next week. One is a partnership with a big local firm looking to do deals like I've been doing for the last couple of years." He paused and looked her in the eyes, looking for a signal from her.

"I'm also giving some thought to going out on my own—you know, doing some consulting work as a boutique real estate consultant. Either way, we won't starve, Mary Kate, trust me. Everything will be fine."

"I love you regardless." She smiled at Mickey and turned to her father, who seemed to be a million miles away, lost in his own thoughts. "Daddy? What's the problem?"

"Well, you may have solved Mickey's issues, but now we have a new one to deal with—my brother Robert. He's just as hardheaded about the feud between the Macgregors and the Campbells. Maybe even more so. He's going to hit the roof when he hears of this."

What the hell was he going to do now? How was he going to tell his brother that Mary Katherine was marrying a Campbell? He couldn't tell him; his brother would just have to find out on his own. That's all there was to it. He would have to just live with it.

Ryan raised his glass for a final salute. "To the Macgregors!" he toasted.

"And to the Campbells!" Mickey responded.

"Long live Scotland," Mary Kate chimed in with the traditional Scottish salute, but for some reason the toast rang hollow that night.

Chapter Twenty-Nine

Everyone was dressed so elegantly for the opera. The lobby was full of eager patrons waiting for the theater doors to open and for everyone to take their seats. Bob brought two glasses of champagne from the bar, and they toasted to a wonderful evening.

Don't blow it, Bob. "Cheers!" he said, raising his glass. "To a new beginning and to *Madama Butterfly*."

Coleen laughed, and it made him feel good that he could coax a smile and laugh from her. When she wasn't looking, Robert stuck his finger inside his new shirt collar to try to loosen it. *It didn't feel this tight in the store,* he thought to himself.

"Thank you for the opera tickets. *Madama Butterfly* is one of my all-time favorites."

"My pleasure."

"And thank you for dinner. A great start to a wonderful evening."

He had made reservations at L'Amour, the best French restaurant in Palm Beach. The food was superb, the wine excellent, the service outstanding. He was shocked when he received the bill for the meal, but looking at Coleen now, it had been worth every penny.

Sitting in the dark, watching the performers on stage, she was engrossed in the classic performance. When Cio-Cio-san sang about Pinkerton, her lost love, with the setting sun behind her, Coleen reached for the comfort of his hand. He held hers, afraid to move. Afraid that if he moved she would realize what she had done and remove her hand. He was engrossed in his own theater, feeling the warmth of her hand, smelling the scent of her perfume; he was lost, lost in love. But much to his surprise, he found that he enjoyed the opera, the singing, and the musical score. It was wonderful.

Later that night, after it was over, and he had walked Coleen to her front door, she turned to shake his hand, kissing him lightly on the cheek and saying, "Oh, Bob, before I forget, I don't know if you'd be interested, but I have an extra ticket to a baseball game tomorrow night. Our company has season box-seat tickets. My daughter, Diane, usually goes with me, along with some other employees and customers, but unfortunately, she can't make it this time. So I have an extra ticket if you'd like to go. There'll be plenty to eat and drink. We have an air-conditioned suite to keep you cool. And, well . . . it's just a very nice evening. I would hate to waste the ticket."

He smiled. "I would love to go."

"Great," she said cheerfully. "Pick me up, say, at six o'clock. And bring your appetite. There is usually so much food there you won't believe it." She kissed him on the cheek and went inside. They stood motionless on either side of the door, neither wanting the evening to end.

Where is this going?

When he picked her up the next night, she commented, "Wow, I don't see you for years on end, and now I see you two days in a row."

"Yeah, hard to believe, isn't it?" he said.

The baseball game was wonderful. The food was great, and he was able to spend four uninterrupted hours with her. She cheered for the home team, booed the umpires for all the bad calls, and was on her feet for every home run. She was a die-hard fan. The only bad part was that the Yankees won, again. They both had a great time. She wore a casual business outfit to the game but changed into a pair of form-fitting white jeans and sneakers once at home.

Afterward, they sat on the wicker sofa in front of the outdoor fireplace at the rear of her house, sipping from a glass of amaretto, now her favorite after-dinner drink. Thanks to Bob. They talked and talked, then laughed, both amazed that their conversation came so easily. She sat close to him, she said, because the weather had gotten cooler. He removed his jacket and placed it around her shoulders, wrapping his arm around her. He had to admit, he loved holding her close.

The flames crackled as he asked her, "Unless you're getting tired of me, would you like to see *Fiddler on the Roof* at the Broward Center tomorrow? I just happen to have two extra—"

She placed her finger on his lips to silence him. "Shhh, I would love to go with you."

Chapter Thirty

Saturday morning, as Eian turned off Atlantic Avenue and approached his street, he saw cars parked everywhere, including on the sidewalk, in front of fire hydrants, and double-parked on the street. He slowed to see what the commotion was and recognized Miguel waving at him. He had parked his bicycle in front of the vacant lot and stood guard, waiting for Eian to show up. "Over here!" he shouted, and waved his arms. "I saved this spot just for you, Mr. Macgregor, Coach."

As he got out and closed the car door, Miguel approached him. "I wanted to make sure you had a parking spot. So I got here early."

"What's going on here? Who are all of these people?"

Miguel's face showed some concern. "You said it was okay for me to bring some of my friends. Correct?"

"Yeah, sure," he said, looking at the kids and parents beginning to crowd around him. "But . . ."

"Well, I told some friends, and they told some of their friends, and then they told . . ."

"Okay, okay, I get the picture." He looked around at all the young kids, some barely as high as his kneecaps, looking at him, waiting to hear from the famed Eian Macgregor. The parents huddled off in the distance. He took a deep breath. "Pitchers to the mound with me. Catchers line up in a single file. Fielders take your places. Okay, let's play some ball."

There were six pitchers lined up for instructions, two of them left-handers. Miguel was at the front of the line. His eyes never left his new hero.

"All right, everybody, form a circle around me," Eian said, kneeling down in the center. He waited until the voices became silent, and he knew he had their attention. "Listen up. Before we start, remember, baseball is a game. If you just want to make a lot of money, do something else. However, play baseball because you want to; no, play baseball because you love the game. I would do it for free. Anyone who disagrees with that should go rejoin your parents on the sidelines." No one moved. "Okay, I'll throw the first pitches after I work with the catchers for a bit. Each pitcher gets five pitches, then you hand off the ball to the next player in line behind you. Then go to the back of the line. Your goal today is accuracy and precision, not speed. And remember that the catchers are just as new to the game as you are. Anybody who hits a catcher with a ball is out for the rest of the day. Got it?"

"Got it!" they all yelled, putting their hands on top of his before grunting and yelling their salute. He worked with the catchers, then the outfielders, then the first and third basemen. Two young girls approached him to jeers and catcalls from the players, but one look from Eian silenced them.

"Coach," the taller girl stammered, "we know how to play, and I was wondering if it's okay . . . for us to . . ."

He looked her over, then the other one; she was athletic, and they each carried old, worn claw-mitt gloves.

"I need a shortstop. You want the job?"

"You bet," she yelled, and ran off to join her new teammates. Turning to the other one, he told her, "We'll try you in the outfield." She smiled and yelled, then took her position in center field.

"Play ball," he yelled, donning his old team's baseball cap. He spent the next three hours working with them, directing them, coaching them. It felt good to have a baseball in his hand again, to hear fans shouting for players, encouraging them. No, it didn't feel good—it felt great.

After four hours on the makeshift ball field, they were done for the day. Eian noticed that two big trucks had pulled up and men were beginning to unload picnic tables, food, and drink. Families appeared with containers of home-cooked meals and sodas, and soon began to play music from nearby speakers. The food smelled delicious.

"Okay," he shouted, "everybody gather around." He looked at his group of ball players, their faces filled with excitement and anticipation. A group of young boys and girls crowded around him.

He looked at each one of the thirty or so kids before saying, "You did real well today." They beamed. "You played hard, you listened, and you followed directions. Now you need to take that to the next level and keep practicing."

Miguel, always the leader, stepped forward. "Are we good enough to form a neighborhood team?"

Eian looked around at the determination on the young players' faces. "Yes, I think you are."

"Can you coach us?" Miguel pressed.

He paused, not knowing what to say. It had been a long time. "We'll see."

Groans followed.

"We'll see how you do next week. All right? Next Saturday. Same time, same place."

They yelled and screamed in excitement, running off to join their friends and family. It was then he noticed some of the fathers standing behind them, watching.

A short, stocky man with a thick black-and-gray mustache approached him. "I am Cesar, Miguel's father. I apologize for him.

Sometimes he is very headstrong and pushy, but he means well. No disrespect." He pointed to the crowd of women feeding the crowd of boys. "His mother spoils him."

"No problem. He's a good kid and a good ballplayer."

The man smiled. "Would you like to join us for some lunch?" he asked, pointing to the picnic tables now overflowing with food. "Nothing fancy, but it's all homemade Cuban food. Hot and spicy, but the best Cuban food you'll ever taste outside of Havana. And the desserts . . . whoa, they are outstanding!"

He glanced at his watch. He would be late for his meeting. *Hell with it.* "I would be honored to join you. Thank you for the invitation."

The fathers were soon peppering him with nonstop questions and, of course, the inevitable suggestions about how he could better use their own kids in the game. It was then he realized how much he missed the game, the spirit, the true love of the game of baseball.

Chapter Thirty-One

"Mother? Mother, are you there?" Diane shouted. Coleen's daughter's voice echoed in the hallway of the big colonial house. *This house is way too big for her now,* she thought, walking inside.

"Mom?" She heard some movement upstairs and headed in that direction and found her mother in the bedroom, singing. A very rare occurrence, to be sure.

"If I were a rich man, ya ba da ba da ba da ba do, if I were . . ."

"Mother?"

Startled, Coleen jumped at the intrusion. "Diane, when did you get here?"

"Just a few minutes ago. I called, but there was no answer."

"Oh." Her mother returned to the mirror to finish putting on her makeup, still humming softly and dancing around the room. Her hair was coiffed, and she was dressed in a black cocktail dress and her favorite gray pearl earrings.

Diane wanted to find out what was going on in her mother's life. Coleen was happier than she had seen her in years. She was singing when she thought there was no one around to listen, and dancing to some unheard tune. Diane was determined to find the cause of her newfound happiness. Their business partner, Perry, had said to leave it be, but she had to know.

"And where, might I ask, are you off to, my dear?" Diane asked as she sat on the bed to survey the situation before her.

"Well, if you must know, I'm going to the Broward Center to see *Fiddler on the Roof* this evening."

"By yourself?" she pushed, edging closer.

"No," she said, pausing before saying, "with a friend."

"Who?"

"An old friend."

"And who might that be?"

"An old friend. You don't know him."

"Did you say *him*? Mother, are you going out on a date?" Diane asked in a surprised, teasing tone. She was happy for her; it had been almost five years since her father had passed away, five years since Coleen had enjoyed the company of a man. It was time for her to enjoy herself with something other than work.

Suddenly Coleen felt a twinge of guilt overcome her. Her first date since . . . Hal died. Her shoulders slumped, and the smile left her face. "Yes. But it's not really a date," she said nervously. "And besides, I think . . . this . . . is the last time I plan on seeing him."

Diane saw the look on her mother's face; the smile was fading. *That's it—open mouth, insert foot.* "Mom, I shouldn't have said what I did. Go out with him. Have a good time. Enjoy it. You deserve some happiness." She paused for a moment before adding, "Where do you know him from?"

"I know him from school, growing up. A big, gawky kid. We ran into each other recently after he lost his wife and . . . he said he had extra tickets to see *Madama Butterfly* and offered them to me."

"Wait. I thought you said you were going to see *Fiddler on the Roof*? Which is it?"

"Tonight is *Fiddler*. We saw *Madama Butterfly* a few days ago."

"So," Diane said, leaning back on the bed, propped up by her elbows, "this is your second date?"

"Third. We went to the ball game together."

"Oh, is that why my ticket mysteriously disappeared?"

Silence.

"Tell me more. Is he cute?"

"I told you, as a kid he was tall and awkward. He's a very nice man. An old and dear friend. And it's strictly platonic, mind you."

"Is that why you're all dressed up?"

"No, this is what I always wear to the theater. Speaking of which, why are you all dressed up on a Saturday night?"

"Oh . . . Perry and I are going to dinner to go over some of the numbers for our meeting next week. We can never seem to find the time at the office, so he suggested dinner. Strictly business."

"I see . . . pretty fancy duds for a business meeting, if I do say so myself."

"Wait a minute, Mother, let's not change the subject. Tell me about this guy, this old and dear friend. Is he so old you have to push him around in a wheelchair?"

"No." Coleen smiled to herself. "He's quite strong and . . ."

The phone rang on the bedside table. Diane was closer and reached over to answer it. It was the front gate guard.

"Evening, ma'am, I have a Mr. Macgregor here to see you."

"Send him right in, Ralph." She stood as her mother made one final check in the mirror, smoothing the creases from her dress and checking her makeup for the third time.

Diane said nonchalantly, "I would like to meet this old and dear friend of yours." *The one who makes my mother sing and dance . . . and smile.*

Bob drove up her long driveway and was impressed by the sheer elegance of the lush green lawn as he approached the old colonial house with its tall white columns. He knocked on the door and was greeted by a much younger version of Coleen.

"Hello."

"Hi, I'm Mac. You must be Diane?" he said, turning to her with a boyish grin.

"Why yes."

"You look just like your mother. And that's a compliment." His gaze lifted, searching to somewhere behind her; his eyes glimmered when he saw Coleen standing there, smiling, waiting.

When he walked inside, he seemed at first almost shy, then laughed; then Diane turned to look at her mother. Coleen's smile had returned, and Diane knew immediately . . . her mother was in love.

"All ready?" he asked.

"Yes," she told him, then, turning to her daughter, said, "Good night, dear. Have a good meeting." And with that they were out the door.

"You look very nice tonight," Robert said as they walked outside.

He opened the car door for her and extended his hand to help her easily slide onto the seat. Her hand lingered in his as she smiled at him.

"Thank you, Bob."

He caught a faint whiff of the sweet scent of her lilac perfume.

Before starting the car, he handed her a small blue box with a pink ribbon on it. "Happy birthday," he said. "Sorry, it's a belated gift. It's not much."

"Bob, I can't take this," she said, handing it back to him. "Really, I can't."

"Too late. The store I bought it at doesn't take returns." He had that determined look on his face.

When she opened the box, she found inside a gold puffed-heart pendant with a small ruby in the center, hanging on a thin gold chain.

"Bobby, it's beautiful!" she said as she hung it about her neck, softly touching it. Coleen kissed him on the cheek, affectionately feeling the golden heart and the warmth of the ruby. She glanced to her side at Robert; he was always full of surprises. "Thank you, Bob, I love it."

"I'm glad you like it," he said with an oversize grin.

Coleen began to hum a tune from the show, but now she was truly filled with mixed emotions. She was torn. The memories of her late husband began to surround her. *Is it too soon for all of this? It's been five years, but am I ready? Most people would say it is well past time, but . . .*

"*Fiddler on the Roof.* It should be a wonderful production," she finally remarked, filling the silence. She admired his profile. His straight jaw, his wonderful nose, and, of course, his smile. *Damn! What the hell am I going to do now?* she thought.

She looked out the car window at the houses passing by. It was beginning to rain. She knew she would have to tell him. In her counseling programs, it was easy for her to tell other people to move on with their lives, but she clung to the past. But tonight she would tell him . . . she did not want to see him again. It was for the best. She looked at him as he turned to her and smiled. Damn him and his Robert Redford smile.

"Everything okay?" he asked.

She managed a weak smile. "Yes, everything's fine. Just tired, I guess."

He reached over and squeezed her hand, sending shock waves through her body. She wished he wouldn't do that, especially now . . . tonight of all nights. She should never have led him on. It was wrong. Tonight . . . she would . . .

"Maybe it's the rain, that's all," he said, trying to comfort her. But not even he could do or say anything to help her. Not tonight. By the time they reached the Broward Center for the Performing Arts, the rain had stopped. He parked the car, and they walked the rest of the way to the theater in silence.

The musical was wonderful. She hummed many of the songs under her breath. He could see her smiling in the darkened concert hall, clasping her hands in the excitement of the moment. He was really beginning to enjoy attending the theater and opera with her, much more than he had ever thought he would.

He had seen the uplifting movie about a father marrying off his daughters, and each one breaking with more and more of the family traditions. When the show was over and the actors took their final bows, he knew she was right; it was a great musical.

Robert loved the show, and he had loved seeing it with her. He could hear her whisper the now-familiar refrains. Such wonderful music. He loved the music. He loved her intoxicating scent. He loved touching her. He just loved being with her. He loved . . .

"Did you enjoy the musical?" she asked as they walked back to the car.

"Yes, I really did," he said enthusiastically. "I know you have seen it many times before, and I've seen the movie, but this is the first time I ever saw it live onstage. It was great."

Now's the time, she thought, gulping. *It's for the best,* she thought. "Robert, we need to talk."

The words sounded ominous. "Sure," he said. He knew that those were never good words to hear, and he detected a certain tone in her voice, one he had not heard before. It gave him chills.

She slowed her walking pace. "We are both widowed. You know we each have families. We each have businesses to run. And . . ."

Now he knew. *Think fast, you stubborn Scotsman.* He blurted out, "Yes, just like Tevye in the musical tonight. He and his wife, Golde, had been married for years."

She smiled at him but was determined to end it. "Yes, but Bob—"

"I loved it when they sang 'Sunrise, Sunset,'" he said as he began to waltz around her.

She smiled at his enthusiasm.

He sang the first word, "Sunrise . . . ," and looked at her, holding out his hand.

She smiled again, finishing the first line, singing, ". . . sunset." They laughed together as he repeated it again and again.

He danced faster, as if doing an Irish jig, and said, "And I loved it when he sang 'If I Were a Rich Man.' It was great; remember the words? 'If I were a . . .'!" They both laughed and continued their walk to the car. He reached for her hand, but she moved away.

Robert swallowed hard and then said, "But my favorite part is when they know their children were all getting married, and they begin to reflect on their own marriage, their life together, and he tells his wife, 'Golde, it's a new world out there. Do you love me?' And his wife responds with something like 'Well, I think—'"

Coleen kept walking but said, "No, no, she said, 'Do I what?'"

"Do you love me?" Robert repeated.

Coleen said the response from the show in a singsong fashion while mimicking the musical. "For twenty-five years I've cooked your meals, I—'"

"Yes . . . but do you love me?" He stopped walking and looked at her, the smile gone from his face. "But do you love me?"

She turned to look at him, standing there waiting for her response. He was serious. He was asking her a question.

"Do you love me?" he repeated slowly.

She walked to him, slowly. "Robert . . . Mac, that's not fair . . . to ask me such a question . . ."

He took her hand and slowly placed it over his heart. "All I've ever wanted is someone to love. Coleen, life has rhythms, just like the sun and the moon. The stars in the sky. The oceans rolling in and rolling out. Rhythms, rhythms of life. My heart is beating for you. Can you feel it . . . can you feel the rhythm of my heart? Can you?"

She could feel his heart beating, pounding, beating for her. *Life is not fair.* She quivered, standing before him, not knowing what to say.

"Coleen, can you feel my heart?" he asked her again. "Can you feel it beating? It's beating for you." His eyes told her the story she wanted to hear.

"Yes," she whispered slowly, "I can feel it."

He took her hand in his and asked, "Do you love me?"

Don't look up; your eyes will betray you. He will know. Don't. Whatever you do, don't look him in the eyes.

"Coleen? Look at me . . . please. I need you to look at me." He repeated, "Like Tevye asked in the musical . . . do you love me?"

She raised her eyes to look at him, and the words came tumbling out, "Yes, Bobby . . . I love you. I've always loved you. Oh my God, I love you."

He took her in his arms and kissed her, a long-awaited kiss. Tomorrow would have to wait another day. Today was their day. They listened to their hearts as he kissed her once more and held her and hugged her. Life was good again for Robert James Macgregor. Life was whole again.

Chapter Thirty-Two

Saturday night the dance studio was empty as Ryan opened the door and walked inside the dimly lit dance hall. He had to admit to himself that he was looking forward to seeing her again; he had told his brothers it was purely professional, but there was just something about her . . . something.

"Alexi? Hello? Anybody there?"

"Ryan? I'll be right out." A few minutes later, she came out from behind a curtain drying her hands on an old blue towel. "Hiya, Doc," she said with a smile. A splotch of white was visible on the tip of her nose.

He laughed.

"What?" she asked.

He touched his nose, then hers. "You have a large white spot on your nose, right here," he said as he touched the errant spot. She rubbed it with her rag until it slowly disappeared.

"Don't ask me why I'm painting just before we close," she laughed. "And I seem to have gotten more on me than on . . ." Her voice trailed off as their eyes met. They stood there, alone, in the quiet. "Let me wash up," she stammered. "I'll just be a minute." She once again disappeared behind the room divider. He could hear her singing in the distance.

When she reappeared, she asked him, "Ready to dance?" turning on some music.

"Yes," he said as he watched her dance solo across the floor, unable to take his eyes off her. She was very graceful as she danced, showing him the next move she wanted him to learn. Her long dark hair flowed behind her, but it was her eyes that sought to draw him in close. Dark, flashing eyes. Penetrating eyes. Eyes that followed him everywhere. She glanced at him, and he returned her gaze. He walked to her and extended his hand, preparing to dance, and slowly drew her close. The music faded into the background as they began to dance.

He could tell she was nervous.

"Your brothers were in yesterday and finished up their final lesson. They don't dance as well as you, but they sure try hard to do what I . . ."

"Shhh . . . just dance with me," he whispered, and held her in his arms.

They began with a rumba, slow, in rhythm with each other, their legs and thighs touching, moving to the beat of the music. He could feel her breasts pressing against his chest. He felt her heartbeat and the rhythm of her heart as if it were his own. The scent of her perfume was intoxicating, drawing him closer. He was lost in her embrace.

Her breath quickened. She danced with him as he held her close. *Just dance, girl, dance as if no one is watching and no one cares.*

They danced for over an hour, and as they danced, his hand slid down from her shoulder to around her waist. She began to feel warm. Finally she broke away from him. "Do you mind if we finish another time? It has been a long day for me. I think you've learned the slow Latin dances pretty well."

He looked at her, stepped back, and said, "Are you sure?"

"Yes," she replied. "Besides, I'm a little tired . . . and very hungry."

"Okay, I understand. We can do it another day." He started to walk away but did not want to leave. He turned and asked, "Would you like to have dinner with me tonight? You said you were hungry. If you like Thai food, there's a great Thai restaurant called the Thai Asian Bistro on Military Trail not far from here."

She vacillated for a brief moment, then smiled and said, "Yes, I would love to have dinner with you. I love Thai food. Let me change my shoes and lock up. I'll meet you out in front of the building. I have to set the alarm."

It was a short ride to the restaurant, and as they entered, it was quiet, since the mad rush of the dinner crowd had long since passed. He asked for a booth so they could be comfortable.

"Very nice. Do you come here often?" she asked as she looked around the quaint establishment.

"Not as much as I used to when my wife . . ." He stopped himself. "Sorry."

"It's okay. It's only natural. How long ago did your wife pass away?"

"Almost two years ago. She was killed in a biking accident. Hit-and-run. Police arrested one person, but it turns out he had a solid alibi. No one else."

"I'm so sorry. Your daughter told me some of the story when she bought the dance lessons for you and your brothers." Their waiter brought two menus and poured two glasses of ice water.

"Thanks. The first couple of months were very rough, but my brothers and friends keep telling me to get on with my life and that it does get easier with time. They just never said it would take such a long time." He picked up the menu and said, changing the subject, "Everything on the menu is good. I've never had a bad meal here."

They sat across from each other, the aroma of spices and herbs filling the air. Cumin, ginger, garlic, krachai, lemongrass, sesame, turmeric, and all the others blended together, welcoming them. A young boy took their order and then brought a pot of tea and two cups to their table.

"Well, I have to tell you, it sure smells great. So, your daughter told me you were . . . a psychologist."

"No, I'm a psychiatrist, a medical doctor. I share the practice with another doctor by the name of Dr. Mary Gladings. She's on a cruise with her husband, so we cover for each other. I see some of her patients when they have an emergency."

"Wow, that sounds interesting."

"I always wanted to help people and wanted to be a psychiatrist. I believe it helps patients to heal when they can share their thoughts and feelings with a trained professional. Most psychiatrists no longer use talk therapy anymore, but I still like to. However, sometimes patients take it the wrong way."

"What do you mean?" she asked, leaning in toward him.

He looked around the deserted restaurant and whispered, "Just this week I had a patient get very emotional in a session in my office. I can't mention any names, due to patient confidentiality, but he pulled a gun on me in my office."

"Oh my God!" she gasped. "What did you do?"

"I told him that I would have my secretary clear the rest of my schedule to spend more time with him. Then I used a code with my secretary, alerting her that there was trouble."

"What did she do?"

"She called the police right away, but by the time they got there, he was already gone. I think he was a little upset with me."

"Were you scared?"

"Yes, with a patient like that . . . you just never know. But it's true what they say, you do see your life flash before your eyes and wish for . . ." He smiled. "I'm rambling again, sorry."

"I like it when you relax and ramble," she said with a smile as their waiter delivered their dinners.

As they tried several dishes, they talked. She was easy to talk to, he thought, like his Gracie. They ordered a glass of wine, then another. He watched her laugh; it was infectious. Their hands briefly touched on the table. He felt something, something that he thought had died with Gracie. He had a strange look in his eyes.

Upon her insistence they split the dinner tab, and he drove her back to the studio parking lot. The night was cool, and the moon shone high above them through the clouds as they walked to her car.

"You still have a partial lesson. When would you like to . . ."

He kissed her awkwardly, then stepped backward. "I don't know what came over me. I'm so sorry."

"I'm not," she responded, as she draped her hands around his neck and moved closer to him. Again their lips met. This time they lingered together, and it was a feeling he had missed so much. He kissed her again. She tasted of honey and roses.

She ran her hand through his hair, and then kissed his cheek, his ear, and his lips. It was something she had wanted to do since she had first met him. "I better go," she finally said, her voice hoarse with passion.

Ryan opened the car door and helped her inside. "I would like to see you again."

"I would like that also. What did you have in mind?"

"Well, we could go to a nice fancy restaurant and . . ."

She shook her head and scrunched her face to show her disagreement. "How about a picnic? At the studio, we'll call it practice. Then maybe have some champagne and candles to celebrate your dance-class graduation." She smiled broadly.

He wanted to ask her something but did not know where or how to begin. He felt even more awkward than when he had first kissed her. *Here goes.*

"Alexi . . ." He stumbled, feeling like an awkward schoolkid. "Alexi, I know that this is short notice and all, but you know that my daughter Mary Kate is getting married next week?"

"Yes, I recall she had mentioned that was the reason she wanted you to brush up on your dancing."

It had been years since he had asked anyone out on a date. "Well . . . I don't have a dance partner . . . or a date for the wedding . . . I was wondering if you . . . I mean I would like to . . . would you be available to go . . . want to go . . . with me . . . to . . ."

"I would love to," she said, then kissed him, then again. "It should be wonderful. I would be happy to go with you."

He left and could still smell the sweetness of her perfume. *Just go with it, Ryan. Just go with it.*

Chapter Thirty-Three

Ryan smiled at the thought of Alexi, watching her drive away, and began to hum a soft song as he pulled out his car keys in the parking lot. The detectives who had been shadowing him all day must have stopped for the evening, because he did not see their ever-present police car. Jeff was probably long gone by now, he thought to himself.

It was getting dark, and he could not wait to see her again. *A picnic? At a dance studio? Candles? Wine? Only Alexi would ever think of something like* . . . He didn't see him until it was too late.

The gun felt sharp against his ribs, and the voice was impatient. "Don't move, Doc. I've been waiting for you. Come on, I want you to join me on a little trip. You're coming with me." It was Mary's patient Jeffrey Long.

They began walking; the gun was pointed directly at him. "Don't do anything stupid, Doc, like you did before. You drive," he said, jumping into the passenger seat. "Drive up Congress toward Interstate 95, then head north."

Ryan put the car into gear and slowly pulled away. He drove down Glades before turning off onto I-95N. "What's this all about, Jeff?"

"Just drive, Doc." They continued in silence. A few miles later, a state trooper pulled up beside him in slowing traffic and glanced their way.

"Remember what I said, Doc? Smile for the nice policeman," Jeff told him, putting the pistol on his lap, pointing at Ryan. "And nobody'll get hurt."

The cop pulled away into the fast lane.

"Turn off on the next exit, Southern Boulevard. Head east toward the warehouse district." He made the turn off the highway and, following directions, made a left onto Dixie Highway.

"Slow down, Doc. Obey the speed limit. Don't want any traffic tickets, now do we?" Jeff leaned forward, looking for his destination. "Here, turn here."

They passed deserted old warehouses left over from the time when the city was a thriving seaport and shipping area. Now they were just old derelict structures waiting to be redeveloped into shiny new waterfront condominiums.

"Pull over and park here, Doc," Jeff grunted. "You're about to get your wish."

"What wish?" There was a chill in the dense night air, and he rubbed his arms, then wrapped them around himself, trying to keep warm.

"You'll see. Walk," he said, shoving the gun into Ryan's back.

Broken beer and whiskey bottles, along with discarded syringes and hypodermic needles, littered the parking lot.

"This door, Doc," Jeff said, pointing using a high-powered beam from his flashlight. It was dark as Ryan made his way inside, down some steps, and into the holding bay of the huge warehouse. He heard the sound of mice scurrying away from the approaching light.

A leaky roof caused puddles on the littered floor; his foot sank inside one, filling his shoe with stale rainwater. It smelled of old fish. The flashlight moved from left to right, causing light and darkness to flash and fade. Soon Ryan could make out the outline of a figure ahead, sitting in a chair. They walked around to the front of the metal chair, and in the middle of the old warehouse was a blindfolded man sitting there naked, obviously shivering from both fear and cold. Another chair farther away was piled with clothes.

"Here you go, Doc. The man who killed your wife. Then he ran away, leaving her on the side of the road, alone to die. Then he had his wife and his best friend lie for him. He admits it. Tell him, Rick; tell him now!" Jeff said, raising his voice while poking him with the gun.

"I did it," the man screamed. "Yeah, it was me. I did it, but I didn't do it on purpose. It was an accident. I swear to God. You gotta believe me. I'm so sorry, really I am. I never meant to hurt her." He stopped to catch his breath before continuing, "I didn't see her on the side of the road. I had a couple of drinks before I left home. My wife and I had a fight, and I left in a rage. Then she felt guilty. That's why she lied for me; she felt guilty, like it was her fault." His voice quivered.

"But there's not a day that goes by that I don't think about that accident. My God, I hit her and . . . killed her. I live with that every day." He bent over in the chair, still constrained by the ropes. He began to cry.

"Okay, Doc. You got the guy, dead to rights. He admitted it. Now make him pay for what he's done. Here." Jeff handed him the gun. "Finish him."

Ryan held the cold piece of steel in his hand and walked toward the terrified man sitting before him, blindfolded. His jaw tightened, his temper rose. The killer of his beloved Gracie sat before him. The man who, in an instant, had changed his life forever. *Goddamn him, goddamn him to hell.* Then it was gone. The wrath and fury that had been building up inside him—was gone. Now before this helpless naked man he stood there, drained.

Forgiven. Redemption.

"Let him go," Ryan ordered as he threw the gun far off into the dark, murky distance. He heard it hit with a sharp metal sound on the concrete floor and echo in the darkness as he began to untie the man.

"Get me his clothes, Jeff. This man's freezing." He turned around and Jeff was gone, like a shadow in the night. Ryan immediately retrieved his cell phone from his pocket and called 911. Jeff was a danger to the public and had to be caught before he hurt somebody else. He needed help.

He knelt before the shivering, naked man and slowly peeled away the bandanna covering his eyes and said, "Let's get out of here before he comes back. I'll take you to the authorities, and you tell them exactly what you told me." For some reason he felt a tremendous weight had been lifted from his shoulders. He finally knew what had happened; he now had closure. *Time to get on with living.*

Chapter Thirty-Four

It was a gorgeous South Florida Sunday morning. A perfect chamber-of-commerce kind of weekend, one it would call a picture-perfect day. Ryan sat at the breakfast table with his brothers having bagels and orange juice. They were all unusually quiet, each lost in his own world until Ryan broke the silence.

"I was kidnapped last night."

"What? What the hell are you talking about? Are you okay?" Robert was on his feet.

"Yeah, I'm fine."

"Who did it?"

"It was the same guy who was in my office with the gun. He came back."

"When did all this happen?" asked Eian.

"Last night after my dance lesson. When I came back to my car after dinner with Alexi, he was there waiting and . . ."

"Wait a minute. Did you say you had dinner with Alexi last night?" asked Eian.

"Yes . . . and it was very nice and . . ."

Robert interrupted, "Hey, bro, let's go back to this crazy guy."

"When I got into my car, the patient who held me at gunpoint in my office was waiting there for me. He had me drive him to a warehouse in West Palm at gunpoint and had the guy who was responsible for Gracie's death sitting in a chair, naked. He handed me the gun and told me to shoot him." Ryan took in a deep breath.

"But as much as I loved . . . and still love Gracie, I couldn't do it. I told him to let the guy go. I called 911, then took him to the Delray police station and filed a police report about what had happened with Gracie. Then I filed a report against Jeff. That guy is very strange. Dangerous. One minute he was there, and the next he just disappeared. It was crazy." For once, the two older brothers had nothing to say.

Ryan sat back in the chair and looked out the kitchen window at the calming water in the pool and the ocean beyond. "I couldn't do it. I couldn't shoot him. He admitted he killed Gracie, but for some reason I couldn't kill him. Suddenly, I felt a tremendous weight lifted from me."

"It's called letting go, little brother," responded Robert. The room became quiet again.

A few minutes passed before Robert spoke to no one in particular. "I've been seeing an old friend from when we were kids. You guys probably don't remember her. Her name was Coleen McGrath back then, but now her name is Coleen Callahan. Nice lady. Husband died a few years back."

Both Eian and Ryan sat in silence, stunned at his revelations.

"I was wondering where you've been spending your evenings here lately. Is she the one you bought the theater tickets for the other day? When you were out dancing in the rain?" asked Ryan.

"Yes, the one and only," he said, smiling broadly. "We're going to a violin concerto tonight at Lynn University. I am actually enjoying all of this culture. You guys should try it. And I asked her to be my date at the wedding next weekend." He stood to pour more coffee, refilling everyone's cup.

"You did?"

"Yep," he said, "and I put a contingent sales contract on a house in Boca Raton. So you'll be getting one of your bedrooms back soon. The place has its own lake behind it—with fish! Very nice. It's not far from the office. It's a fixer-upper, but that's what I love to do. I told Bobby I'm going to take some time off after I close on the house, and we'll see what happens. Who knows?"

"Good for you, bro," said Ryan.

"I miss my house," said Eian to no one in particular. "I loved it there. Don't get me wrong, I love it here with all you guys, but . . . that was home, really home for me."

"What's going on with that?"

"It's with the attorneys. They told me I never should have left. Spousal rights. Squatter rights and a bunch of other things. But I didn't want to cause . . ." He lifted his coffee cup and sipped it in silence.

Ryan coughed to break the mood. "Well, I also have an announcement. I too have a date for the wedding; Alexi has said she'll go with me."

"Whoa. Way to go, little brother. That leaves just Eian without a date. What about it, Eian? Big shot? Got a date yet?" They both turned to look at him.

"No, not yet."

"You're running out of time, brother. The wedding is next Saturday afternoon, or have you forgotten?"

"Well, I don't know . . . I'm supposed to go out of town on business to California starting on Tuesday for a few days."

"I can't wait to hear you tell Graw about that. Whew. I can hear her now," Robert said.

"We get fitted for our tuxes tomorrow with Mickey and then pick them up on Friday. So you don't have a lot of time. Better get crackin'," said Ryan, looking outside. "It's so warm today. I think I'm going to take a swim in my pool. I haven't used it in . . . years."

Just then, the phone rang. "Macgregor residence," answered Robert, trying to sound so official. "Oh hi, Alexi. It's Robert. Yeah, I'm good. You looking for Ryan? He's right here. Hold on; I'll get him." He covered the receiver and said, "For you. It's Alexi." He smiled and raised his eyebrows a few times to show his approval.

"Hey, I was just talking about you. Me and my brothers were finishing a late breakfast, and I was getting ready to put on my swim trunks and jump in the pool for a swim."

"Really? Great minds think alike. I know we said we'd do a picnic at the studio," she started, "but it's such a nice day—would you want to go to the beach down near Caffe Luna Rosa instead?"

"Sure, that sounds great," Ryan chirped with glee.

"Meet me at the beach at Atlantic and A1A. One hour? I'll bring everything we need. See ya."

"Great! See you soon." He hung up the phone and ran for the stairs. "Going to the beach. Have a good day," he shouted, leaving his brothers behind.

It was warm and sunny, like most days in South Florida. The beach at downtown Delray was crowded for a Sunday afternoon. Where else but Florida could you go year-round for beautiful beaches, warm sun, and gorgeous weather?

Ryan saw Alexi halfway down the beach waving to him. He returned the wave and rushed to where she had laid out a beach blanket. As he approached her, he could not help but admire her sensuous curves outlined in her swimsuit. She was beautiful! And sexy.

She kissed him on the cheek and handed him a glass of champagne. He toasted, "Cheers!" and set down the glass as he stripped to his swim trunks.

"Have you been working out there, Dr. Macgregor?" she said jokingly.

"Every morning. Keeps me healthy. Do you like?"

"I like. Here, have some grapes or cheese and crackers. I got them fresh from the market."

They sat on the blanket and talked. She was easy to talk to, like his Gracie. The sun began to warm the sky as they ran into the ocean to cool off before settling back onto the oversize blanket she had brought with her. They lay side by side under the warm sun, not saying a word, just enjoying each other's company and the bubbly champagne.

Finally he said, "You know last night after I walked you to your car? Somebody was waiting for me at my car . . . with a gun."

"What? What happened?" she sat up and faced him. Afraid for him.

"It was that patient that I told you about, the one with a gun in my office. I think he thought he was trying to help me; he captured the guy involved in the hit-and-run with my wife, Gracie. He took me to the guy he had tied up in some old dingy warehouse. He had the gun trained on me the whole time. I was so scared of what could happen next. But, you know, a lot goes through your mind at times like that. Makes you think. About people. Places. Values. Friends. Family, a lot. I see myself making some changes in my life. Maybe even take some time off. See the world. My clinic partner comes back from her cruise soon, and I may do just that, travel. Take off and go somewhere."

"Really?"

"Yeah, why not? I really need the time off."

"How about Paris?"

"What?" he responded.

"I said, how about Paris?"

He had a puzzled look on his face, and then said, "Paris would be great. Perfect. That's one place on my bucket list I would love to see. The Louvre. The Arc de Triomphe. The *Mona Lisa*. I'd love to see it someday."

Alexi moved in front of him. "I don't know how to say this. It's not something I'm very good at, so let me get it all out before you say anything. Please."

"Okay," he said, putting his champagne glass into the sand. "This sounds serious."

She cleared her throat and took in a deep breath. "Here goes. We have only known each other for a really short time, yet I feel incredibly attracted to you." He reached for her hand.

"Ryan, I felt that way from the moment I saw you. And then when we danced, I don't know, it was almost a fairy tale or something. You make me feel wonderful . . . again. It has been a long time since I have felt that way. When we're apart, I feel empty, and I can't wait to see you."

"I feel the same way, Alexi. Really I do. I want to get to know you even better. I want to have more picnics like this, just the two of us. It's just that . . ."

"Then come to Paris with me," she blurted out.

He fell backward, nearly falling into the sand. "What . . . what do you mean? Come to Paris with you? Now? What's going on?"

"I was helping my brother paint the studio because he's renovating it. I have a six-week class at one of the most prestigious dance schools in the world, The International Dance Academy, in Paris. I leave next Sunday. Come with me. I used to live there for years, so you could see the world of Paris through my eyes." She was nearly in tears, excited, holding his hands, pulling him closer to her. "Please, say you'll come. Please. It would be wonderful."

She looked so fragile, so sexy, so alluring, so wanting, and he wanted the same thing . . . he wanted her. But even a few weeks off would be tough on his practice and his patients—but he deserved it. He remembered kneeling on the floor in front of the gunman in his office and then sitting in his car with him, so scared that he had promised himself that if he ever got out of the mess he was in, he would change his life. Change it for good. In Paris? See the most romantic city in the world . . . with her.

Ryan looked in her eyes again. He saw picnics along the Seine, walks along the Champs-Élysées, the Eiffel Tower, bike rides in the south of France, and he could spend time with her and have it all. *Now is the time, Dr. Macgregor. Make a decision. What are you waiting for? What are you going to do?*

"I told you I'm not very good at this. Maybe I shouldn't have sprung this on you like this, but . . . ," she said. "Come with me. I think we can make some great memories together, our memories." She pressed his hand to her chest. "Will you come with me? To Paris?"

"Yes . . . yes, I'll go with you."

Chapter Thirty-Five

Robert drove to Coleen's house and knew the entrance guard well enough that he did not even stop him or ask to see his ID. She looked radiant in her black dress, simple gold earrings and, of course, the gold puffed heart he had given her for her birthday. She touched the ruby in the center for good luck. It was like a fairy tale, and she did not want it to end. Coleen had no idea where it was heading, but she listened to Diane. Her daughter had said, "Mom, just let it happen. Hang on."

The violin concerto at the Lynn University Conservatory of Music was one of the best she had ever heard. With her eyes closed, she held his hand, and she was in heaven. It was a sold-out performance, but, more important, it looked as though Robert really enjoyed it too.

"Wonderful," he said as they walked to the car. "You are making a real connoisseur out of me."

"Is that an objection I hear?"

"No, not at all. How about an amaretto at home for a nightcap?"

"Sure. But we'll have to stop somewhere to buy some. We drank what little was left the other night after the musical. I'll look for a store on the way home."

As they pulled into the parking lot, he turned off the engine and said, "I'll be right back. What brand was it again that you liked?"

"I know the label by sight, but I don't remember the name. Wait, I'll go into the store with you."

Coleen found it immediately on the shelf, and as Robert was paying for it, he dropped his wallet. She stooped to pick it up and glanced at the picture inside. She looked closer.

He whispered, "That was my Tess. It was one of the last pictures we had taken together."

She could not take her eyes off the picture and was silent on the way home. As he pulled up in front of her house, she touched his arm and said, "I think I'll call it a night. I don't feel so well. I may be coming down with something. Do you mind?"

"No, of course not. I hope you feel better." *She was fine earlier. Was it something she ate? Could it be something in the picture that upset her?*

"Good night." She kissed his cheek and was gone.

Once inside, she closed the door behind her and slumped to the floor in tears. *Why? Why? Why? Was everything he told me a lie?*

Chapter Thirty-Six

The phone rang on his desk. "Hello. Eian Macgregor."

"Hey, Mac, it's Paula. Are we still on for tomorrow? Are you still coming to California? I hope so; I'm really looking forward to it."

"You bet," he replied.

"Great. I'll pick you up at the airport. Can't wait to see you. We'll go back to my place and get reacquainted. Okay?"

"Yeah. See ya soon." However, for some reason his enthusiasm had waned since he had first talked to her, and he didn't know why. *Hope it's not the flu or something. Shake it off, bro.* Tonight he was going out with his two brothers and with his new future in-law, Mickey. *Yeah, that should be fun.*

Eian sat behind his desk inside his newly remodeled office and glanced outside. It had felt warmer today than yesterday when he had come into the office. *That's why everybody wants to live in South Florida. Gorgeous weather, gorgeous beaches, and gorgeous women. But it is too nice to be inside. Hell, I'll call my brother and see if I can borrow his convertible for the day.*

"Ryan? Eian. Do you mind if I borrow your convertible? I thought I'd play hooky today and drive down the coast, to Lauderdale."

"Sure, man, you're welcome to use it anytime. It just sits in the garage all the time and really should be driven. Enjoy it, bro." He paused before hanging up the phone and said, "Hey, Eian, I almost forgot . . . I'm going to Paris for a couple weeks . . . with Alexi."

"What? When the hell did all this happen?"

"Yesterday. Alexi is going to France for a class there and invited me to join her. It's been a while since I've taken a vacation, and I figured— what the hell."

"Oh . . . when do you leave?"

"Sunday, the day after the wedding."

"Wow. Hey, who's going to make me breakfast while you're gone? You know you make the best chocolate chip waffles. And I love your omelets. And who's going to clean up the place? Bob's no help."

"You're a big boy, Eian. You'll manage . . . somehow. I thought you'd be happy for me . . . getting on with things in my life and all."

"I am . . . but . . . it's just that . . . I've kind of gotten used to having you around, you know?"

"I'm not moving. I'm just going away on a short vacation. A long-overdue one, I might add."

"Hey, maybe I'll go too? And Bob? He's never been to France."

"It's not that kind of vacation, bro. It's just the two of us, Alexi and me."

"Oh," Eian said, sounding disappointed. "I guess we'll manage . . . somehow or another. You said I could use your convertible?"

"Sure, the keys are in the kitchen drawer. It's all gassed up. Enjoy. What's mine is yours, bro."

Too nice to be working inside but a great day for a ride in a convertible. A great day just to spend outside, relaxing with someone. Rose? Yes, Rose.

He dialed her number and was excited when he heard her voice, but it was her voice mail: "Sorry I can't take your call at the moment, but if you leave your name and number, I'll call you back." *Beeeeeep!*

"Hey, Rose, Eian here. Just thinking of you and thought maybe . . . well . . . call me when you get this message."

Eian spun around in the chair like a twelve-year-old, going faster and faster. Then looked outside with random thoughts running through his mind. The phone rang and he answered, "Eian Macgregor."

"Eian, hi . . . it's Rose. I got your message. What's up?" she added tersely.

"Hey, Rose. I'm glad you called."

That was it, more than she could tolerate, and finally she said, "That's more than I can say about you." She sounded mad. "You said a week ago that you'd call me. I waited for you. You said we were going dancing, and you never even so much as picked up the phone to say hello or good-bye or kiss my ass. I thought we were going dancing." Disgusted, she finally said, "Good-bye Eian," then hung up the phone.

What the . . . ? he wondered.

He redialed her number. "Rose . . ."

"What?" she said, nearly shouting at him through the phone.

"I'm sorry, Rose. I screwed up. I'm really sorry."

She could not be angry with him, but she also did not want to let him off the hook. *Let him squirm.* "Well, you should be . . ."

"Forgive me?"

"Well, I don't know . . ."

"Let me make it up to you."

"How?" she asked.

"First, can you get away?"

"Yeah . . . I guess. Why? You're still in the doghouse, buster. You're not getting off that easy."

"Rose, I thought it was such a nice day, too nice to be inside. It's a great day to be driving a convertible down the coast and maybe have lunch near the beach. I know a place that makes great margaritas. I called my brother, and he said I could use his convertible, and well . . . you were the first person I thought about. Sorry."

She melted. She could not resist him. "Okay, okay. Pick me up at home, twenty minutes. I gotta change clothes."

"No need. Whatever you're wearing I'm sure will be fine. You always look great." *Damn him.* Now she was really like putty in his hands. *Hold on tight, girl. This is going to be one helluva ride!*

"Twenty minutes, at home." She wanted to look perfect. "And you better be there this time." Then she softened and said, "See ya soon," and was out the door.

He was there in nineteen minutes and watched her lock her house behind her. Eian looked at her as she ran to the car like an excited schoolkid. Rose looked great in her snug white jeans, pink silk top, thin sandals, beige scarf, and ever-present sunglasses. He thought she looked like a movie star.

"You look great," he said as she slid into the seat beside him. It was a dark-green two-seater British sports car, and the engine responded with a growl at the slightest touch of the gas pedal.

"Thank you," she said with a smile, giving him a slight peck on the cheek. She smelled wonderful too. "And thanks for thinking of me. What a wonderful idea. Where are we going?" she asked as the car pulled away from the curb and he drove east toward the ocean.

"You'll see."

They turned onto Ocean Avenue, and Eian said above the roar of the engine and the whistling wind, "I thought we would head over to the Coast Highway and drive south toward Lauderdale. There is a nice little restaurant on the beach I love to go to. Kind of special. It has a bar upstairs, which overlooks the ocean, and they serve great frozen margaritas and even better seafood. It won't be crowded at this time of the day. I thought we'd try a little bit of tapas, a little of this and a little bit of that from their menu. What do you think?"

I think life is grand and just keeps getting better, she thought. "Perfect," she said as they turned south onto the two-lane Ocean A1A road. She tightened her scarf and leaned back to enjoy the day, the sun, the surf, and . . . him. She looked at him, completely at ease, and asked herself, *What's happening here?*

He turned on the radio to a Miami mellow Latin jazz station as they passed through the different villages along the ocean and made their way south. Some towns, like Highland Beach, consisted of magnificent, multi-million-dollar oceanfront estates, with their broad dark-green lawns, lush landscaping, tall fences, and tall entry gates. Other towns, like Boca Raton, featured rows upon rows of high-rise condominium buildings with Spanish-sounding names: Boca Del Rio, Aqua Del Mar, Del Boca Costa, and many others. In between the towns, over the dense sea grape shrubs, they could see the surf crashing onto the beach as cruise ships set sail to exotic destinations.

The traffic slowed as they drove through small towns such as Deerfield and Pompano Beach, which were filled with long boardwalks, restaurants, bars, and T-shirt shops overflowing with tourists carrying big chairs and umbrellas to the beach.

Once in Lauderdale-by-the-Sea, the narrow two-lane road was lined with big homes with acres of vacant land stretching as far as the eye could see, mixed with lofty condominium buildings.

Eian pulled into the parking lot of the restaurant with its faded red-and-blue sign welcoming all to the Sea Watch Restaurant.

He led Rose up the two flights of old wooden steps, then outside to the covered deck. It was deserted at that time of day, so he chose one of the choicest tables overlooking the ocean.

"How's this?" he asked.

"Wow!" she said as the vista unfurled before her. Two huge sailboats glided out to sea, and windsurfers skimmed the waves near the shores. Farther down the beach, they could see paragliders riding high above the blue ocean waters. It was picture-perfect.

They sat beside each other on the bench seat so they could both watch the ocean and the beach activities. She felt warm next to him. She felt safe.

"What can I get you two lovebirds?" asked the tall, skinny waitress. It felt awkward and somehow broke the mood.

"Rose?"

"I'll have a frozen margarita, with salt, please. You made it sound so good."

"Make that two."

"I have some menus for the two of you. We close for lunch at three thirty and reopen at five for dinner. If you get your order in before three, you should be fine. But we serve small plates and tapas all day."

"Leave the menus here. And we'll order things as we go along," he said. It was a wonderful afternoon. They sipped their drinks in silence and watched the boats go by as the tall dune grasses swayed in the gentle breeze.

Over the next hour they leisurely ordered some crispy calamari, and then two bowls of conch chowder and a plate of hot fish fritters.

Rose looked at him. "You were right; this place is wonderful. Thanks for bringing me here." Then she paused for a moment before asking, "But why . . . why here . . . why me?"

He dabbed his mouth with the cotton napkin and said, "It was such a nice day, and I didn't want to spend it alone. I really needed somebody to talk to . . . and I thought of you."

She didn't know what to say or how to respond. Until she finally asked him, "What's wrong?"

He shoved the drink aside and told her, "I played baseball with a bunch of young kids the other day on a building lot. I coached them, I played some ball with them, I taught them how to hit, how to catch, and how to field. And, Rose, it was the best feeling in my life."

"So what's the problem?"

"I liked it so much that I've decided to leave the station and try to put together a South Florida little league to get kids involved in baseball again. I want to try to get them out of their rooms, away from their computers, away from the video games and everything else. I don't need the money I'm making now. Hell, I've made enough money to last me two lifetimes. I've invested well since I've left the major leagues, and now I'm ready to do something I really enjoy. Am I crazy?"

"No, you're not, Eian. Do it. Why would you hesitate? Both of us are not getting any younger. Don't wait." She laughed and then became serious. "Eian, this is something you love to do. I can tell it in your voice and see the way your face lights up when you talk about it. Do it, otherwise you'll regret it the rest of your life."

He smiled that smile she had always loved.

"You're right. Thanks, Rose, thanks a lot." He hugged her, and in all the excitement, he kissed her on the lips. He didn't know what to say. Or do. They sat on the windswept wooden bench, looking at each other, old friends—seeing each other differently for the very first time.

Awkwardly he glanced at his watch. "I think we'd better go. I have to meet my brothers tonight. Then tomorrow, real early, I head out to California for a few days for the grand opening of a new training center." He paused to help her up from her seat, and she stumbled and fell into him. She looked at him and could not move. He helped her steady herself, then looked around for their server. "I'll call you when I get back, and we can . . . talk some more. Okay?"

"Okay," she whispered, and then wisecracked, "It seems to me I've heard that line once before, somewhere."

Eian chuckled. "I mean it. I will." He kissed her on the cheek, his lips lingering longer than before, as he whispered, "I promise."

Once at Rose's home, he went to get out of the car, but she stopped him and said, "I can take it from here. Eian, I had such a nice day. I can't thank you enough." She smiled, then kissed him on his cheek. "Talk to you soon?"

"You bet."

She laughed, then closed the door and watched him drive away. *Now what? What the hell am I going to do? He's my best friend,* she thought.

Chapter Thirty-Seven

The two brothers waited impatiently outside the tuxedo store for Eian and Mickey to arrive.

Robert looked at his watch. "He's late again. Damn him." He nearly spit out the words.

"Bob, he'll be here. You can count on it. Free food. Mary Katherine said Mickey's paying for dinner." He continued to pace around the front of the small storefront at Duke's Tuxedo Shop. "Wait, here they come. Both of 'em," said Ryan nervously. How was he going to let Robert know that Mickey was a Campbell? Robert seemed agitated for some reason. *Why?*

"Hey, guys, look who I ran into," said Eian.

"Hey, Mickey, good to see you again. Let's go inside and get measured," said Ryan as they all shook hands and quickly went inside. He was anxious to keep everything moving. No time for small talk.

Robert was measured first, then Mickey. Eian was followed by Ryan, who tried his best to keep Mickey away from Robert.

The portly salesman who did double duty as the tailor told them, "Gentlemen, your tuxedos will be ready Friday, or you can get them

Saturday, the morning of the wedding. If you have any questions, feel free to call me."

"I hope we have better luck here than the first tuxedo place," said Eian.

"You mean the one that went out of business?" said Ryan.

"Yeah. That one." They all laughed.

Dinner was held at a nearby Irish pub, and when the evening was finally over, they said good night to Mickey and said they would see him at the rehearsal. On their way home, Ryan said, "Nice fellow, isn't he?

"Yeah . . . for a Campbell."

What? He knew. He must have known all along.

"Robert, put it behind you, all of it. Let it lie."

"Never. He's a Campbell, and that's all there is to it, but I wasn't about to shame our family tonight and say something about it."

"When did you find out?"

"At the tuxedo store. I overheard Mickey say something to the tailor about being a Campbell and how he would love to wear the traditional Highlander kilt—the nerve. I'm surprised at you, hiding all that about him. And disappointed. Good night, Ryan."

Chapter Thirty-Eight

It was an early-morning flight. Eian had not been able to get a direct flight to California and had to change planes in Cleveland and was delayed there due to bad weather. He waited an hour, until they said the flight would not leave for another three hours. He was going to arrive in California late. He should call Paula, he thought to himself, and let her know so she would not worry. His phone rang. "Hello?"

"Mr. Macgregor, this is Gentry, I work for our general manager, Todd Andersen. You and I spoke on the phone, and I was the one who arranged the tickets for you to come to the grand opening of our new training facility here in California."

"Oh yes, Gentry. I'm stuck at the airport in Cleveland, but I should be there for the opening tomorrow."

"Well, that's what I was calling about. We had a minor glitch."

"What's up?"

"We had some terrible weather here, with lots and lots of rain. It caused the roof of the new facility to cave in and flood everything. We're going to have to push back the opening by at least a month. I feel really bad."

Eian, for some reason, felt relieved.

"I'm sorry, but we're going to have to postpone your visit. I'll be back in touch just as soon as we have a new date. We'll make it up to you, I promise."

"No problem. Call me." He was off the hook. Now to call Paula. He dialed her number, and suddenly he didn't know what to say as he heard her voice. "Hey, I was just thinking about you. Where are you?"

"Cleveland. My plane was delayed by about four hours."

"Well, okay . . . call and let me know when you think you'll be here. We'll still have plenty of time. My husband doesn't come home for at least a week."

"Husband?" he nearly shouted as he squirmed in his seat. *She has a husband?*

"Yeah, you remember, I told you I got remarried but kept my maiden name. At least I thought I told you."

"No, you didn't. You told me you were married before but it didn't work out."

"It doesn't matter; I'll tell you all about it when you get here. In the meantime, I have the champagne on ice, chocolate-covered strawberries in the fridge, and my black-lace nightie on . . . all waiting to be unwrapped by you."

He heard a loud announcement in the background, but it wasn't about his flight.

"Was that your flight?"

"Yes," he lied. "It's been canceled. Next flight is out tomorrow." Then he thought about what he was saying and finally said, "Hey, Paula . . . I have to tell you . . . I don't think this is going to work out. You and me. Maybe it would have in another time, other circumstances. You know? I'm sorry."

"What? Eian, are you saying you're not coming?"

"Yeah, I guess I am."

"I had some really nice things planned for us to do. I mean, really nice. I spent a lot of time . . . and money putting it all together, just for the two of us. Nothing I can say to change your mind?"

"No, I'm sorry, Paula."

"Me too, Mac. You don't know what you're missing."

He smiled to himself. Yes, he did.

"You take care of yourself," she said before the phone connection went dead.

He caught the next flight back home to Florida, and as he left the airport, he dialed Rose's phone number. He could not wait to hear her voice.

"Hello? Mac?"

"Hi, Rose. My trip was canceled."

"Where are you?"

"Just leaving the West Palm Beach airport. You know, I was thinkin', I'm starvin'. Do you want to join me for some dinner? We can finish our conversation from yesterday."

"Yeah, I would like that."

"Pick you up in an hour?"

"Sure."

"Great. See you then." He started to hang up but shouted her name, "Rose?" Nothing. "Rose?"

"Yeah, Mac? What'd you forget?"

"Forget?" His voice dropped to a low tone, one she could hardly hear. "I forgot to ask you . . . do you want to go to my niece's wedding, with me . . . Saturday?"

"This Saturday? Mac, that's hardly any notice at all."

"Yeah, I know, I'm sorry. You probably already have plans for this weekend, and it's short notice, and I'm a real jerk for waiting so long to ask you. I understand, but I thought . . ."

"I'd love to go with you, Mac. See you in an hour."

"Great. See you then."

He was now the happiest man alive. He was going to the wedding—with Rose!

Chapter Thirty-Nine

"Mother?" Diane hollered from the first floor, looking up the steps. She was worried about her, as she had appeared distracted at the office. Something was troubling her. "Mother?" she said with a certain insistence that only daughters could muster. Still no answer. "Moth—"

"Out here, Di," a voice sounded from the kitchen. She walked through the house and sniffed the air. She could almost taste the flavor of fresh-baked cookies and warm bread. Her mother was an excellent baker, though baking was something Diane had never been able to master.

The huge kitchen was filled with stacks of cookies, loaves of bread, and croissants that filled the counter. Six pies of various sizes and flavors were on a nearby cooling rack by the open kitchen window. Apple-cinnamon crusts, blueberry scones, and strawberry tarts were scattered about the country kitchen. Diane grabbed a couple of cookies. Delicious and still warm.

The room smelled heavenly. Copper pots and pans, long spoons, and spatulas hung from a ceiling rack above Coleen's work area. In the center of the kitchen was a long granite countertop perfect for baking and rolling cookies. It was something she had had installed years earlier.

"Mother, what on earth are you doing? What's going on? What is all this? Are you opening a bakery or something?"

"No," her mother said, stopping long enough to take a sip from her glass of white wine before she opened the oven door and retrieved a fresh batch of lemon sugar cookies from inside. "Just keeping busy, that's all. Just need to put this last load of cookies in. Pour some wine for yourself and pull up a chair."

Diane had seen her mother like this once before, when her father died; she had fallen to pieces and gone on an eighteen-hour baking marathon. She dutifully opened the refrigerator and poured them each some wine.

"Okay, tell me what's going on," she said as she unbuttoned her suit jacket and kicked off her high-heeled shoes. "What's going on here?"

Her mother sat down on a stool next to her. "It's about Mac . . . he lied to me."

"What do you mean he lied? He doesn't seem like the type. What happened?"

"You know he gave me a gold puffed heart with a red ruby in the center?"

"Yes, I know, you wear it all the time and . . ." Her daughter noticed it no longer hung about her neck.

"When we were out the other night, he dropped his wallet, and when he picked it up he showed me a picture of his deceased wife." She stopped and could not go on. Diane hugged her to encourage her, to release the pain she was obviously feeling.

"She had on the heart. He gave me the same heart he gave his first wife. I saw a picture of her wearing it. He said I was special, but he lied to me." She was nearly in tears as she drained her glass of wine and reached for the bottle to refill the glass.

"He made me feel different," she said between her tears. "I felt I was the only one in the world. He told me that I was his heart and soul and I could feel the rhythms of his heart. He even put my hand on his chest for me to feel it beating. Now I wonder if he said the same things to her? And who else has he said it to?" Tears were running down her cheeks; her makeup was a river of black lines on her face. "Diane, what am I going to do? I love that old Scotsman, and I thought he loved me, but now . . ."

"Mom, I'm sure he does. Just in his own way, that's all."

"Well, I have to tell you, I haven't talked to him since Sunday. And I miss it, I miss him, but I just can't bring myself to call him. I just can't do it. What am I going to do?"

Diane plucked some tissues from the box and handed her a few. "First, clean up your makeup. Second, pour some more wine. Third, call him . . . just don't do it today. Sleep on it, and then call him tomorrow. For now, let's cut up one of these wonderful pies! Oh, and Mom, check the stove, I think I smell something burning."

Chapter Forty

"Claret! Woman, what's with all those bags on the floor here in the bedroom?" he bellowed, glancing at the suitcases stacked by the hallway door near the top of the steps.

"Angus, I told you before, I'm going to my son's wedding with you . . . or without you. Today is Thursday, the rehearsal is tomorrow, the wedding is Saturday, and I plan to be there for it."

There was no one more stubborn than a hardheaded Scotsman, unless . . . it was a determined Scotswoman, and Claret was one of the finest. She loved him and respected him, but sometimes she had to remind him who really was the boss in the family.

Angus turned and walked away. He returned an hour later holding up his tuxedo in one hand and his kilt in the other. "Which one should I bring, dear?"

She walked to him, gently smoothing the snowy-white hair on the side of his head. "Bring them both, dear heart."

"I'm sorry, you were right," he said meekly. "I love you, Claret."

"I love you too—you obstinate Scotsman," she said, gently touching the gold puffed heart that hung around her neck, the one he had given her so many years earlier. "Remember, he's our only son, and he craves your love and respect. Don't be afraid to give it to him and to those he loves. I don't want to lose him. We've already lost one son; I don't want to lose another." She kissed him and draped her arm around his neck. "I love you," she repeated.

He held her tight. This would not be easy, but he knew what he had to do. He loved that boy like his own. He would make it work, if not for his sake, then for everyone else's, especially Claret's.

Chapter Forty-One

Robert picked Patti up at home and drove to her see his new house. He wanted his daughter-in-law's opinion of the new place before he signed the final papers.

She slowly exited the truck. Her back was aching, and it was becoming more and more difficult for her to stand up straight. She paused and took in a deep breath, massaging her lower back. She stood and admired the house. It was a two-story home surrounded by tall banyan trees, which provided welcome relief from the hot Florida sun.

"It's a nice house, Dad. Mom would've loved it," she said as they walked through the graceful home, set back from the street. They walked through the entire house, and the more she saw of it, the more she thought it was perfect. The upstairs was cozy, with a bedroom, bathroom, and den. Back downstairs, she looked through the rear window and saw the lake outside.

"Oh, and the lake is lovely," she said, holding her belly. She had walked too much and now glanced around the room, searching for a chair so she could sit down and rest her aching back and feet.

Robert was quickly at her side. "Come here in the kitchen and sit down. I don't want anything to happen to you . . . or my future grandson." He pulled the chair from the table and helped her sit down.

"Better?" he asked as she eased into the chair. She was the daughter he had never had, and he appreciated that she always said exactly what was on her mind. He loved her and would do anything for her.

"Much better. Thanks, Dad," she responded, watching him. "What's wrong? You've been distracted since you picked me up."

He was quiet for minute and then said, "No one else knows yet but . . . I'm not going to Graw's wedding, that's all."

"Why the heavens not?"

"He's a Campbell, the same clan that tried to obliterate the Macgregors from the face of the globe for hundreds of years," he said quietly.

"What? What do you mean?"

"The king of Scotland, James the Sixth, issued an edict that proclaimed that the name of MacGregor was to be abolished. It meant that anyone who bore the name of MacGregor must renounce their name publicly or be hung." He paused to catch his breath.

"Campbell clans took the lead and hunted the MacGregors in the moors, in the mountains and the valleys, and then murdered them like wild animals. The MacGregor clan was scattered to the four winds, with many being forced to take other names like Murray or Grant. Even the horrible Scottish parliament got involved and abolished the name of MacGregor and shunned all those who bore it. The Campbells were behind it all. But can you believe it, even with all of that, the MacGregors still fought for the king of Scotland during the Scottish Civil War?"

"Dad, I know my Scottish history. That was in 1603, and I'm sure Mickey was not around then, and neither were you. He had nothing to do with it. Let it go, please. You're still alive, aren't you, and you certainly don't look over a hundred years old?" she said, trying to make light of it. He needed to see it as it was—an old feud. "Mary Kate means a whole lot more than some festering feud that happened hundreds of years ago. Mickey seems like a real nice guy, and they love each other. That's all that counts. Isn't it?"

He was quiet.

She paused before saying, "You do what you want, but I know that it would break Mary Kate's heart if you weren't there for her wedding." His mind seemed made up, and she knew she could not alter his perception of reality. Changing the subject, she said thoughtfully, "Dad, this is a lovely house. You have four bedrooms, an unfinished basement downstairs that you can build out if you like, and a nice workshop in the garage. The yard is large enough so we can have family cookouts here and Thanksgiving dinners, the way you always like to do. And during the holidays, you can throw a big Christmas log onto the fireplace. Yeah, it'll be real nice."

She patted his hand. "Everything will work out fine, trust me. It's perfect. It has everything you need."

"Everything except someone to share it with," he added quietly.

He pulled out his phone and dialed a number, and after a few moments he hung up and tossed his phone on the kitchen counter. His face said it all. "I guess she's out. Somewhere."

"Coleen?"

"Yes." He was silent, and she could tell he was struggling.

"Something happened when we were last together. I must have done something wrong or said something wrong or . . . gee, I don't know. And now I can't even get through to her. At the office, they say she's unavailable. At home she won't take my calls. It's been days, and I've heard nothing from her. I miss her."

She could tell he was in pain. She reached out to hold his hand. "I'm sure there's a simple explanation for it all. Wait, you'll see."

He smiled at her, then stood watching some young boys at the back of the property fishing from the old wooden boat dock. He saw them bait the fishhooks and cast their lines far out into the lake. He watched them fish as he began to pace in front of the window.

Finally he said, "Will you be okay here if I go out and talk to them for a few minutes? I just want to see what kind of fish they're catching and what they use for bait."

"Sure, I'll be fine. You go ahead. I'm just going to sit here and watch."

"I won't be long. I'll be right back. Five minutes."

Patti saw him walk down the hill toward the lake and wave at the kids as he approached them. Once there, he sat on the grass as he watched them fish and talked to them.

She took off her shoes and began to massage her swollen, aching feet. Nothing helped; she could never get any relief no matter what she did. Her feet always hurt, and her back ached no matter how she slept or walked or sat. *Everything* ached.

The baby kicked, and then kicked again and again. *Oh no. Not now, not here, please.* She sat perfectly still, rubbing her belly. "It's okay, everything will be fine, dear heart," she whispered. "Take all the time you need . . . but I'm sure ready whenever you are."

The house was quiet as she sat and looked around. It had a warm, comfortable feel to it. *This will be a good house for him,* she thought as his phone rang and vibrated across the countertop. It rang again. She turned to look for him; he was still engrossed in discussion with the young boys down by the lake. She picked up the phone and looked at the caller ID; it read COLEEN CALLAHAN.

"Hello?" she answered.

"Hello? Mac?"

"No, I'm sorry, he's not here at the moment. He just stepped out for a minute," she said, trying to stand to wave at him but thinking better of it and sitting back down.

"Oh," came the disappointed reply.

"This is Patti, his very pregnant daughter-in-law. I'm sure he'll only be a few minutes. He just went outside."

"Hi, this is Coleen. I'm an old friend of Mac's."

"Hi. Nice to meet you. He has spoken very fondly of you, which is not something that he does about most people. Some call him crotchety, but I just love him to death." She heard her laugh.

"Well, he's never been crotchety with me. As matter of fact, he's been nothing but kind, sweet, caring, and . . ." Her voice went silent. "I miss him, Patti; God knows I miss him."

"Coleen, I can tell you he hasn't been the same over the last couple days. I would have to say he misses you too, but I don't want to get in the middle of whatever is going on between the two of you." The phone went silent again. She heard a sigh on the other end.

"Patti, he gave me a gold puffed heart for my birthday, one with . . ."

"A small red ruby in the center?" Patti finished the sentence for her.

"Yes! How did you know?"

"It is a very special Scottish symbol to give as a gift to someone you love."

"Well, I saw a picture of his wife, and she was wearing the same gold heart. He always tells me about how I am the rhythm of his heart, and now I start to imagine him saying the same things to her. I felt special before, but now I feel betrayed, like . . . he was lying to me. I don't know what to do."

Patti took in a deep breath, and said, "Robert Macgregor is a good man. One that you can count on when the going gets rough; you know that he'll always be there for you, no matter what. Mac gave you the heart because that is the only way he knows how to tell you that he loves you." She stopped. Was she going too far? She didn't want to interfere.

Coleen was quiet. Patti pressed on cautiously.

"For a Scotsman, it's a symbol of him giving his heart to you. Think about it . . . what more can he give you?" She became silent.

"Coleen, he's a good man, one of the best that I know"—she paused to chuckle—"but like most men, he's just not that creative or original when it comes to matters of the heart . . . but he means well." She looked out the window and saw him stand and begin his trek up the hill, back to the house, and she knew she did not have a lot of time. "He's on his way back."

Coleen sounded desperate. "What do I do now? I've been avoiding his phone calls and not talking with him or seeing him. He must think I hate him."

"I don't think so at all. My suggestion would be to hang up and call back in a few minutes and talk to him. You'll know what to say. Just don't tell him about our conversation. Okay?"

"Okay. Thanks, Patti. I can't wait to meet you at the wedding. Bye."

She hung up and set the phone back on the table just in time to see him walk through the door.

"Hiya."

"Catch anything?

"The boys caught some bass and sunfish, and then threw them back into the lake. Catch and release. But there's some good fishing here, I can tell." Robert glanced down at the phone before saying, "Howya doing? Feet okay?"

"No, but that won't change for a while. It's my back that's killing me, carrying around all this extra weight," she said, rubbing her back, then her belly. "Won't be long." She was hurting more than usual, and differently from before.

"You want some hot water to soak your feet? Or maybe some Epsom salts?"

"No, but I may need some help in getting my shoes back on."

"No problem." He grabbed her shoes from the floor and was handing them to her when his phone rang. He looked at the caller ID, then at Patti before he answered it. She nodded for him to take the call.

"Hi," he said tenderly, and as she watched him speak, she saw his body language change. He covered the mouthpiece and whispered to her, "It's Coleen."

Patti watched him as he listened to Coleen on the phone and heard him say, "That's awful. Are you feeling better now?" He motioned to Patti that he was going outside for some fresh air and to finish his conversation. "Something you ate? Oh, that must have felt terrible . . . ," she heard him say. She smiled and watched him through the window as he walked around the patio. A few minutes later, he came back inside with a huge grin on his face.

"Can you believe that? She got food poisoning and was sicker than a dog for the last few days? Didn't feel like talking to anyone. Poor girl, but she said she's feeling much better now. I think I'll send her some get-well flowers."

"I think that's a wonderful idea, Dad." She smiled. "Are you ready to go?" she asked as she finally managed to shove her foot inside her shoe.

"Yeah. I think I'll buy this house. It has a good feel to it."

She hugged him and wrapped her arm around his. "I agree. Good choice. You're so wise. I guess that's why I love you so much."

"I'm just a lovable kind of guy, that's all. Come on, let's go."

They walked outside and he took one last look around at the house and the lake. "Yes, this will be a good house for the family. I'll put a swing right there and swing with my new grandson, Robert."

She looked at him. "Dad, about the name thing . . ."

He saw the look on her face and said, "Or whatever you decide to call him. It'll be fine with me. As long as he's healthy. That's all that matters." He smiled and they walked away arm in arm from the soon-to-be Macgregor homestead.

"And I think I'll put a Macgregor coat of arms right there on the fence, for all to see."

"Great idea." But she was worried. It would not be the same without him at the wedding. He was the elder of the family, the rock of the Macgregors, the glue that held everything together. She knew in the coming years everyone would regret it, including him. *How can I talk him into it? What can I do?*

Chapter Forty-Two

"Where's the money, Calley?" His voice boomed from inside the bedroom and echoed throughout the small house.

"What money, Phil?" she asked from the living room.

"The spendin' money we keep in that old metal box in the bedroom. That money. The box is empty. Where is it?" he shouted, his voice now at a fever pitch in the kitchen.

"The grocery money?" she asked fearfully.

"Yeah, that money. Where is it?" She could hear him in the kitchen cabinets, searching the shelves for any other money she may have hidden away.

"I used it to buy groceries," she said, getting off the couch and turning off the television. Calley had heard that tone in his voice before and knew what it meant. He was going to hurt somebody, and that somebody was usually her. Phil had been drinking again all day, and now he would take out his anger on her.

She could hear Oscar begin to bark in the yard outside, responding to the repeated shouts emanating from inside the house.

"Calley! Damn it!" he shouted.

Run! She ran to the bathroom and locked the door. He was steps behind her. He pounded on the door; it shook violently and barely held him outside. She slid to the floor and began to cry, her back to the door to hold him at bay.

A strange, deep voice chilled the silent air. "I'll be back, my sweet, and when I am . . . I'm going to take care of you. Do you hear me, girlie, I'm going to take care of you once and for all. I've had enough of this . . . and of you." The floor creaked in the dining room, and she heard him open the drawer there in the armoire—*oh my God, no, now he has the gun.*

Through her tears, she began to pray, something she had not done in years, as her body shook in waves of fear. Then she heard the front door open and shut, the car door slam, and the car tires churn up the gravel in the driveway behind him.

Calley went to the front window and saw the car race away, soon followed closely by a dark sedan. Her hands shook; she could not stop the tremors racing through her body. She knew what she had to do and ran into the bedroom. She grabbed clothes, shoes, her makeup bag, and whatever else she could find, throwing them into her old suitcase. She took the money from her secret hiding place underneath the floorboards and ran for the door. He would be home soon from the liquor store, and then the hurting would begin all over again.

She opened the door, and standing before her was Oscar, his snarling pit bull, guarding her escape exit. He snapped, and then lunged at her as she stepped backward. *Trapped! Oh my God, what do I do now?*

Chapter Forty-Three

"Well, brothers, I got my date for the wedding," said a chipper Ryan. "Eian, you got a date yet?"

The other brothers watched him in anticipation.

"Yes, I do, as a matter of fact."

"No groupies. Remember what Mary Kate said," chuckled Robert.

"She's no groupie. I asked Rose, Rose Gilardo, to come with me. And she said she would be honored to join me."

"You're kidding, right? Rose is going with you?" asked Ryan as they all sat on his living-room sofa, the TV on in the background with the sound muted. For once they were more interested in each other than in watching some foreign soccer game.

"I predicted it," said Robert, stretching out on the couch.

Eian threw a pillow in his direction. "You what? I didn't even ask her until yesterday."

"I predicted it right here last week."

"Like hell you did. You always want to take credit for everything," laughed Eian.

"Well, one thing I can't take credit for is my Bobby's barbecue-grill idea."

"What's that?"

Robert sat up on the sofa and turned to them. "He rented the open space next to the store and converted it to a barbecue-grill shop. New grills, books, accessories, the works. At that store, you buy it from us, we assemble it, and then we deliver it to your home, free of charge. It just opened a few weeks ago, and it's going like gangbusters. The store has all of the newest barbecue equipment. Can you believe it? I'm so proud of him; I can't begin to tell you. I told him I am going to finally semiretire. At the end of the month he'll take over running the business."

The three of them sat there in a rare moment of silence.

Ryan broke the silence by saying what they all were thinking. "Who would have believed this? Our business lives are doing well, Eian is embarking on a new baseball venture that he loves. I'm going to take a long-needed break to France with Alexi. And now Bob is retiring."

"Semiretiring, bro," the elder brother quickly chimed in.

"Sorry, semiretiring. And once again, we all have women in our life that we care about. And we can salute Mary Kate for pushing us into action. We can all really celebrate at her wedding."

Robert was quiet and suddenly withdrawn.

"What's wrong, bro?" Ryan asked.

"I'm not going to the wedding," he said darkly.

Agitated, Ryan was on his feet. "Is this because of that Campbell feud stuff? Give me a break, Bob. Get over it."

"Yeah? I have believed and lived my life all along as a Scotsman and a Macgregor. Always. And no self-respecting Macgregor would go to a Macgregor-Campbell wedding. It's just not done. It's like in Ireland during the bad times, unthinkable for a Catholic marrying a Protestant. Or someone in India marrying outside their caste. That's all there is to it. I'm not going to the wedding, so drop it."

"I'm not dropping it. What else is going on here?"

He paused and his eyes turned hard. "You don't remember this because you were away at school, but a Dr. Neidlin Campbell was father's attending physician. To this day, I think he let him die. I don't think—I know—he let him die. He gave him too much morphine, and he died within an hour."

"Father was in so much pain, he was dying of cancer, for Christ's sake, Robert. I remember the doctor—tall, distinguished, plain face, dark glasses? I'll never forget him. Well, I think he was only trying to make Da comfortable during his last hours on earth. And his name could have been Macgregor, Murphy, Smith, or Parker, or whatever, but it had nothing at all to do with him being a Campbell." Ryan paused to look at his two brothers. Silence. Tonight was a night for secrets.

"My daughter and I are expecting this wedding to be a celebration of her marriage and the joining of two families, not about some old Scottish feud."

Silence.

"I can't believe this. My one and only daughter is marrying a fine young man, and you're going to boycott the wedding?"

Eian looked up slowly and spoke softly. "If my brother isn't going . . . then count me out too. I stand by my brother."

Ryan's Scottish temper flared as he attacked them. "Both of you are not going to attend Graw's wedding? I can't believe this. How dare you! She loves the both of you. You were there for her birth, and now you won't be there for her wedding? Unbelievable!"

They nodded in silence as he strode back and forth in front of them.

He stopped pacing. "She will never forgive you . . . nor will I," he yelled. "What would Tess say about this? Or Alice? They would be ashamed of you, both of you." Silence.

"Which one of you is going to tell Graw? You?" he asked Robert, who lowered his head. Silence.

He turned to look at his other brother. "Then Eian, I guess it'll be you, right?" Silence. "And what about Mickey? You're going to hold his last name against him? I, for one, think he's a great guy, a better man then either one of my brothers, apparently."

The brothers were quiet in their shame but remained firm as the youngest of the three paced in front of them. Finally he turned to them, asking them one last time, begging that they reconsider. "I have never asked anything of you two before in my life, but I'm asking now . . . no, I'm begging you . . . please rethink your decision."

Eian gulped and spoke first. "I stand by my brother. Through thick or thin."

"I've never asked anything of either of you, and now you won't attend my family's wedding, Graw's wedding? I spit on you." Ryan spit on the floor in front of them. "You should be ashamed of yourselves." He turned his back on them, his fury spent.

"Aye, younger brother. You don't know what your elder brother has done for you," Eian began to say until Robert gently touched his arm. "Quiet, Eian. This conversation is over. Don't go any further. Let it be," said Robert. *Please*, his eyes begged him.

"It must be told. He needs to know."

"What? What do I need to be told?" Ryan asked, glaring at both of them.

Eian started to say something, but Robert interjected. "Nothing," he said, glaring at his sibling, saying, "Perhaps we should leave now. We have enjoyed the generous hospitality of our good brother long enough. He needs to get on with his life. Thank you for having us as your guest in your home, good brother. We will leave now."

Ryan stood before them. "Wait. Tell me now what I should know, or so help me God I will . . ."

"Sit down," said Eian, waving away Robert's hand as he tried to silence him. "Sit and listen." He took in a deep breath. "You were young when Father became ill and died. Mum went to work to earn money cleaning houses, and somehow we managed. She worked hard, but she wanted her youngest, her brightest, to go on to college. To this day, I think all those hours killed her. Up at four a.m., and then finally falling asleep at midnight. It was too much for her."

Robert nearly shouted, "Eian, stop."

"No, he must be told."

Robert slumped into his seat, quiet.

"Well, as your mother lay on her deathbed with Da gone, she made the two of us promise that you would finish college. Your brother Robert dropped out of school to work to support the family and put you through college. He bought used clothes at secondhand stores and flea markets. He fixed up old run-down cars with hundreds of thousands of miles on them and then sold them to make money. He bought powdered milk and eggs and mixed it with water to help stretch the budget. Anything to make money, all for your schooling. He believed in you, and he made a promise to Mum and Da to take care of you."

"Eian . . . ," Robert started. "Stop."

"No, Robert, he's gotta know what you did for him. He put me through school as well, giving up his college dreams so we could have ours. When I went on to play baseball, I sent money home to help out, but at the time, I wasn't making much money at all in the farm clubs. Brother Bob shouldered most of the burden by himself. Then when you were accepted to medical school, he kept his frugal ways, all to put you through medical school. To make your dreams come true."

"I never knew. You never told me," Ryan said, his voice cracking.

"That was Bob's idea. He didn't want you to know. You had this idealized dream that Mum and Da saved the money for you and paid for everything. Well . . . Robert didn't want to shatter your dreams. He wanted to keep your dreams alive."

"I always thought Dad had set aside money for my schooling. I had no idea that the two of you paid for it all." He plopped down on the sofa next to them.

"Ryan, you had to know, so for you to say that your brother—"

"Brothers," Robert interjected.

"Thank you. So to say that your *brothers* have never done anything for you is wrong. Very wrong. If my brother, who I love dearly, is saying he is not going to our wonderful niece's wedding . . . I have no choice but to defer to his judgment . . . I'm not going; I owe him that for everything he's done for me."

Ryan looked at both of them and then stared at the silent television and said, "I'm not going either."

They all sat there together, in silence, the three Macgregor brothers—always brothers, until the end. How were they going to tell Mary Katherine? Or more important, who was going to tell her? And what about Alexi? Coleen? And Rose? Their dates. The gravity of the situation and their decision settled on their shoulders. They were looking for a way out, but unable to change the truth of the situation. What to do? How to change reality? They sat there in the quiet not saying a word.

The front door swung open wide, and in walked Patti. "What the hell is going on here?" she asked. "Did somebody die and I not find out about it? Come on, will somebody help a pregnant lady out here, or do I have to do this all myself?" she asked, holding a freshly baked pie in each hand. "There are more pies outside in the car," she said as she disappeared inside the kitchen with the three of them in hot pursuit.

"What's going on?" asked Robert as Ryan and Eian went outside and soon returned with more pies and two large brown paper bags.

She took comfort on one of the counter stools. "Ahhh," she said in relief as she settled onto the stool. "This one is an apple pie, and this is peach. All freshly baked. In the one bag are fresh croissants—delicious, I might add—and the other bag is filled with delicious cranberry scones."

"You baked all of these?"

"Good heavens, no. Coleen baked them. She dropped by the house earlier today, and we had a long girl talk at my place. We drank some coffee, some tea, and she brought plenty of pies. She baked me an absolutely delicious boysenberry pie."

Patti glanced at the time on her phone and said, "Gotta go. Lots to do before the wedding. Bye for now, guys. Enjoy the goodies." The brothers crowded around the fresh-baked goods.

She grabbed her purse and started walking for the door when she turned and said, "Oh, Uncle Robert . . . by the way, that Coleen of yours is such a lovely woman. We have so much in common. She's Scottish," she said with glee. "Did you know her mother's maiden name was . . . Campbell? Small world, isn't it? A Campbell? Gotta go. People to see and places to visit. Watch out, pregnant lady coming through," she shouted and was gone. As Robert watched her walk to the front door, he smiled.

Ryan poured them each a glass of milk as Eian cut one of the pies and slid the pieces onto plates. As they ate the delicious pies, Robert said to no one in particular, "Hmmm, Mickey's last name is actually Thompson, isn't it? So he's really not a Campbell at all," he mused before saying, "Delicious pie, isn't it?"

"Wonderful," chimed in Ryan.

Eian ate in silence as Robert said, "Eian, they called and said my tux would not be ready until Saturday morning, something about the alterations on my tux taking longer than expected. Since you're going to be near there with your new baseball league, would you mind picking up my tuxedo for me?"

"No problem, bro. Happy to do it."

"Should be a grand wedding. A good old-fashioned Scottish wedding," said Ryan.

"Aye, that it should be, little brother, that it should be," responded Robert. "Good pie. That Coleen of mine is a great baker. Aye? And Scottish at that, what a bonus. She's a good lass, that Coleen."

They all laughed at the irony of the situation. *One crisis averted,* thought Ryan. *Let's just get through the rehearsal, the dinner, and finally the wedding. Then peace and quiet, hopefully.*

Chapter Forty-Four

The phone rang on the bedside table; it was after nine on Friday morning as Mickey rolled over in bed. *I could get used to this life of the unemployed,* he thought. *Friday morning and not a care in the world.* The phone rang again. *Better answer it,* he thought. "Hello?" he said, still half-asleep.

"Where the hell are you?" It was Angus. He was perturbed.

"In bed." Then he thought for a minute. *Why is he calling me?* "Where the hell are you?"

"In your office, that's where. It's nine o'clock, and if you don't get your ass in gear, you'll be late for your ten o'clock meeting."

"What ten o'clock meeting?"

"Your meeting with Fabian Rumpe. That meeting."

Ten o'clock meeting? What?

He was about to hang up and said, "Hey, wait a minute, I don't work for you anymore. I quit, remember?"

"You can quit a job, Michael . . . but this is family. You're always going to be family. You never can quit that. Now get dressed and get a move on. We have a lot to discuss. Hurry . . . please."

Angus Campbell was there waiting for him and took him into the conference room. He was all business. Bashir, as was his way, stood in the corner watching and waiting. He nodded and bowed at the waist, happy to see Mickey again, removed from his self-imposed exile. "Good morning, sir," he said to Mickey. "Good to see you again. Tea?"

Mickey nodded. "Yes, please." He was happy to see his longtime friend and companion.

Angus spoke first. "I went through all of your notes, and detailed analysis. You were right on the money. But I do have a couple questions for you." They sat, talked, and reviewed the notes repeatedly until the older man finally said, "Now I think it's time to see what Mr. Rumpe is made of. Are you ready? It's your meeting, and this deal is your call."

"Yes, sir."

"Let's go, then." They walked down the hallway, two generations of Campbells, shoulder to shoulder. Angus, the tall, stocky, aging Scotsman with the thick white beard and equally thick mustache, wearing a Campbell tartan plaid tie, and Mickey, the thin younger man in his Italian-cut suit and brightly shined English oxford shoes, walked to meet Fabian Rumpe. They were ready to do battle or do business with the brash New Yorker. They knew he had talked to some of their banks and the unions and had tried to turn them against the firm and, more important . . . against the family.

They turned the corner and saw through the glass walls that Fabian Rumpe was sitting in the main conference room. He seemed surprised to see both of them.

"Angus, I didn't know you would be here," he said with a swallow. "How good it is to see you again, sir. How are you?"

"I'm fine, Fabian, but I'm only here as an observer. I'm in town for my son's wedding, and he asked me if I would care to join you. You see, although it has not been announced officially, I will be retiring soon, and my son, Michael, will be taking over as president of the company once we move our headquarters to Florida. I am here strictly as an observer. But please don't let me hold up your meeting."

Mickey tried to hide his amazement. One surprise after another. *Retiring? Me as president? Moving the corporate headquarters?* This was all news to him. *Focus, Michael, focus.* His father always moved quickly and was constantly full of surprises.

Mickey took control of the meeting as his father sat off to the side on the sofa. Bashir brought him his tea and moved to wait in the corner.

"Fabian, after our last meeting," Mickey started, "I looked over the financial numbers for our project and the plans we have made for the future. We are seeing tremendous growth in population and businesses here in South Florida, and that is why we will be moving our corporate headquarters to this building. I presume you are seeing the same growth prospects that we do and are excited by the possibilities."

Once again, even the unflappable Rumpe seemed surprised. "I see an opportunity here to expand the Rumpe brand to the backwaters of Florida," he bellowed. "I have long believed that in South Florida there is a tremendous . . ."

"Cut it, Fabian. There are no cameras or reporters here today. We're all businesspeople here. So let's get down to it. It's a good marriage between our companies to work together as equal partners. I say we both share in the risk, the glory, and the profits . . . or the losses. If you want in on this deal, it's a fifty-fifty deal or nothing else. Your end will cost you a little over three hundred million dollars. The lawyers can hammer out the details. All I want today is a simple yes or no. What will it be?"

Rumpe turned frantically to Angus on the sofa, sipping his tea. The old Scotsman smiled, held up his teacup, and said, "Great tea, isn't it?"

The New Yorker was cornered. He knew it was a great deal that Mickey had crafted, and he finally put his hands in the air and said, "I give up. It's a good deal. Count me in. Let's do it."

They shook hands on it. "Oh, and Fabian, we will make a joint announcement . . . together . . . here . . . to the press . . . once the lawyers are done with the legal paperwork. Agreed?"

"Agreed. Good to do business with you, Michael. I think this will be the start of a long and fruitful relationship." He nodded to Angus and said, "Good to see you again, sir." He saw Bashir in the corner and gently nodded in his direction before leaving and returning to his helicopter for his trip back to the airport.

Angus stood and shook his son's hand. "Well done, Michael. Now let's go have an early lunch with your mother." He grabbed his briefcase and added, "I know it's short notice, but . . . perhaps your future bride, Mary Katherine, would care to join us?"

"I think she would like that, Father, I think she would like that very much." He glanced at the old man and knew he was trying to make an effort to change; he smiled and patted his father on the shoulder. "Shall we go? Don't want to keep Mother waiting."

Chapter Forty-Five

Mary Kate reread the note she had given to her boss and saw his response written at the bottom in his distinctive and elegant handwriting:

MK—

Have Ms. Terrell call me and I'll see what I can do about helping her find a job.

No promises, but I'll make some phone calls.

Sonny

She smiled; she knew she could count on him. Calley had to have a job. *What good would it do to get her out of her situation at home and not be able to support herself?* She knew that one way or another she could rely on Max to get her out, but she was getting worried. It had been days since she had last met with him, and she had heard nothing. *Should I call him? No, that is probably not a good idea. Wait one more day.*

Her phone rang. It was Mickey. "Hiya. What are you up to, Mr. Thompson?" she asked giddily.

"Not much, Mrs. Thompson," he said with a chuckle. "I just met with Fabian Rumpe, and we're doing a business deal together, on my terms."

"You're going to work for Rumpe?"

"No. I'm back with the company."

"Ahhh . . . really? What does your father think about all of this?"

"He was the one who set up the meeting with Rumpe and sat in on it, but only as an observer. I got my job back and a promotion. I have so much to tell you, I don't know where to start, but first . . . do you want to do lunch? With my parents?"

"Your parents? They're here?"

"Yes."

"When?"

"Now or as soon as you can get away. Casual attire."

She had so much to do to prepare, and so many details left to handle, but she so wanted to meet his parents before the rehearsal dinner that night. "Okay, sure. I took off work today to handle the last-minute details of the wedding with Gloria, but we're just about done here. Where do you want to meet?"

"They're staying at the Breakers. Angus is on his way back to the hotel, so he suggested having lunch there, say in ninety minutes?"

She glanced at her watch; that time was tight but workable. "All right, see you there." *What do you wear to meet your wealthy future in-laws at the most exclusive resort in Palm Beach? Maybe I should just put on a bathing suit and tell them we should have lunch by the pool near the ocean. Ugh. Casual chic? What an oxymoron.*

"Gloria, help!" she shouted.

Chapter Forty-Six

"What a wonderful restaurant, Dr. Ryan," Alexi said jokingly.

"I'm glad you like it. Great food and great atmosphere, and you can watch the boats go up and down the Intracoastal and see them open the drawbridge every hour."

A waiter approached them. "Welcome to Prime Catch. I'm Jeff, and I'll be waiting on you today. Our lunch special today is blackened grouper or bronzed swordfish served with our signature Maytag salad."

"Maytag salad?"

"Yes, sir . . . it used to be called the Stilton salad."

They both looked through the menu, and finally Alexi closed hers and proclaimed, "I know what I'm having—grouper and the Stilton salad. Sounds wonderful."

"Me too. But in the meantime I want to show you something." Ryan reached inside his jacket pocket and pulled out some papers. He held them up in the air and proclaimed, "Passport—check. Airline ticket—check. Hotel reservations—check. Car rental—check. That's so we can go out and see the French countryside if we ever get tired of Paris. Who said the phrase, 'He who tires of Paris, tires of life'? Voltaire?"

"I don't know."

"Alexi, come on now."

"Well, I believe the phrase was 'He who tires of London, tires of life,' by Samuel Johnson. But they were both right." They laughed.

"So you have everything you need for our adventure?"

"Yes, and I'm really looking forward to it and spending quiet time, alone with you—in Paris, no less. What could be better?" As if on cue, his cell phone rang. He ignored it.

"Perhaps you better answer it? It could be important," she said.

"No, I am off work starting today, and the family can get by without me for an hour. What are they going to do when I'm thousands of miles away in France?" The ringing stopped. Then it began again.

"I think you should answer it, please."

"All right," he said as he reached for his phone. From the caller ID he could tell it was Robert. "Hey, what's up, bro? I'm at lunch. Can I call you back later . . . ?" He listened intently. The color drained from his face. "I'll be right there."

He turned to look at her. "I'm sorry. I must leave. It's Patti—she was rushed to the hospital."

"Go, call me later," she told him.

"I'm sorry, Alexi," he said as he kissed her cheek. "I'll make it up to you."

"Go. We'll have plenty of time for lunches, in Paris."

She saw it in his eyes; it was subtle, but something had changed. She watched him walk away, and a strange chill engulfed her. *What do I do? I'm falling in love with him.*

Chapter Forty-Seven

Mary Kate made it to the famed resort in record time, and as she pulled up to the security guard at the drive-up entrance, he approached her with a smile. "Good morning, ma'am, welcome to the Breakers. May I help you?" Mickey always told her, "If you look like you belong, you can gain entrance anywhere."

"Yes, you may. I'm meeting my fiancé for lunch with his parents. They are guests here; their last name is Campbell."

He looked up and down his clipboard. "Ah yes, you must be Ms. Macgregor. They are expecting you in the Seafood Bar overlooking the ocean. Just drive straight ahead and stop under the portico, and the valet will take care of your car for you and direct you to the restaurant."

"Thank you."

"You're quite welcome, ma'am. Have a nice day," said the young security guard with a smile.

The Breakers was located on the "island" of Palm Beach, one of the most exclusive and expensive locales in the country. The Breakers Hotel Complex, destroyed by fire in 1925, was rebuilt by Henry Flagler in 1926 as a place for wealthy Northerners to get away to a luxurious home away from home and escape the horrible winters up north. They liked what they saw and stayed, building huge, expensive estates.

The "island" of Palm Beach was divided between millionaires, with their luxurious mansions on the Intracoastal Waterway, and the billionaires who built their extravagant estates as second homes facing the ocean.

Mary Kate noticed the main entranceway was lined with pots of richly colored flowers hanging over the sides, and as she drove up the brick driveway, she saw the two large cupolas on the top of the grand hotel with flags flying high above. She noticed children playing croquet on the lawn off to her right, while their parents sat in the coolness of the shade on the patio in oversize wicker chairs, enjoying their mint juleps.

The beige-and-off-white ten-story building stood at attention to welcome her as she drove her car underneath the covered portico. Beautiful multicolored flowers were everywhere. Graceful ivy draped the walls below.

As her sports car rolled to a stop and before she could even reach for the door handle, one of the very attentive valets opened it and reached out to help her from the car.

"Welcome to the Breakers, ma'am. Will you be staying with us?"

"No. I'm joining some friends for lunch."

"Very fine, madam. Which restaurant would that be?" asked the young-looking attendant. "We have eight. Or I would be happy to check with the concierge if you like."

"Thank you, but that won't be necessary. It's the Seafood Bar. I've been here many times before, and I know my way, thank you."

He handed her a parking stub and said with a smile, "Have a nice meal, and enjoy the view."

"Thank you," she said, discreetly handing him a tip for his service.

The young attendants watched her stroll by, and one held the entrance door open for her as she passed. She was wearing dark sunglasses, white linen slacks, a sheer silk blouse, a gold-and-pearl necklace, and her latest designer handbag. She and her parents had been there many times in the past when her mom was still alive, and she felt as if she belonged there.

She loved this place, she thought as she walked inside, making a right, past the sofas in the grand lobby filled with hundred-year-old tapestries hanging from the wall, and with solid wood floors. The smell was one she never tired of; it gave you a warm, comfortable feeling; it had the subtle suggestion of old money. It was a nice place to visit, but she liked where she was living—Delray Beach was home to her.

Mary Kate looked briefly at the shops as she passed by. They sported designer jewelry and clothes, along with beach and sundry items. She turned left and saw the champagne bar in the enclosed outdoor plaza, with sounds of soft Latin jazz music coming from a nearby guitar player.

She stopped by a mirror to check her makeup and, after seeing the reminder sign posted in the lobby, turned off her cell phone. She took in a deep breath; she was as ready as she would ever be, ready to face the lions. Her hands shook slightly, but as soon as she entered the room and saw Mickey, her fears faded. He had that way about him.

He kissed her on the cheek and turned to introduce her with a huge smile as he continued to hold her hand. "Mom and Dad, I'd like you to meet Mary Kate Macgregor."

"Mr. and Mrs. Campbell, I am so happy to meet you at last, and I am so glad that you were able to make it here for the wedding."

His mother beamed with delight, came to her side, and said, "Oh, please, child, nobody calls me Mrs. Campbell. Please call me Claret." She shook Mary Kate's hand and then hugged her. "And maybe at some point, you'll feel kind enough about me to call me Mom."

She turned to her son. "Mickey, dear boy, you never told me what a sweetheart you have here."

Angus stood by awkwardly until Claret, with her arm around Mary Kate's shoulders, turned her to face him while whispering loudly for all to hear, "And this old grump here, who looks like he eats nails for breakfast, is my loving husband, Angus. Don't let him scare you."

He shoved his hand forward. "Pleased to meet you, Miss Macgregor."

Claret's piercing evil eye and arched eyebrow penetrated his heart, and he got the message. He stumbled awkwardly toward her, then dropped his hand and went to hug her. "Welcome to the family." He was a big man and nearly smothered her as he hugged her.

"Nice to meet you too, sir."

"Sit, sit," he said. "I ordered champagne to celebrate. Dom Pérignon." She looked at him and then at her; they were going to get along just fine. After the celebratory toast, they ordered lunch.

Claret reached out to clutch her hand and smiled. "Now tell me all about yourself. My dutiful son has neglected to tell me anything at all about his future wife. So tell me everything."

She liked Claret, a lot. As they talked, Mickey and his father discussed business. Then she heard them both laugh and knew everything would be fine. She felt very comfortable with Claret and was warming to Angus. He had a hearty laugh.

As the waiter brought coffee, Claret said, "Now I understand that tonight we have the rehearsal at the church, then a dinner with the rest of the family?"

"Yes, the church is down the block from here. It's called the Chapel-by-the-Sea, and the dinner is at Testa's on Royal Poinciana Way," said Mary Kate. "It was one of my mom's favorites." She paused for a minute. "And tomorrow is the wedding, with the reception back here at the hotel at the Breakers."

"I hope there's a good band; I love to dance."

"Yes, ma'am. So do I. It's a very good band. You'll have a great time, I promise you."

Claret leaned in and whispered, "And your wedding dress? Tell me about it." Mary Kate smiled; she saw that she was just a little girl at heart.

"It's white with rows of beads and pearls down the side. It's beautiful. The rear bodice is laced with white ribbon. I can't dress myself, so Patti, my cousin, is coming over to my dad's house tomorrow before the wedding to help me dress. The front is filled with French lace."

Claret whispered, "The front . . . is it . . . cut . . ."

"Cut low? Heavens no, Miss Claret. It's very conservative. Would you like to see some pictures? I had some taken on my cell phone during one of the fittings."

Her face beamed with a smile. "I would love to see them."

Mary Kate reached over and pulled out her bag and found the pictures on her phone. Mickey looked up from his conversation with his father. "What are you two girls talking about over there?"

Claret hid the phone from him so he could not see the pictures of Mary Kate in her wedding gown. "Just you never mind," she scolded him. "You just keep having your silly conversations with your father. It's bad luck for the groom to see his bride in her wedding dress before they're married. You just go on now," and she shushed him away with the back of her hand. "Go on."

Claret smiled at Mary Kate as if the two of them had their own little secret. They were both having a good time talking together; Mary Kate was what she had always wanted, someone dear and close to talk to.

Mary Kate excused herself to find the ladies' room, and when she was returning to her table she heard a familiar voice on a newscast coming from the bar adjacent to the restaurant.

It was Max being interviewed by a TV news reporter. She stopped to listen to him.

"We were making our rounds and drove through a parking lot and saw some suspicious activity inside a local liquor store. Then we received a silent alarm and noticed it was a male perpetrator robbing the store at gunpoint." She moved in closer to be able to hear everything he said.

"We parked our patrol car, and when he exited the store, we ordered him to drop his weapon. He refused, and then pointed his gun at my partner, firing at him twice. I then discharged my service revolver, striking him with one fatal bullet. He was pronounced dead at the scene. We just happened to be in the neighborhood and were glad we were able to assist before anyone else got hurt."

Max's picture faded from view, and the announcer said, "That was police detective Max Haines of the Delray Beach Police Department responding to a serious situation. The dead suspect was later identified as Phillip Terrell of Delray Shores. In a related story, earlier today police were called to Mr. Terrell's residence and were attacked by a pit bull at his home. The animal was killed by the responding police officer. Now back to your local news after a word from our sponsors."

She stood watching, engrossed by what she saw. She didn't know whether to be happy or sad, but now she knew that Calley was no longer in danger.

After she returned to the table and they said their good-byes, Claret tucked her arm inside Mary Kate's as they walked with her to retrieve her car. Claret kissed her on the cheek and said, "This was wonderful. Thanks for coming on such short notice. I guess I'll see you in a little while at the rehearsal." Then, leaning in closer, she said, "I think we're going to be really good friends. Good-bye, Mary Katherine. See you soon."

"Good-bye, Claret. I had a wonderful lunch, and it was so good to meet you."

As she drove away, she stopped at a stoplight and retrieved her phone from her purse to check her messages. She was surprised to see six missed calls and three texts: one from her father, one from Robert, and one from Bobby. She read her father's text first. Her hands began to shake and tremble as she read it:

```
Graw—
URGENT—
Patti was rushed to Saint John's hospital
with a high fever.
Not good. Hurry. See you there.
Pray.
Dad
```

Mary Kate sat there staring in disbelief at her phone until a waiting car behind her honked its horn and brought her back to her reality. She sped away, heading to Saint John's Hospital as fast as she could drive. *God, I hope she's all right. Please God, please keep her well. Please.*

The reception desk at the hospital gave her the floor number, and she took the elevator to the fifth floor. The family was all there, waiting. Robert, Dad, Bobby, and the others, all desperately waiting for news.

She saw them first, pacing in the waiting room. "What happened?" she asked her father frantically. "Is she okay? What about the baby? Oh my God . . . what about the baby?"

He took her in his arms and said, "We don't know yet. We're waiting for the doctor to come out and tell us what's going on."

Bobby stood next to them. "She was really lethargic as she got out of bed this morning. Then when we were having breakfast she said she was feeling tired and went back to sleep. I did the dishes and took a shower. When I came in to kiss her good-bye before I left for work, she was hotter than a coal fire. I couldn't wake her, and then she moaned about something, half-asleep. I brought her here since it's the nearest hospital to our house. A doctor examined her, and her obstetrician was consulted; now we're just waiting."

They turned around as a white-coated doctor entered the waiting room. "Mr. Macgregor?" he said, searching the room for a response.

"Yes, Doctor," said Bobby.

"I'm Dr. Sanders. Your wife is safe for the present, but we were unable to bring her temperature down, and in her current condition, it's not a good thing. The longer her fever remains high, the worse it is for her and the baby. She's comfortable now. We're running more tests and will let you know more as soon as we get the results. But please wait here and be patient."

"Is she awake, Doctor?"

"She is in and out of consciousness. I'm sorry I don't have better news for you."

"Is there anything we can do?"

The doctor looked at all their faces and responded, "Pray. It may be a long night."

"Thank you, Doctor."

"Hang in there," he said as he returned to his duties.

They huddled in a corner . . . and waited. Half an hour later, Mary Kate's phone rang. It was Mickey.

"Hey, girl. Great lunch. My parents loved you." He was almost bubbly in his conversation, which was unlike him. "Let's get together after the rehearsal dinner, and I'll fill you in on all the changes at work, but you did real good. I am so proud of—"

"Mickey," she interrupted and said, "I'm at Saint John's Hospital with the whole family. Patti has a very high fever, and it doesn't look good. I gotta go. I'll call you later."

Forty-five minutes later she saw him walk into the room, followed by his parents.

Mickey was the first to speak. "You said the whole family was here. Once I told them what had happened, they insisted on coming."

His father greeted Mary Kate and said, "Well, girl, you're now family, we're all family here, and we stick together. We came here to support you, come hell or high water."

Robert and the rest of the family approached Angus. "I'm Angus Campbell, Michael's father, and this is my wife, Claret."

Robert stuck out his hand and said, "I'm Robert James Macgregor. We welcome you to join us. Thanks for coming. It means a lot." The two men locked hands, and each understood, family came first.

They all sat and waited. The minutes turned to hours, and still no word.

Robert stood and stretched his legs. "I'll be back," he said. He walked toward the elevator, and once downstairs went inside the chapel, only to find Mary Kate and Claret there engrossed in their own prayers.

He knelt and prayed to his higher authority, the only one who could now help Patti. *Lord, protect her. She's the soul of the family and the light of my eye. Keep her safe, but if you must take her, so be it, but if you could let us have her for just a little while longer, I would much appreciate it. Please, Lord.* Tears streamed down his face. He felt someone next to him, it was Coleen. She squeezed his hands and knelt down quietly beside him. They both knew there was nothing more they could do. Bobby sat in the seat in front of Robert.

At six p.m. the doctor returned. His face was troubled.

"Mr. Macgregor?" he said. The two of them talked as the brothers stood by, ready to be tested by the news. The rest of those in the waiting room slowly roused to hear the report from the doctor.

"We have the results of the ultrasound tests. It shows her fever is being caused by an abnormal ovarian cyst; however, we do not know yet at this point what kind of a cyst it is."

"Uncle Ryan, can you join us, please? My uncle is a physician—Dr. Ryan Macgregor—and I would like him to listen to the prognosis."

"I understand completely." Ryan nodded as the doctor continued. "A cyst that contains a simple sac of fluid on ultrasound is more likely to be a benign neoplasm than a cyst with solid tissue in it."

Ryan asked him, "Can you tell if the cyst is solid or filled with fluid?"

"No, not yet. We're going to do some further tests. The ultrasound appearance also plays a role in determining the level of suspicion regarding an ovarian tumor."

"Tumor? Cancer?" Bobby asked, hearing the words of dread, nearly losing his balance.

"I'm sorry; it's just too early to tell. Ovarian cancer is rare in women under the age of forty. But after age forty, an ovarian cyst has a higher chance of being cancerous than before age forty, although most ovarian cysts are benign even after age forty. Blood testing with RUT-3, using CA-125, can be used as a marker of ovarian cancer, but it does not always represent cancer, even when it is abnormal, and it may be normal in the presence of malignancy."

"RUT-3?" asked Ryan.

"It's a new test for cancer, and we have found that CA-125 is a protein that is elevated in the bloodstream of women with advanced ovarian cancer. If the cyst is filled with fluid, that could be a danger to the baby, if and when the tumor bursts. However, we can always drain it or deliver the baby if we have to do that. We ordered a rapid amnio test to see if the baby's lungs are mature enough for delivery. We're also waiting for those test results. At this point, her obstetrician does not want to perform a cesarean section to deliver the baby. Time will tell. Please be patient as we wait for the results of the blood test. I will let you know as soon as I know anything at all. I was scheduled to finish my shift at seven," the doctor said, glancing at his watch, "but I will stay here until I receive the results."

"Thank you, Doctor," was the chorus from the crowd of Macgregors now listening to his every word.

They returned to their corner refuge, now filled with stacks of empty coffee cups, pizza boxes, newspapers, and candy wrappers. All they could do now was wait.

Standing at the coffee machine, Ryan said to his daughter, "I'm sorry, Mary Kate, this is not how I thought we would be spending tonight."

"Me too, but I called the others and told them to go ahead with everything and just e-mail me the video from the rehearsal. I'm glad you insisted on an earlier rehearsal last month. At least we won't look like total bozos walking down the aisle."

Eian came up behind them. "Do you have any change to lend me? For some coffee?"

Ryan looked at Eian; then father and daughter both said at the same time, "Some things never change." They laughed for the first time that night. Time dragged on—eight, nine, ten o'clock. It was well after midnight before the doctor reemerged, this time smiling.

"You got the test results?" Bobby asked him.

"Yes, it was a fluid sac. We drained the fluid, and she is out of danger, with her fever receding. It was a large fluid sac, and the marker test results came back negative. She is resting comfortably now."

"And the baby?"

"The baby is fine. No delivery, which is good. However, I do want to keep both of them overnight for observation, as a precaution." He turned to Bobby and said, "In the meantime, she would like to see you."

Bobby smiled for the first time. "Can I go in now?"

"We're moving her, but you can visit with her soon. But please stay only for a few minutes; she needs her rest. I'll send an aide out to bring you back to her room."

"I understand. Thank you, Doctor."

"And for the rest of you, go home and get some rest. She's going to be just fine." He went to talk with another group in the room that was also waiting for news from him.

The family gathered together in a circle. "Well, that's good news," Ryan said to them. "Very good news. I suggest we all head home now . . . we have a wedding to go to tomorrow."

"I'm not going to a wedding tomorrow," Robert said.

Oh no, Ryan thought, *Not again.* "Robert, I thought . . ."

"It's after midnight. The wedding is today. See you all tonight, because now we have two things to celebrate." He shook Angus's hand and said, "Thanks for coming, Mr. . . . Campbell. It meant a lot to the family . . . and to me."

"That's what family is all about. See you at the wedding. And the name is Angus . . . Robert." He smiled a knowing smile.

"Yes, it is."

Mary Kate looked worried. *No rehearsal and no Patti. Patti was supposed to be there to help me get dressed. This should be fun, trying to get this dress on by myself. Maybe I can ask . . .*

Claret walked beside her and draped her arm around her shoulder. "Mary Kate, since Patti won't be there, I would be happy . . . no, I would be honored, to help you prepare for your wedding and help with your dress. If you like."

"That would be wonderful," said Mary Kate.

"And appropriate," said her father. "Gracie would have approved."

"Well, I'm heading home. I have a baseball practice with my new team in a few hours," said Eian.

"You better not be late for my wedding," admonished Mary Kate.

"Aw, Graw, you know I'd never miss your wedding. Funny you should mention that, though . . ." He paused and looked around at his brothers but said nothing further.

"And don't forget to pick up my tuxedo, bro!" said Robert.

"I won't. You can count on me."

"Yeah, like a forest fire, blowing with the wind. I never know what's going to happen with you."

Chapter Forty-Eight

There were twice as many boys this Saturday as the prior week. They would need a bigger field, he thought to himself. *I could always sell this property and buy some other parcel, larger and better suited.* But he still would need a place to live; he could not stay with Ryan for the rest of his life. *I'll worry about that later,* he thought; right now he had to figure out the teams. There was no saved parking spot for him this week because he was late after picking up Robert's tuxedo. Duke's had called that morning after it finished the alterations. He had to park three blocks away.

"All right, let's play ball," he shouted in the traditional fashion. He glanced at his watch; he had to be home by one o'clock. No later. He had promised Graw he would not be late.

Her wedding day! Mary Kate poured more champagne for the women in the wedding party—Alison, Gerri, and Mattie. They were her best friends in the whole world. Her wedding planner, Gloria, was shouting instructions and directions to the photographer and videographer. The hairdressers and makeup artists had a production line for the women's hair and makeup, to get them ready for the big event. She missed her mom. It was a sad day, but a happy day. She thought about everything that had happened over the last week.

Mickey had made peace with his father. He was going to be promoted to president of the firm when it moved to Florida. Exciting! Patti had called her from the hospital and wished her well. Wonderful to hear from her. Her father had found Alexi, someone he was happy with, as Uncle Robert had found Coleen, and Uncle Eian had found Rose. Outstanding. She was quite pleased with herself. She heard the front doorbell ring.

"Can someone get that? Please?"

Alison, her coworker and bridesmaid, opened the door, then walked toward her holding a long, thin white box tied with a yellow ribbon.

Mickey had sent her one yellow rose. A Scottish sign of love and respect.

> *Graw—*
> *My love, soon we will be one and our life will never be the same.*
> *I want to grow old with you, to hold you, to cherish you.*
> *I love you always,*
> *Mickey*

"Oh, how romantic can you get?" Her friends swooned.

"That's my Michael," Claret whispered, smiling at her new daughter. They hugged. "This is the best day ever."

Robert walked inside carrying the corsages for the bridal party and Claret. He also had boutonnieres for the groomsmen, for Angus, and for her father and two uncles.

"I guess it's time for me to get dressed and let them take some pictures," said Mary Kate. She looked around. *It is nearly one o'clock. Where is Uncle Eian? He promised he would not be late.*

"Yes, indeed," responded Claret.

Claret helped Mary Kate with her slip and her dress, and then patiently tied the intricate bodice in the rear. When she was done, Mary Kate turned to face her new mother-in-law, who gasped. "My God, you're a beautiful bride. Your mother would be so proud of you."

They hugged. "Don't make me cry, Mom," Graw said. "I just had my makeup done."

She called me Mom! Claret began to tear up; she was so full of emotions. "Time for me to get dressed and for you to make your grand entrance downstairs to see your father," she said, dabbing a handkerchief to her eyes. "Go on now."

She shouted from the top of the steps, "Don't look, Dad. Turn around and look away, I'm coming down. I'm ready for the pictures, but don't look yet, and promise me you won't cry."

"Me? Never."

Mary Katherine came down the steps accompanied by ohhhs and ahhhs from those waiting below, then walked up behind him and touched his shoulder. When he turned around, he was overwhelmed. Standing before him was his little girl, the little one he had walked to school, the one he had taught how to swim and ride horses. The one he took to ballet classes, and chauffeured to the junior prom with the neighborhood boy who had all the braces. Today she looked like an angel; she looked just like her mother on their wedding day, so many years ago. He could not hold back the tears.

"Daddy, you promised me you wouldn't cry," she said, herself starting to tear up.

"I couldn't help myself. You're so beautiful. He's a very lucky man. I love you, Graw, and I am so proud of you."

"I love you too, Daddy." As she walked to join the others, she glanced at her watch. It was after three o'clock. *Where is Uncle Eian? I don't need this today.* "Daddy, can you call Uncle Eian? Please! I'm a little worried. He should be here by now."

Chapter Forty-Nine

The game was over, and Eian was about to make an announcement to the crowd of young ball players and their parents sitting around the picnic tables enjoying lunch and talking about the game.

Miguel stood and tapped two metal spoons together to get everyone's attention. "Please, quiet. Quiet, please. Coach Macgregor has something to say." Eian stood and looked around at all the people listening. He took in a deep breath and said to the waiting crowd, "You all played well today, and many of you show great promise." He nodded to each and every one.

"You all need practice, practice, and more practice, but always remember something that I nearly forgot over the years. This is a game. And later in life, if any of you are lucky enough, and good enough to be paid for something that you love to do, well, that's a real bonus." They all clapped.

"Practice and coaching is what works best, and then team play. To that end, I want to let everyone know, I have quit my job at the radio station and have filed paperwork to form the South Florida Youth Baseball League for Delray Beach, Boca Raton, Boynton Beach, and Deerfield Beach. I'm sure there will be other teams for us to play in this new league. For any of you that are interested, I have left some applications here on the table for you to fill out and return to me within the next two weeks. It should be fun and exciting because they have a youth World Series every year held in Fort Lauderdale. And we want to be part of that." The group stood and clapped.

A young girl in the rear raised her hand. "Coach, is the new league . . . open to girls?"

"Yes, absolutely, open to everyone." Then he remembered and looked at the time, and he knew he was going to be late. He had promised Graw he would be there.

"I know you will all have a lot of questions, so we can talk briefly and then I must leave." The parents cornered him and peppered him with questions for the next forty-five minutes until he told them, "I really must go now. My niece is getting married today, and I am already late." They waved good-bye as he rushed to his car. Late! He hated to be late, and especially today. Three blocks away he turned the corner and crossed the street, reaching in his pocket for his car keys and cell phone. *I'll call Robert to let him know I am on my way and I have his tuxedo.* His phone rang, an unknown caller.

"Hello?"

"Hi, Eian. It's Laura, your daughter," she said in a voice so sweet it would have attracted bees.

Laura? His stepdaughter. The same Laura who threw him out of his house and home two weeks ago? The home he loved and still missed. That Laura.

"Howya doing? It's been over a week since we talked last." Something wasn't right; she was acting too sweet.

"I'm fine, but in a hurry to get to a wedding. What's up?"

"I have a favor to ask."

"Yeah? And what's that?"

"I need you to sign a document for me. I just need to clear up some odds and ends with the estate. That's all."

"What's this all about, Laura?" he asked, his suspicions now aroused.

She let out a deep breath. "Well, you know my dear mother always wanted me to have the house she was living in and . . ."

"And me."

"Yes, of course, of course, and you. We both know mom was not herself there toward the end," she went on.

He did not respond, but took in a deep breath, his anger building.

"Apparently she had her attorney file some type of document, called a life estate trust, giving you the deed to the house. I just need you to sign this over to me and rescind this silly paperwork. My name is on the house. You understand, don't you?"

"Yes, I understand completely. The house is mine, for as long as I live," he said, stopping at the corner and looking for his car. "This is something your mother and I talked about for years; I just didn't know she filed the papers. Good for her." He could tell she was getting frustrated.

"Well, Mother told me four years ago she was going to do that, and we fought about it, and I thought she had changed her mind."

"Obviously she did not. Tell you what, mail me the document, and I'll take a look at it this week or next."

"Just sign it, will you? Eian, it's my house. I'm her daughter. I need the money."

"So you were planning to sell it? Sell your mother's home? My home? On second thought, let me think about it. I'll call you later."

"Just keep the stupid house; I never really liked it. Who wants to live on the water anyway? Too many mosquitoes. Finally, don't call me, I'll call you. Eian, you'll never change," she said, nearly screaming at him before she hung up.

Perfect! Ryan will be very happy to hear that news. He was going home. He had to smile as he looked around for his car. *I know I parked it right here, under this tree. Where is it? Where's my car?* he asked himself. He turned and looked around; this was right where he had parked it. *It's gone! Stolen. Oh no! What am I going to do now?*

Chapter Fifty

"I have to go and get Eian," Robert said as he ran out the door.

"It's almost time for pictures. Where are you going?" Mary Kate hollered, chasing after him. *No, not now. Please not now,* she thought to herself. *Brother stuff.*

"I'll be back. Talk to your father."

"Oh no, this isn't happening," she said, nearly in tears.

She felt a calming hand on her shoulder. "It'll be okay, pumpkin."

"Daddy, what's going on? We don't have a lot of time," she said almost frantically. "We need to take pictures, and Uncle Bob and Uncle Eian have to get dressed and ready. I knew something like this was going to happen, I just knew it."

"Uncle Eian's car was stolen while he was at the ball game. Bob went to pick him up. But don't worry, he'll be ready, I'll make sure of it. Say good-bye to Claret. Angus is picking her up in a few minutes."

He always knows just with to say, she thought. She gave him her fake stern look. "I'm counting on you."

The doorbell rang, and when Alison opened it, Angus appeared in a Campbell Black Watch Scottish kilt. "Don't you look handsome," commented Mary Kate.

The old Scotsman nearly blushed. "Well, thank you, my dear. And if you don't look as lovely as a morning sun in Scotland, then I . . . you look wonderful." He smiled and turned to look for his wife. "Come on, Claret; let these youngsters finish up here." He shook Ryan's hand and said, "It should be a grand party, aye?"

"Yes, indeed, it should be grand. See you at the church."

"Wait, while you're here, let's get some quick photos of the four of you," commanded Gloria. "Yes, that would be perfect." The photographer took photos on the steps, in front of the fireplace, and in the formal dining room.

Finally Ryan said, "Enough. These good people have to get to church, and the rest of us need to finish getting ready. See you soon, Angus, Claret." As they left, he saw the white stretch limousine pull into the courtyard in front of the house, closely followed by Robert's car carrying Eian.

Eian and Robert stood in the foyer and started to tell Mary Kate what had happened. It was her wedding day, and she didn't have time for all of this.

Eian told her, "We reported the car as stolen to the police, but . . ."

"Okay, okay, enough! Tell me later. Spare me the details. Just get dressed. Now!" she commanded and stomped away, muttering something under her breath.

"Well, there's a problem," said Robert.

"What now?" she asked, spinning around.

"Well, Eian's car was stolen and—" Robert started to say.

"Yeah, yeah, I know that, so?"

"Robert's tuxedo was in the back of the car—it's gone, along with the car," Eian said.

"Oh no!" she said, with her hands covering her face. Then, turning to her uncles, she said, "No time. Come on, you two; let's get this show on the road. Go upstairs and find Daddy. I'm sure he's already searching through his closet to see if he has any suits that may fit you."

"Fat chance," commented Eian.

"Well, I'll not have you walking down the aisle at my wedding wearing only socks and boxer shorts. No sir," responded Mary Kate.

Ryan stood at the top of the stairs. "I can't find anything that would fit him unless . . ." He was out of sight for a brief moment, then returned. "How about this?" he asked, holding Robert's dress Highland kilt outfit.

"Nay. I'll not be wearing that to this wedding."

Mary Kate spun around to face him. "Why not?"

"Because today is your day, and I'll not be upstaging or taking any sunshine from your rainbow, darlin' Kate, that's why not."

She softened and moved closer to him. "Uncle Bob, you could never do that, and I would be honored to have you wear the full Macgregor colors. Besides, Angus was wearing his Black Watch plaid colors, his Campbell kilt."

"He was?"

"Aye."

"Give us a few minutes to get ready, and we'll be down shortly."

"Hurry, we don't have a lot of time." This was not quite how she had envisioned her wedding day starting off, but she was glad that everybody was here. That was the important thing. *Now let's get to the church before something else happens. Let's get this over with.*

Chapter Fifty-One

The Chapel-by-the-Sea was a small, very quaint, hundred-year-old building set back and secluded from the street, under a huge ancient magnolia tree. In traditional Palm Beach style, the walkway was lined with perfectly trimmed hedges of sea grape bushes. The rear of the chapel overlooked the rolling waves of the Atlantic Ocean. Inside was a small and intimate church with high marble arches. The beautiful blue-and-red stained glass windows cast their wonderful colors on the old stone floor as they caught the warm rays of the Florida sun. It was perfect for a small, intimate wedding.

Angus, dressed in his kilted outfit, walked his wife, Claret, down the aisle, her arm draped over his. She smiled at the assembled crowd. The groomsmen looked handsome in their tuxedoes, as did the brides-maids in their lovely coral dresses.

Robert strode down the aisle with Coleen on his arm. They looked like the perfect couple. He looked so dashing in his traditional but very formal Highland regalia, his subdued red-plaid Macgregor kilt with his belt and ornate silver clan buckle, his fancy hand-tooled leather sporran, the white kilt shirt, and his traditional brogue shoes. Women turned to watch him walk down the aisle.

At the sight of the traditional Macgregor colors, Angus Campbell's eyes flashed red, and his wife noticed the change in his demeanor. As they sat in the pew, she patted his arm to calm him down. But Claret knew him too well, and she most likely would have little effect on him. No one else noticed . . . except for Robert.

The organist began the wedding march music, and Mary Katherine Macgregor walked down the aisle with her father, holding tightly onto his arm until he lifted her veil at the altar. He hugged her and kissed her on the cheek, whispering, "I love you, pumpkin. Your mom would be proud of you." It nearly brought her to tears. Her arms and legs began to shake.

Mickey stood there patiently waiting for her at the altar. She wished her mother could have been there to see it all—she would have been so happy. The wedding was a blur to her; it seemed as if it were over in mere minutes. She remembered the flowers, the scents, the people in attendance, but soon the only person she had eyes for that day was—Mickey.

When Mary Kate reached for Mickey's hand—the trembling stopped. Just from the touch of his hand. She felt safe and secure. Everyone knew her as a strong and independent woman, which she was, but she felt safe with him. Always did. The only thing she remembered was saying the words, "I do."

She felt happy when it was over and then shot a quick glance at her new wedding ring. Touching it made her feel warm. Married. "Mrs. Mary Katherine Thompson," she said softly to herself. It had a nice ring to it.

The photographer kept them for more than an hour taking photographs, but soon they were on their way. When they walked inside the reception hall and were introduced for the first time as husband and wife, the room went wild with clapping and shouts of congratulations, as the band began to play. These were memories she would always cherish, for the rest of her life.

The MC stood with the microphone. "And now we will have the father-and-daughter dance. A waltz."

Ryan took her in his arms, and they waltzed around the dance floor. He held her for one last time in his arms. He never wanted to let go of his little girl.

"Thank you, Daddy, thank you for everything. I love you," she said, nearly in tears.

"I love you too, pumpkin. He's a good man."

When they finished their dance, Ryan returned her to her seat and took the microphone in his hand. "Aye, girl, this is your day, the day of your wedding for both you and Mickey. I give you the ancient traditional Scottish blessing:

> *May the best you've ever seen*
> *Be the worst you'll ever see;*
> *May a mouse never leave your pantry*
> *With a teardrop in his eye;*
> *May you keep whole and hearty*
> *Till you're old enough to die;*
> *May you be just as happy*
> *As I wish you to be.*
> *Today, tomorrow, and ever be.*

"Cheers," the crowd thundered.

Robert stood and took the microphone from his younger brother. "I too have a toast for the two of you, in health and happiness. It's an old Celtic blessing upon you:

> *May the blessing of light,*
> *Be with you always,*
> *Light without and light within,*
> *And may the sun shine*

Upon you and warm your heart
Until it glows
Like a great fire
So that others may feel
The warmth of your love
For one another.

"Cheers to Graw and Mickey. May you live long and love forever."

The crowd clapped and the band began to play again. Now everyone was dancing, including Rose and Eian. Robert and Coleen were lost in each other as they danced around the floor.

As the night progressed, Ryan danced and danced with Alexi, then finally led her to their table. Alexi held his arm and said, "You did real well dancing tonight. I am very proud of you."

"Thank you, my dear."

An old family friend who had had a few too many cocktails during dinner dropped by their table and said, "Nice wedding, Ryan. Like yours and Gracie's. Remember?"

"Yes, I do, Sam. It was a good time. Good to see you again."

Alexi squeezed his arm in support as he walked away.

"He was a neighbor who lived down the street from us at our old house," Ryan explained. "He loved to tease Gracie."

Ryan finished another glass of champagne, smiled, then reminisced, "At our wedding reception, we made a promise to each other that no matter who wanted us to come to their table to visit them, we were going to stay together—no matter what. We had the caterer follow us around with champagne and told him to keep filling our glasses. Our wedding celebration was the best time I've ever had in my life. Everybody was there." He began to talk about his life with Gracie, as he had not ever done before. "I miss her. She would have really enjoyed tonight."

Alexi felt a twinge of sorrow for him and tried a few times to change the subject, but he continued to talk about his life with her and how perfect it had been for them. She could tell he still loved his wife.

Mary Kate sat at the head table having the time of her life as people stopped by with envelopes and best wishes for the both of them. She looked at Angus and could tell something was wrong and turned to Mickey. "What's wrong with your father? He looks upset. Should you go talk with him?"

Before he could answer her, their attention was diverted by a loud voice in the center of the dance floor. It was his father yelling. "Macgregor!" he slurred. "Where are you?"

Robert walked slowly to the center of the room and said just above a whisper, "Aye, brother. We're family now. And I'll not raise my voice against family." He seemed to have caught him unaware. "Angus, it's not Scotsman against Scotsman; it's Scotsmen against our enemies. We are bound together, like it or not, as family, and I'll drink to your health."

"I'll not drink to no Macgregor's health. I'll as soon die as . . ."

The loudspeaker drowned out what he said next, and they both turned to face the head table. The bride stood tall, holding the microphone, eyes and temper flashing. "This ends now! Do you hear me!" she said, looking squarely at the two men. "My name is Mary Katherine Macgregor Thompson. I am proud of my family, both of them. We are here tonight by the grace of God." She paused. "I would like to make a toast to Bobby and Patti Macgregor. And a blessing to all of those who are not here tonight, especially Tess Macgregor, Alice Macgregor, and my mother—Grace Macgregor. And also to Bryce Campbell, may he rest in peace." The old man began to shake at the mention of his dead son.

She continued, "There is a Scottish belief that as long as someone is still loved, they will never die. My mother said that so long ago and taught me the Scottish blessing for those who are not here, written by Mary Frye. It goes something like this:

> *Do not stand at my grave and weep*
> *I am not there, I do not sleep.*
> *I am a thousand winds that blow,*
> *I am the diamonds glints on snow*
> *I am the sunlight on ripened grain.*
> *I am the gentle autumn rain*
> *When you awaken in the morning's hush*
> *I am the swift uplifting rush*
> *Of quiet birds in circled flight.*
> *I am the soft stars that shine at night.*
> *Do not stand at my grave and cry;*
> *I am not there. I did not die.*

By the time she finished, she was in tears. "We will always remember those who are not here, but the time for feuds is over. Let's not forget what we are here for today and tomorrow. All shake hands as family, or heaven help me, I will . . ." Her voice rose to fever pitch. Her father was at her side whispering something that calmed her and brought a smile to her lips. She handed him the microphone.

"Ladies and gentlemen, I know this is a wedding, but I just got a text and a picture. Robert, I have something for you to see." He walked down to join the two men. "I just got this text from Bobby, at the hospital. They tried to call you, but your phone must still be off. Patti and Bobby had their baby! It's a girl. Congratulations, Grandpa." He gave Robert his phone and showed him the picture of Patti holding the new baby.

"Oh my God. I'm a grandpa! Whoa." Robert read Bobby and Patti's message aloud: "Meet your new grandchild—Roberta Tess Macgregor, six pounds, seven ounces." Robert hugged Ryan and said, "Aye! Strike up the band. Let the celebrating continue!"

He turned to Angus and showed him the picture of the newest Macgregor. "Now this is something worth fighting for, my friend. Our children and their future. And in a few years you'll know what I mean."

The old man's face softened, and in his tears, Robert knew it was over. Angus said, "Aye, let me buy you a drink, Macgregor . . . I mean Robert . . . Bob."

Mary Kate and Mickey danced the night away. Waltzes, rumbas—they danced them all. At the end of the evening, they were among the last to leave. She put her arms around his neck and said, "Take me home, Michael Thompson, husband. I love you."

"I love you too, Mrs. Thompson." They walked hand in hand out the door; they had made and kept a pledge: *Hold on tight to each other throughout the night.* Life was good.

Chapter Fifty-Two

The day after the wedding, it was late and they were both quiet on the ride to the airport. Ryan managed a weak smile as they pulled into the parking garage. He looked at the sky above; the darkened skies looked threatening, black-and-gray clouds fighting one another, swirling high above them.

Alexi had not known him for long, but she knew him well. "What's wrong?" she asked, already knowing the answer.

"I can't go to Paris," Ryan stated bluntly as they walked inside the terminal.

"What?"

"I just can't, Alexi. As much as I would like to say yes and run off with you to Europe . . . I just can't. I have my life here, responsibilities. My practice. My family. My brothers. And I have so many memories of . . ."

She let out a painful sigh while still holding his hand. "Ryan, sweetheart, one day you will run out of excuses for why you're not happy. I guess it's just not today. Let me know when that day arrives, my sweet. I can't compete with memories."

"But, Alexi, you don't understand . . ."

She placed a fingertip to his lips and leaned in close to whisper, "Be still, my heart." She kissed him and turned to walk away; she paused to wave good-bye, and then she was gone. Gone from his sight and gone from his life. He missed her already. He ached for her, and for the second time in his life, he had lost someone he truly loved.

He ran up the stairs, up one level to the darkened observation room high above the airport. The lights on the runways and the control tower were an array of different colors, like a kaleidoscope. A soft rain pelted the glass windows. He could see her plane below pull away from the terminal and slowly taxi toward the runway. It was dark as he saw his reflection in the glass looking out over the bustling activity before him and saw the heavens clearing, showing the stars in the sky. Then he thought of his Gracie. He remembered how they would sit on the porch and watch the stars come out at night. He was torn.

She came from the shadows and eased beside him, dressed in her white jeans, pink T-shirt, and sandals. He always loved her in that outfit, so sexy. It was his Gracie.

"Hiya, Mac," she said, kissing him on the cheek while her hand rested gently on his shoulder.

"Hey, baby," he said softly without taking his eyes off the plane. "I've missed you."

"I know. Me too. I will always miss you and love you, but . . . it's time for you to get on with living." They watched together as the plane lifted smoothly into the South Florida sky. "I've come to say good-bye. Get on with your life, Mac. Go find her and hold on to her as tight as you can. Go get her." She kissed him tenderly on his cheek and walked away. Gone. From the darkness he heard her whisper, "And, hey, take your brothers with you."

Chapter Fifty-Three

The sun shone bright and warm as the midmorning traffic roared to life on the springtime streets of Paris.

He first saw her strolling down the avenue toward him as he glanced over the top of his newspaper. She was beautiful. He closed the paper, folded it in half, and set it on the table next to his coffee cup, all the while admiring her. She was walking with purpose toward him as if in slow motion, her beret cocked to one side, her high heels accentuating her strong, athletic legs, a feast for his eyes. She was dressed as fashionably as any of the other Parisians on the street that day, in her sculpted French skirt and patterned silk blouse. He loved the way her skirt clung to her curves, gently swaying with her every movement as she walked.

When their eyes met, Alexi smiled that coy smile of hers, and her hand whispered a gentle wave to him that only he saw.

"Good morning, my sweet," she said as she slowly kissed him on both cheeks, French-style, with her lips lingering longer than for a mere tender hello.

"Morning," he responded as he caught a faint hint of her new French perfume. He noticed the top button on her blouse straining, nearly undone, as she leaned forward to kiss him.

She sat down next to him, smiled, and placed her hand gently on his leg.

He saw a flash of her thigh as she slowly crossed her legs, and he heard the unmistakable sound of her sheer stockings rubbing against each other. He thought of her, all of her. *So tempting.*

Their regular waiter, jovial François, as they called him, dressed in his usual black-and-white uniform and carrying a white towel draped over his arm, approached her as soon as she was seated.

"Bonjour, madame," he said, smiling broadly, eyeing her.

"Bonjour, François."

"Coffee, *madame?"*

"Oui. Café au lait, s'il vous plaît." She looked at Ryan's nearly empty cup and held up two fingers. *"Deux, s'il vous plaît."*

"Oui, madame."

They sat outside at their favorite corner table on Rue d'Orléans just off Avenue Charles de Gaulle on the Left Bank, sipping their coffee and watching the daily life of Paris slowly meander by.

She had finished her classes early, and now she had him all to herself. She leaned close and kissed his neck.

He felt her pressing against his arm as she leaned over to kiss him. He placed his hand on her leg and was amazed at the warmth of her body; he shivered, hoping she would not notice.

"What time is our lunch today?" he asked in a nonchalant manner.

Everyone was to meet for lunch; they would have a wine-and-cheese picnic along the banks of the Seine. Robert and Coleen would be there after their tour of the Louvre. Eian and Rose would arrive early, as usual, to secure their wonderful picnic spot under the graceful weeping willow, after visiting Notre-Dame Cathedral.

"Not until one o'clock," she said calmly. Then she turned to him, smiled, and whispered with a gentle kiss while squeezing his leg, "We have time, plenty of time . . . my love. Let's go. I wasn't that hungry anyway," she said as he reached for her hand.

He laid some coins on the table and waved good-bye to François, who returned the gesture with a knowing smile. "*Au revoir*, François."

He looked at her and said, "Time to go."

Robert and Coleen walked up the steps to enter the museum on that warm and sunny day in Paris.

"I have been waiting my whole life to come here," Coleen whispered in anticipation as they walked down the quiet, wide hallways of the famed Louvre. "And now I'm here, with you. Robert, I'm so excited. I can hardly wait." They walked around the magnificent museum, and then they saw her, under a soft light, highlighting her ever-present smile. The *Mona Lisa*.

"She's beautiful," he said as they stood there looking at her, frozen in time and space.

Coleen hugged his arm, bringing him closer. "Can you believe she is over five hundred years old?"

Bob leaned in closer, tilting his head as he studied the famed portrait. "You know, she doesn't look a day over four hundred."

They both laughed and soon reluctantly walked away to explore the rest of the museum.

"I'm so glad we came," Coleen said. "I've always wanted to come to Paris."

"And now you're here. Don't I always give you what you want?"

"Yes, you do," she said with a twinkle in her eye. She turned and reached into her purse, pulled out an envelope. She handed it to him. "I have something. This is for you. For us."

"What is it?"

"Open it and see."

They stopped and sat down on a bench in front of a serene, soft blue-and-gold Monet countryside painting. He opened the envelope and began to read the contents. His eyes grew wide, his mouth opened. "What? What . . . is this?" he stammered.

"When we leave here for the States on Monday, we're taking a slight detour before we go home—I bought us a five-day side trip to Scotland. We fly into Edinburgh and then tour about the countryside, and you will finally get to see the places you've only read about. We can visit the bonny, bonny banks of Loch Lomond, walk along the pathways followed by Rob Roy MacGregor, pay homage at the William Wallace Monument, see Hadrian's Wall, and visit many other places. Is that good?"

For once he was at a loss for words until he finally said, "Very good. Very good, indeed."

"I love you, Robert Macgregor. And I love saying it."

"I love you too, Coleen . . . Coleen Macgregor?"

She smiled with that twinkle in her eye. "We'll see."

He pulled her close and kissed her, and then kissed her again as unflappable romantic Parisians strolled by, paying no attention. Everyone was lost in their own world.

Life was good. Life was very good, again.

Acknowledgments

I want to thank all of my readers and reviewers, who have provided me with not only their support but also encouragement in my writing. Thank you! I also want to thank Judy Hanses for all her help, Dr. Robert Johnston (Doctor Bob), and Doris and the late Irwin "Sonny" Block, and a special thanks for the inspiration of Bob and Cheryl. Thank you one and all.

—B

About the Author

Bryan Mooney is the author of *Christmas in Vermont*, *Once We Were Friends*, *Love Letters*, *A Second Chance*, and other romance novels, as well as the Nick Ryan thriller series. He spent years traveling the globe for both business and pleasure, and he draws upon those experiences in his writing. Originally from the Midwest, Bryan now lives in sunny South Florida with his longtime wife and childhood sweetheart, Bonnie. When he is not penning romance novels and thrillers on the beach, he and his wife love to travel. Connect with Bryan at www.bryanmooneyauthor.com.